When Savannah's husband Rafe loses his position with the Tennessee Bureau of Investigations, Savannah gets excited about the prospect of them taking their new baby and moving back to their hometown of Sweetwater. Rafe has already received a job offer from the Columbia Police Department, and although he doesn't seem terribly interested in accepting, Savannah would enjoy having her family around, not to mention Rafe's grandmother Mrs. Jenkins.

But before they can make any decisions, Rafe's former boss at the TBI turns up dead. And Rick Goins, the MNPD detective in charge, seems determined to prove that Rafe had something to do with it.

Detective Tamara Grimaldi, former colleague of Goins and now Chief of Police for Columbia, swears that while it might take him some time, Goins usually comes up with the right solution in the end. But with fresh victims dropping like flies, and someone seemingly doing their best to fan the flames of Goins's biases, Savannah isn't sure she can wait for the detective to come to his senses. Because while she'd like to move back to Sweetwater, she doesn't want it to be because her husband is behind bars…

OTHER BOOKS IN THIS SERIES

A Cutthroat Business

Hot Property

Contract Pending

Close to Home

A Done Deal

Change of Heart

Kickout Clause

Past Due

Dirty Deeds

Unfinished Business

Adverse Possession

Uncertain Terms

Scared Money

Bad Debt

Home Stretch

WRONGFUL TERMINATION

Savannah Martin Mystery #16

Jenna Bennett

WRONGFUL TERMINATION
Savannah Martin Mystery #16

Interior design and formatting: B. Gallagher
Cover Design: Dar Albert, Wicked Smart Designs

Magpie Ink

One

Rafe lost his job on the first business day of the new year.

We had no warning it would happen—although if we'd thought about it, I guess maybe we would have seen it coming. And the Tennessee Bureau of Investigations—for which my husband had spent ten years undercover, shedding blood, sweat, and tears, and risking his life on a daily basis—didn't even give him thirty days' notice, let alone sixty or ninety. Just told him they'd give him a two week severance packet, and to clean out his desk and begone.

"How rude," I said, stirring chicken on the stove.

Rafe shrugged. "They don't know what to do with me." He reached up and loosened his tie, before flipping open the first couple of buttons on his shirt.

My mouth started to water, and I don't think it was the smell of the chicken.

He knew it, too, because he grinned. "Hello, darlin'."

"Hello," I managed, as he came closer. And then I forgot about the chicken, and the spatula in my hand, and everything else while he kissed me. It was only his turning me away from the stove that prevented me from setting my posterior on fire.

We'd been married more than six months. We'd been in a committed relationship for more than a year. It was getting on for a year and a half since I'd first found myself in bed with him.

And he could still take my breath away with nothing more than a look.

When the spatula hit the floor, he let me go, and bent to pick it up. I watched the black slacks pull snugly across his butt—much nicer than mine—and surreptitiously checked my chin for drool.

"Here." He straightened and handed it to me.

The spatula.

"Thanks." I moved the couple of steps to the sink and rinsed it. And thought about splashing cold water on my face, but decided that I'd already made enough of a fool of myself.

"Carrie asleep?" Rafe asked, and put that excellent butt against the edge of the kitchen island while he focused on rolling up his sleeves.

I nodded. "Last nap of the day. She'll probably wake up in the next few minutes, and want to eat."

By now, our daughter Caroline was six weeks old, and had a prodigious appetite. She wanted to nurse all the time. The good thing was, I was losing baby weight like crazy. The bad thing, of course, was that I was walking around like a zombie, because I was awake every couple of hours throughout the day and night, feeding the beast. Rafe could still get me stirred up, and probably always would, but between you and me, I would rather have eight uninterrupted hours of sleep right now, than sex with my husband.

Although, since the eight uninterrupted weren't likely to come my way for another six months or more, the sex made for a very acceptable substitute.

But not right now. I was in the middle of cooking dinner, and Carrie was due to wake up any moment. And I wanted to know what had happened.

"They knew what to do with you last year," I pointed out. "It may have taken them a month or two to get around to it, but they offered you a job after you'd blown your cover and couldn't do undercover work anymore."

"Only because Wendell twisted their arm," Rafe said.

Wendell Craig was Rafe's handler during the undercover years. Last December, when Rafe finally succeeded in breaking up Hector Gonzales's South American Theft Gang and put Hector behind bars, Wendell went to bat for him with the TBI, and talked someone into hiring Rafe to train other undercover agents.

"I guess you've talked to him about it?"

Rafe nodded. "First thing after it happened. He quit."

My mouth dropped open for a second, before I hiked up my jaw. "No kidding."

Rafe shook his head.

"He didn't have to do that."

Rafe shrugged. After a second he added, "The boys are done training."

The three young men he'd been working with for the past year, under Wendell's supervision.

"Doesn't the TBI have anyone else who needs training?"

"Not till they see how the first three do," Rafe said, which I guessed made sense.

"So the boys have been given new assignments? Where are they going?"

"The Memphis office for José," Rafe said. "Lotta Latino gangs in Memphis."

And José would fit right in. "His girlfriend is going with him, I assume?"

"I guess," Rafe said. "Clayton's going to Chattanooga."

The towing capital of the world, where Clayton's knowledge of cars, and boosting them, would come in handy.

"And Jamal?"

"Alexandra's pregnant," Rafe said. "I don't know what's

gonna happen to the two of'em—she's just seventeen, right?—but for now, he's stepping up and taking some responsibility. He asked if he could stay in Nashville."

"Good for him." And good for Rafe, who had probably put a little pressure on Jamal to do the right thing. Alexandra Puckett, the mother to be, was by way of being a friend of mine, and since the two of them had met at Rafe's and my wedding, I felt a slight responsibility for what had happened. "Wendell didn't want to be Jamal's handler?"

"Jamal's gonna be in narcotics," Rafe said. "At least for a while."

"Why not gangs?" That was what had made Jamal want to be a TBI agent in the first place. His brother had been killed, and he wanted to make a difference in that area.

"We blew his cover pretty good last fall, remember?"

Now that he mentioned it, I did remember. My husband had taken a last undercover assignment of his own, long after it was safe for him to do so, because Jamal had gotten a tip about a gang war about to go down, and they didn't want to send Jamal into the breach on his own quite yet. So Rafe donned a head of dreadlocks and a fake gold tooth, and became Jamal's cousin Ry'mone for the duration. The thought of it was enough to send a reminiscent shiver down my spine.

"Wendell isn't interested in narcotics?"

"It ain't that he isn't interested. But narcotics is a different field. With different people in it."

"Different department?"

"Different side of the same department," Rafe said. "If Jamal woulda wanted to leave Nashville, they woulda put him into the gang trade in Memphis. That's what McLaughlin wanted to do. But he asked to stay here. So he's gonna spend some time in narcotics."

Fine. I guess it made sense. Although something else didn't.

"Any reason the TBI didn't ask you to be Jamal's handler?" Or José's or Clayton's? "You trained all three of them." And he could use another job.

"I don't imagine they trust me overmuch," Rafe said.

"You can't be serious." He'd sweated and bled for them. "Why on earth wouldn't they trust you?"

He shrugged. "Once a criminal…"

I rolled my eyes and put the spatula down. "Oh, please. You've more than paid for that."

Not only had he spent two years in prison, but he'd spent the decade afterward risking life and limb for the TBI. How dared they not trust him?

"It don't matter." He tilted his head as a soft squeak from the baby monitor on the counter signaled that Carrie was awake. "Want me to go get her?"

"Be my guest," I said. I spent enough of my day carting the baby up and down the stairs and changing her diaper. He was welcome to his share of the baby duties.

So Rafe took himself up to the nursery, and I turned the heat to low under the chicken. When she came downstairs, Carrie would want to eat, and the fact that our dinner would get dry while I nursed her wouldn't mean squat.

I settled into the sofa in the parlor, and waited for Rafe to bring her down. She was all nice and clean and sweet-smelling, and rooted like a piglet when I lifted my shirt. Rafe sat down on the ottoman across the table and watched, his expression partly fascinated, partly amused.

"So Wendell's leaving, too," I said, picking up the conversation sort of where we'd left it. "What's he planning to do now?"

Rafe had a job offer from the Columbia PD. From our old friend, Nashville homicide detective Tamara Grimaldi, who had taken the position of chief of police down there, effective yesterday. Her Christmas present to Rafe this year had been a job offer. But that didn't extend to Wendell, or not that I knew.

"Fish," Rafe said.

Excuse me? "Where?" Was there a living to be made in fishing? In Alaska, sure. But in the middle of Tennessee?

"He's talking about selling his place in Hermitage and buying a shack on a river somewhere. And spending his time fishing and sleeping."

OK, then. To my mind he was a bit on the young side to retire—in his fifties, by my gauge—but after ten years of handling Rafe, maybe fishing and sleeping was exactly what he needed. "Let me know if he needs any help buying or selling."

When I'm not cooking dinner or feeding the baby, I have a real estate license. I don't use it much, but I'm always on the lookout for people I can inveigle into becoming clients. And this would be a double whammy, both a sale and a purchase, which would be extra sweet.

"I'll do that," Rafe said. "But you can tell him yourself. I told everybody we'd have 'em over for a meal on Friday, before they go off."

Today was Tuesday. That didn't give me a whole lot of time to plan a dinner party. "I'm sure I can throw something together."

Rafe grinned. "I'm sure you can. But we can order a dozen pizzas and buy some beer and be just fine."

Of course we could. And everyone might enjoy it a lot more than anything I'd pull together, anyway.

I was brought up to be the perfect Southern hostess, from a combination of my mother's tutelage and attending finishing school in Charleston. Mother would have been aghast at the idea of me serving delivery pizza and store-bought beer at a get-together in my house. I was tired enough from dealing with Carrie to think it sounded like an excellent idea.

"I'll take care of everything," Rafe said. "Not like I got anything else to do."

"They don't even want you to finish out the week?"

He shrugged. "A couple of meetings. An appointment to hand in my gun and badge. Paperwork to sign. But no. No work."

"Huh." I unlatched Carrie with a little pop, and shifted her from one side to the other before she could complain. "What about Wendell and the boys?"

"Wendell's finishing out the month," Rafe said. "They're prob'ly hoping they can change his mind."

"Maybe so." And who could blame them? Wendell had been with the TBI a long time. I had no idea how long, but he'd been around to recruit Rafe back when my husband was eighteen, so it had been a while. The least they could do, after more than a dozen years' faithful service, was to give him his thirty days' notice. Hopefully his severance package was a lot better than Rafe's, too. "And the boys?"

"Getting their affairs in order," Rafe said. "Lots of paperwork for them, too. José and Clayton have to pack and say goodbye to their families."

"It'll be nice to see them one more time."

Rafe nodded.

We sat in silence a moment.

"Have you called Grimaldi?" I asked.

"No," Rafe said.

"But you're going to take the job, aren't you? With the Columbia PD?"

He didn't answer.

"Rafe?" I said.

He sighed. "I imagine so. A man's gotta do something. I have a family to support now. And no skills for nothing else."

"You have skills." A lot of skills. Quite excellent skills, in fact. Although some of them—the ones that made a corner of his mouth curve up—weren't skills I wanted to share with anyone else, even if he could have made a fortune going into the gigolo trade.

"Not those skills," I said. "That's not to say that you aren't very good at certain things. Which I will let you show me later, if you want to. But I was thinking more of ten years undercover, and the fact that you've spent all your adult life in law enforcement."

"Living your life deep undercover ain't exactly law enforcement," Rafe answered. "It's more like being a criminal with a get out of jail free card."

Fine. "All the years you spent as a criminal have made you well equipped to catch other criminals."

"I suppose," Rafe said, sounding dissatisfied.

We sat in silence a moment. Carrie indicated that she had finished eating, so I lifted her up on my shoulder and patted her back. She emitted a very unladylike belch, and a tiny trickle of milk I could feel soak into my blouse. Rafe's lips twitched, but he didn't say anything.

"We should go have dinner," I said.

He nodded, and I think he looked relieved. "I'll take the baby." He pushed to his feet.

I handed her over, and Rafe cradled her expertly. We'd both gotten pretty good at baby-handling over the past month and a half. Neither one of us worried much about dropping her anymore. "Why don't you put her in the bouncy seat until we're done eating, so we'll have our hands free, and she'll be out of the way."

Rafe nodded and moved toward the bouncy seat. With it in one hand and the baby in the crook of his other arm, he headed for the kitchen. I rearranged my clothing and followed.

I bided my time, and let the subject lie until bedtime. By then Carrie was asleep, and couldn't be used as a distraction. And Rafe didn't seem interested in the other usual distraction, namely making love to me. Since I was more interested in sleep than in sex anyway, I was OK with that. But I was willing to sacrifice a few minutes of rest for a conversation. "What's going on?"

"Nothing," Rafe said.

"Are you upset because they let you go?"

He shrugged. I guess that was a yes. Or a provisional yes, given that the boys wouldn't be there, nor would Wendell. So at least he wouldn't be missing much by not working for the TBI anymore.

Except a job and a steady salary.

"You do have another job you can go to," I reminded him.

He made a noise. It wasn't quite a grunt, but something like it.

I turned my head to look at him, what little I could see in the semi-dark. There was a night light on in the hallway, for when I'd have to get up in the middle of the night to pick up Carrie, so I wouldn't run into the wall or pitch headfirst down the stairs. And the door was open so I'd be able to hear her start to cry. I could see the light reflected in Rafe's eyes. He was staring up at the ceiling.

"Don't you want to work for Grimaldi?" I asked.

Another shrug.

"I thought you liked her."

He glanced over. "I like her fine."

I thought for a second. "Is it because she's female?"

He'd never struck me as someone who'd have a problem with female authority, but maybe I was wrong. He's quite the alpha, of course, and so is Grimaldi, so I guess I could see why that might become a problem.

"No." I could hear the smirk in his voice.

"You wouldn't have a problem working for a female boss?"

"I wouldn't have a problem working for Tammy," Rafe said.

I turned all the way toward him and went up on one elbow. "Are you sure? She'd have to give you orders, and you'd have to follow them."

"I don't have a problem taking orders," Rafe told the ceiling.

I didn't say anything, and after a second he glanced over at me, lips twitching. "Maybe that ain't exactly true. I've been doing my own thing for a long time. Having somebody else tell me what to do could take some getting used to. But Tammy and I've worked together before. We get along."

They did. And I'd never sensed any kind of problem between them. At least not when they were on equal footing.

"So if it isn't that, what is it?"

"Nothing," Rafe said.

I waited, and eventually he sighed. "We talked about this over Christmas. Who in Maury County's gonna accept me as the law? They all know who I am."

"They knew who you were," I corrected. "A long time ago. You're not that person anymore."

"They don't know that."

Perhaps not. But— "They'll find out."

He was silent another minute. So long that I started thinking he might have fallen asleep. "I dunno about this, darlin'."

That was obvious. "Tell you what," I said, as my own eyelids got heavier. "You don't have to figure it out tonight. Maybe someone at the TBI will change their minds. Maybe they'll keep you on after all."

He made a noise. This time it was definitely a grunt.

"Or maybe not. We'll be fine either way. If you can't work for the TBI and you don't want to work for Grimaldi, we'll figure something else out. We live cheaply."

In Rafe's grandmother's house, that had no mortgage or rent. Or we could move to Sweetwater, to my mother's house. The mansion had been built right around 1840, and had been in the Martin family since, so there was no mortgage or rent due there, either.

Rafe still didn't say anything, and I suppressed a yawn. "You could go to work for Yvonne at Beulah's Meat'n Three. She'd hire you in a heartbeat, and you'd look cute in one of those little aprons. Or maybe we can renovate houses together. I can find them, you can renovate them, and then we can sell them again. You renovated this."

"Maybe," Rafe said, his voice far away. "Go to sleep, darlin'."

"You, too," I said, or maybe I didn't. I'm not quite sure. I was asleep by then.

Rafe went to the TBI the next day, to sign paperwork and hand in his badge and gun. He also had a meeting with Doug Brennan, who was Wendell's boss, and who was not happy about the situation, but who hadn't anything even resembling a reasonable solution to the problem.

"He said I could maybe work in the gym," Rafe told me over dinner. "Said I was in good shape, and maybe I could teach the agents a thing or two."

"That's pretty rude," I said, as I twiddled pasta around my fork.

Rafe didn't answer, but I figure he thought so, too. "When I told him I hadn't gone through everything I did to help the real agents with push-ups and chin-ups, he offered me a desk job."

"What kind of desk?"

"I didn't ask," Rafe said, his tone deeply disgusted. "I figured he'd say security."

"Mr. Brennan sounds like he's pretty clueless."

"He ain't the sharpest tool in the shed," Rafe agreed. "Although he's less of a problem than the upper brass. Brennan would be happy to keep me working. It's the folks above him that wanna see results before they'll agree to give me anybody else to train. Hard to blame'em for that."

I guess. "It isn't fair to just fire you without warning, though. And after all these years, too!"

He shrugged.

I hesitated. "So is it time to discuss Tamara Grimaldi's job offer yet?"

"Thought we did that yesterday," Rafe said.

And of course we had discussed it yesterday. Just without coming to any conclusions.

"If we stay in Nashville, what do you plan to do for a living?"

"Like you said," my husband said, "we could renovate houses together."

We could do that. I might not be great at finding or keeping clients, but I could manage to find my husband a house to renovate. However— "How would we pay for it? If you're out of work and I'm a stay-at-home mom with a real estate license and very little income?"

"Home equity line on this house?" Rafe said.

That would be a great idea, if not for one small fact. "Isn't it your grandmother's house? I don't think anybody's going to give you a home equity loan on a house you don't own."

And while we could dust off his grandmother, who lives with her niece—Rafe's second cousin twice removed or some such, who also happens to be my mother's best friend—in Sweetwater, and bring her to Nashville, no banker worth his salt would give Mrs. Jenkins a loan. Not only does she not have a job either, but she's very far from *compos mentis*. Half the time she doesn't even know who Rafe is, and thinks he's his father, her son, instead.

"And anyway," I said, "you tried this last year, remember? After you finished up being undercover before Christmas, and you had those couple of months with nothing to do." Nothing but making love to me and finishing fixing up Mrs. Jenkins's house, which he had started doing in the fall. "You went absolutely crazy with boredom."

He didn't answer. We ate in silence for a few minutes.

"I can tell you want me to take the job with Tammy," Rafe said.

I opened my mouth to deny it, and closed it again. And opened it again. "I don't want you to take the job unless you want to. But you don't have a job here anymore. And I'm going to miss Grimaldi now that she's living down there. Same with your grandmother. And with Mother shacking up with the sheriff, the mansion will be sitting empty. Nobody else wants it." My sister and brother and half-sister all having their own places to live. "You and I could just move right in. You know as well as I do that it would be safer for Carrie down there. Here, I can't even take her out to play in the yard without worrying about driveby shootings."

OK, so this was a bit of an exaggeration. Not only was Carrie much too young to go outside and play, but we didn't have a big problem with driveby shootings. Word had gotten around that Rafe worked for the TBI, with a gun and the power to arrest people, so most of the evildoers in the area gave our house a wide berth. So far, the only trouble we'd had, had been from people who were after us for personal reasons, and not just because they were committing crimes in the neighborhood in general.

That would probably change now, too.

Rafe made a face when I mentioned it, but he didn't argue. He must have come to the same conclusion.

"But it's totally up to you," I said. "I know you don't have warm feelings about Sweetwater. If you can't face going back there, I understand. Carrie and I just want to be where you are. And if that's here, then we'll stay here. Or we can go somewhere else. Somewhere that isn't Sweetwater."

Like the little town where we'd spent our honeymoon six months ago. On the Florida gulf coast. Rafe had enjoyed it there. Maybe the chief of police would give him a job.

On second thought, maybe not. She'd been extremely attractive, and I felt like a hag these days. At least if he went to work for Tamara Grimaldi, I didn't have to worry about her batting her eyes at him, seeing as she's more interested in my brother than in my husband. At least in that way.

"It just seemed somewhat fortuitous," I said. "That Grimaldi offered you a job, and a week later, you lost the job you had."

After a beat, I added, "You don't think…?"

He shook his head. "Wendell didn't know till I told him. If he didn't, I don't see how Tammy coulda."

I didn't, either. So it must just be fate.

"It would be nice to have some help with the baby," I said wishfully. "If we lived in Sweetwater, my sister would babysit sometimes. Or my mother. Or Darcy." My half-sister. "Or Audrey and your grandmother. Lots of people who'd take Carrie and give us a chance to spend a little time alone once in a while."

We weren't at a point where that was an issue yet. Carrie was so young, and we were so new at parenting and so crazy about every little thing she did, that we didn't mind spending every waking moment with her. But as she got a year or two old, I had a feeling that that would change. We'd welcome the chance to eat a meal like grownups again. And when we did, it would be nice to have people around who could provide a couple hours of babysitting.

Not to mention that it would be nice to have people around who had gone through child rearing, and who I could ask questions of, when something came up. Just last week, I'd had to call my sister in a panic and tell her that Carrie was hiccupping and wouldn't stop, and did I need to take her to the emergency room? (No. It was normal and would go away on its own. Which it did, an hour later. An hour I spent sitting next to the crib watching my baby to make sure she didn't hiccup herself to death in her sleep.)

And yes, it was nice that I had someone to call. But it would be even nicer to have Catherine close enough that I could actually take Carrie over to her house if I wanted to.

Rafe made a noise. It was somewhat agreeable. Or at least not disagreeable.

"You could drive down and talk to her," I said, "maybe. Grimaldi, I mean. She offered you the job and you said you'd think about it, but you didn't actually talk to her. Not that I know."

He shook his head.

"It might help to get some kind of idea exactly what she has in mind. I mean… if she's planning to put you in a uniform and send you out on patrol, I can see why you wouldn't be interested in that. But if she wants you to do detective work, that'd be different."

He nodded.

"We could run down tomorrow morning. You could see Grimaldi. I could too, for that matter. See how she feels about her new job after the first couple of days. And we could see Mother and the sheriff, and your grandmother and Audrey and everyone else."

And then we could either drive up again tomorrow afternoon or evening—it's just over an hour, so no big deal—or we could spend the night in Sweetwater, and leave Friday morning, and still get home in plenty of time to set up for the party.

"Would you like to do that?"

"I suppose," Rafe said. He still sounded dissatisfied, though.

"At least if you talk to her, you'll have more of an idea what she had in mind. And if you turn it down, you'll know exactly what it is you're turning down."

He nodded.

"So do we have a plan?"

"I suppose," Rafe said.

The lack of enthusiasm was annoying. But he'd agreed to do something, and that was more than he had when we'd sat down to dinner, so I counted it as a win, and devoted myself to my spaghetti. Talking about it more would only muddy the waters.

Two

We set out around nine the following morning. Rafe had no appointments at the TBI, and I had nothing to do, either. So we waited until Carrie had woken up, and spent the couple of hours she keeps awake looking at her and tickling her tummy, and when it came close to the time she'd go down for another nap, we piled her and all her paraphernalia into the Volvo, crawled in after her, and set off for Sweetwater.

With a quick stop at the gas station on the corner of Dresden Street and Dickerson to put gas in the car before we hit the interstate.

We'd only been driving for a few minutes, but Carrie was already getting drowsy. I stayed in my seat while Rafe got out to do the honors.

As sometimes happens, the credit card machine was on the fritz, and Rafe ended up having to go inside to pay. And spent a couple of minutes talking to the kid behind the counter before he came back out. His name is Malcolm, and he lives up the street from Mrs. Jenkins's house.

"Did you tell him you lost your job?" I said when he was sitting beside me again, and had turned the key over in the ignition.

He shook his head. "Don't figure it's any of his business."

Aside from which he might still be hoping that what's-his-name—Brennan—would be able to pull some strings and change things. No need to give up hope quite yet.

"I guess that'll put a kibosh on Malcolm's plans to join the TBI when he's old enough, anyway."

Rafe shrugged. "He might could change his mind about that, anyway. Not like he's doing much to make himself more likely to be hired."

No. He'd been working at the gas station since he left high school, and didn't seem in any hurry to leave there to go to college. And the TBI, like every other employer in the state, seemed to prefer someone with a secondary education to someone without.

If Rafe had had a college degree, he might still have a job.

"He'll figure it out," Rafe said, and turned the car onto Dickerson Pike in the direction of the interstate. "And if he don't, none of my business."

None at all. I settled into the seat and glanced over my shoulder at the baby. Her eyes were closed, with long eyelashes fanning against her cheeks the way her father's did. Her little pink lips were pursed and making sucking motions. I reached over and rescued the pacifier that had fallen into her lap, and stuffed it back into her mouth before she could realize that it was gone and start crying.

Rafe glanced over at me. "She OK?"

I smiled. "Perfect."

"Sleeping?"

I nodded.

"You comfortable?"

I was.

"Why don't you take a nap, too? I'll wake you when we get there."

I squinted at him. "Are you sure?" I could use the nap, sure. I'd been up several times overnight. But— "You don't want the company?"

"You'll still be here," Rafe said. "Just not watching how fast I'm driving."

Ah. "Have at it. Just remember that if you get pulled over now, you won't have a TBI badge to get you out of the speeding ticket."

"I won't get pulled over," Rafe said, cutting onto the interstate in front of an eighteen-wheeler carrying gas. We weren't dangerously close, and in the second it took the driver to lay on the horn, we'd already traveled far enough that the deep, angry toot was far behind us.

Rafe laughed. I smiled, and closed my eyes.

When I opened them less than an hour later, we were just pulling up outside the police station in the town of Columbia in Maury County. I blinked at the clock. "Here already?"

"I told you I was planning to go fast," Rafe said.

"Sure, but…" It wasn't worth asking him if he'd flown—he had to have been, to have gotten here in the time we had—so I didn't. Instead I glanced over at Carrie. She was still asleep, the pacifier making tiny in-and-out motions as she sucked on it in her sleep. "I'll stay here with the baby."

"Bring her," Rafe said, opening his car door. "I'm sure Tammy'll wanna see her."

I wasn't. Tamara Grimaldi isn't exactly the warm and fuzzy type, and I couldn't imagine she'd care one way or the other whether I brought the baby in to see her.

Not that she minds children. She seems to get along with Dix's daughters well enough. But she has a pretty pragmatic approach to them. She doesn't gush or coo or tickle their feet. When they're old enough to be talked to, she talks to them like small adults. Or so I've determined from seeing her interact with Abigail and Hannah.

On the other hand, I wasn't all that keen on being left in the car. This could take some time. It was cold. And I wanted to see

Grimaldi, and ask how she was doing. So when Rafe told me to bring the baby, I brought the baby, car seat and all.

He held the door for me, and let me walk into the lobby first. I made a beeline for the reception desk, where a young woman in uniform was taking up space. "We'd like to see Tamara Grimaldi if she's available, please."

She looked from me to Rafe and back. A little slowly. Her gaze lingered on him a lot longer than it did on me. He usually has that effect on women. "Who should I tell her is here?"

"Savannah Martin," I said, and added, a second later, "Collier. And Rafe. And Carrie."

She nodded and picked up the receiver. A red fingernail tapped buttons on an old-fashioned phone. After a second, she said, "Chief Grimaldi? Someone to see you."

A beat passed, then she rattled off our names. Rafe's first. Then she put down the phone and told him, "She'll be right out."

He nodded. I rolled my eyes. She didn't notice, since she was still looking at him.

"You can wait in the sitting area over there." She waved a vague hand in the direction of the sofa and a couple of chairs on the other side of the lobby.

"I don't imagine it'll be long," Rafe told her, "but thanks."

She nodded, and watched him walk away. She even got halfway up from her chair to get a better look at his butt.

I ought to be used to it by now.

Correction: I am used to it by now. Women always look at Rafe. I look at him myself. He's nice to look at. As I think so myself, it's hard to blame other women for thinking the same. But when he was standing in front of her with a wife and small baby, the blatant appreciation was a bit too much.

Nothing I could do about it, though, so I followed Rafe—and his excellent butt—over to the seating group. And no sooner had

I put Carrie's carrier on the low table, than the door to the inner sanctum opened, and Tamara Grimaldi strode through.

The first time I met Tamara Grimaldi was a couple of hours after Rafe and I had stumbled over my colleague, and Alexandra's mother, Brenda Puckett's butchered body in what was now the house we were living in on Potsdam Street. Brenda had essentially cheated Mrs. Jenkins, Rafe's grandmother, out of it, and put it on the market for a lot of money—money she didn't plan to share with Mrs. J. But she'd gotten herself murdered in the middle of the deal, and when Rafe and I showed up, we found her with her throat cut in front of the fireplace in the library.

It's a long story.

We called 911, of course, and ended up being taken into downtown, to police headquarters, for an audience with Tamara Grimaldi, who was the homicide detective on call that weekend.

She intimidated me from the get-go. She's everything I'm not. Brisk and capable and businesslike and not in the least concerned with my feelings.

That's not to say she goes out of her way to hurt me, or for that matter anyone else. She's actually very nice. As I've gotten to know her over the past year and a half or so, she's become a good friend—maid of honor at my wedding—and I can't count the number of times she's talked me off some ledge or other, at least in the early days, because I was worried about Rafe's safety, or about whether he truly loved me.

We owe her a lot. But she's still everything I'm not, and she still manages to intimidate me from time to time.

This was one of them. With any other friend, I would have squealed and given her a hug. Grimaldi doesn't invite to that kind of thing. She shook hands with Rafe and nodded to me— and gave the sleeping baby a glance—before she turned back to the door. "Come on back."

She keyed in the code that would let us back into the sanctum while Rafe picked up the baby carrier with one hand and put the other on my back. "Go on, darlin'."

I went, following Grimaldi down the hallway behind the door, while he and Carrie brought up the rear.

We went past a lot of offices and an open area full of cubicles, to the back of the building. Through one of the open doors I saw a detective I recognized, although it took me a few seconds to come up with the name. It wasn't until Grimaldi had ushered us into her office, with a big window looking out the back of the building, and gestured to two chairs in front of her new desk, that I said, "I see Jarvis is still here."

Grimaldi gave me a look as she seated herself behind the desk. It was already covered with paperwork, and it was only her third day on the job.

Or maybe this was how she'd found it—maybe the paperwork had piled up during the months Columbia had been without a police chief—and she was working on clearing it off. At the moment, I couldn't even see surface on much of the desk.

At any rate, she gave me a look. "Any reason he shouldn't be?"

"None I know of," I admitted, as I seated myself and folded one leg over the other. Next to me, Rafe put the baby carrier on the floor—Carrie was still sleeping—and took a seat in the other chair.

"You knew enough to mention it," Grimaldi pointed out.

I shrugged. "I just remember him from a couple of months ago, when Rafe was down here to help the sheriff with the Skinner investigation. Jarvis was in charge of exhuming Beulah Odom."

Not himself. The city or county did that. But Jarvis had been the detective standing next to the digger at Oak Street Cemetery.

Next to Beulah's sister-in-law and niece, whom I suspected of having done away with her.

Not that any of that was Jarvis's fault. At least I didn't think so. Patrick Nolan, who also worked for the Columbia PD—and for Grimaldi now—and who happened to be dating my sister Darcy, had said that while Detective Jarvis was just as fond of clearing cases as the next cop, he wasn't a bad guy. If Jarvis thought, or suspected, that Mrs. Otis Odom and her daughter had done something to hasten Beulah's demise, Nolan was pretty sure Jarvis would do something about it. He certainly wouldn't stand by and be quiet.

"I haven't had much to do with him yet," Grimaldi said, getting comfortable behind the desk. "He's working on cases he was working on while Sheriff Satterfield was running the department. So far, he hasn't asked for help or input. And I haven't started interviews of my new department yet. This week I'm just getting the feel for how things work, and clearing the paperwork off my desk."

"There's a lot of it."

She nodded. "Most of it is just busywork that's been piling up while the position's been empty. It'll take me a few days, and then it'll be done. Not much got done around here between the time the old chief left and when I came in."

"Sheriff Satterfield could probably only do so much," I said, "as he had his own sheriff's department to run, too." Not to mention my mother to propose to.

Grimaldi made an agreeing sort of noise and switched her attention to Rafe.

"The TBI fired him," I said, and Grimaldi turned back to me, her eyes wide. "Tuesday morning. As soon as he came in to work after the holidays."

"You wouldn't know nothing about that, would you?"

This was Rafe's contribution, of course, delivered in a

deceptively even tone, the kind that sounded a lot like the noise a knife makes when it's drawn from a scabbard.

Grimaldi recognized the tone, as well as what it meant, I'm sure. She shook her head. "Of course not. If I'd known they were thinking about letting you go, I would have mentioned it. Not let them spring it on you without warning."

"The boys are being promoted," I said. "From rookies to real undercover agents. They're all leaving this weekend. Chattanooga, Memphis… And the TBI decided to wait and see how they do before they take on anyone else. So Rafe's out of work."

Grimaldi turned back to him. "I had no idea. I figured the boys'd go off soon. It's been a year. But I didn't think they'd let you go. That wasn't why I offered you a job."

"Why did you?"

"Isn't it obvious?" Grimaldi said. "I have a department of people I don't know here. My whole support network's gone. You and I work well together. I'm going to miss you, now that I'm here." She glanced at me, lest I misunderstand and think she was talking about him, not both of us. "And I thought Savannah might appreciate a chance to come back to Sweetwater, now that the baby's here."

Rafe didn't answer.

"You were good at your job," Grimaldi added. "I thought that might translate to you being good at mine."

"Detective?"

She nodded. "I wasn't going to ask you to put on a uniform and patrol the streets. I didn't figure that would go over well."

She didn't specify whether she thought the not going over well applied to Rafe or to the people he might meet in his uniformed patrolling. Maybe both.

"Most of your patrol officers prob'ly have a better education than I do," Rafe told her, the corners of his mouth curling.

"You have ten years of undercover work and a year of employment at TBI headquarters. Not to mention that we've collaborated on a lot of cases in the past year and a half. I'll take that over a college degree any day."

So would I. Not that anyone asked me. But I could have married Todd Satterfield, with his law degree and job at the D.A.'s office, and I'd picked Rafe.

Not that that had any bearing whatsoever on what we were talking about. I'm just mentioning it because formal education isn't everything, and in Grimaldi's shoes, I would have been thrilled to have Rafe, too.

"I can offer you a halfway decent salary and full benefits," Grimaldi added, and mentioned a sum that, while not exactly exorbitant, would be more than enough to live on if we didn't have to pay rent. "You'd get the use of an unmarked car if you needed it. Twenty days paid vacation. I know better than to tell you that you'd get weekends off, and you know better than to believe me, but there's a rotation, so unless you were on call, you'd get to sleep in on the weekend. And you'd have lots of time to spend with Savannah and the baby. And your grandmother, now that she's here."

Rafe nodded. I did, too.

"If you'd agree, I'd want to put you in the criminal investigations department. It's either that or narcotics. I figured you'd be more comfortable in criminal investigations."

Rafe shrugged. "I ain't uncomfortable with drugs."

Grimaldi shot him a look, and he smirked. "Not something I'm supposed to tell the chief of police?"

Grimaldi shook her head. "If you'd prefer narcotics…"

"I ain't even sure I want the job yet. All I'm saying is I haven't had much experience with either. No more with murder investigations than with drugs, really."

Grimaldi nodded. "If you decide you want the job, we'll

figure it out. Both departments are divided in two. The narcotics and gang intel unit in narcotics, with a K-9 unit for support. I don't imagine I have to explain what each does?"

Rafe shook his head. It was pretty self-explanatory, even to me. The narcotics unit dealt with drugs, and the gang unit was under narcotics because there's often drug activity involved in gangs. It sounded similar to the TBI, at least if Jamal's being partnered with a handler in narcotics meant anything.

"The criminal investigations unit consists of general investigations—that's your murder, robbery, assault, rape—and a special victims unit, which is mostly domestic abuse."

Rafe nodded.

"In addition to investigations, we've got a patrol unit and support services. K-9 is a support service. So is training, and record keeping, and hazardous devices—" the bomb unit, I assumed, although what a small town in Middle Tennessee needed with that, I had no idea, "and evidence room clerks, and crossing guards, and SWAT."

My husband's lips curved.

Grimaldi gave him a stony look. "Really?"

Rafe's smile widened.

Grimaldi sighed. "Sorry, but I'm not putting you in Special Weapons and Tactics. You'd be wasted there."

I wasn't sure I agreed. I've seen my husband in SWAT black, and he's quite a sight.

On the other hand, I could see Grimaldi's point, too. He has abilities in other areas, as well, and I couldn't blame her for wanting to make use of them.

Silence reigned for a minute, while they watched each other. I looked from one to the other, wondering who would break first.

"Are you serious?" Grimaldi wanted to know, her voice exasperated. "I'm going to have to bribe you with SWAT to get you to come to work for me?"

"Let's call it an added inducement." Rafe leaned back on the chair and folded his hands across his stomach. His very flat stomach, under a nicely snug T-shirt paired with faded jeans.

No, he hadn't bothered to dress up for what was essentially a job interview. I guess he knew he didn't have to. She'd grab him if he was willing to work for her, however he was dressed. He was the one who had to decide.

And obviously the Special Weapons and Tactics unit had appeal. In some ways, he's a typical guy.

The upside to it, as far as I was concerned, was that in a place like Columbia, population under 40,000, the chances of the SWAT team getting much of a workout, especially on anything dangerous, were probably pretty slim.

"I'd rather you take a nice, safe, investigative job where you'd be home at five every afternoon," I told him. "But if SWAT would make you happy, go for it."

"You make me happy," Rafe said, with a glance from me to Carrie and back. "But a man's gotta have a little fun sometimes, too."

And since he'd married me and given up the other sorts of fun he might have had without a wife and baby at home, I guess I couldn't very well deny him the chance to join the SWAT unit if Grimaldi agreed.

She sighed. "If the only way I can get you to work for me, is if I put you on the SWAT team, I'll put you on the SWAT team. But it wouldn't be my first choice."

Rafe nodded. "Coming back to Maury County ain't my first choice, either. Guess we both gotta figure out if it's something we wanna do."

Grimaldi nodded back. "Think about it and let me know. If the TBI fired you, you have to do something. And you could do worse than come here. At least there are people here who care about you."

"And plenty who'd be happy to see me six foot under," Rafe said.

"But surely that's true everywhere?"

He turned to me with an arched eyebrow, and Grimaldi smothered a laugh.

"I just mean," I said, "that you did undercover work in a lot of places." Nashville, Memphis, Clarksville, Knoxville, to name a few. "And you made sure people were arrested in all of them. There are probably people all over Tennessee who'd like to see you dead. Being here isn't any different."

Rafe shrugged. I guess he had to concede my point, however badly put. "Maybe I should join Wendell in that shack on the river. We could fish all day and eat what we caught and not have to work anywhere else."

"It'd be tight in that shack with all four of us," I pointed out, and saw the corner of his mouth lift.

"Maybe we'd just get a shack of our own."

"You've already got the choice between two mansions," Grimaldi pointed out, looking from him to me and back. "Your grandmother's house in Nashville and Savannah's mother's house in Sweetwater."

No arguing with that. Mrs. Jenkins's Victorian might not be a mansion in the sense that Mother's house was, but it wasn't too far off, either.

"What's this about Mr. Craig?" Grimaldi added.

"He quit," I said. "When he found out that Rafe had been fired. But unlike Rafe they're giving him his thirty days notice."

Grimaldi's eyes had gotten wide again. "Mr. Craig is leaving the TBI?"

"The end of the month. He wants to sell his place in Hermitage and buy a shack on a river somewhere, and spend his time fishing."

Grimaldi got a calculating look in her eyes. Maybe she was thinking of hiring him, too. Or maybe she thought, if she could convince Wendell to put his shack on the Duck River, Rafe would be more likely to want to come to work in Columbia.

Into the silence the phone buzzed.

"Excuse me," Grimaldi said and pushed the button for the speaker. "Yes?"

"Chief Grimaldi?" It was the voice from earlier, that belonged to the young woman in the lobby. "Sergeant Tucker would like a word when you're finished with your current appointment."

"Tell him to wait five minutes," Grimaldi instructed, and added a "Thank you," before she hung up. Or pushed the disconnect button.

"We should go," I said, with a glance at Rafe.

He nodded.

"Any other questions?" Grimaldi looked from him to me and back.

I shook my head. I knew all I needed to know. But this wasn't my decision to make. If it had been, I would have already made it. I'd been inclined this way as soon as Grimaldi offered him the job. When he lost his position with the TBI, as far as I was concerned, it was a done deal. But obviously Rafe was less sure.

"Can't think of any," he said. And thought of one. "You available for dinner?"

Grimaldi arched her brows, but nodded.

"I figured maybe we could talk somewhere that ain't the local pokey." He looked around as if the office—and by extension, the rest of the building—made him uncomfortable.

"I can't imagine that bodes well for you going to work in the local pokey," Grimaldi said dryly, "but sure. When and where?"

"I heard Beulah's was gonna open after the holidays. Six-thirty?"

Grimaldi nodded, and pushed back from the desk. "I'll see you out."

She came around the desk while I got to my feet and scooped up the carrier with the baby, who had slept through the whole interview. "Thanks for your time."

Rafe rolled to his feet, too. "I'll take her." He reached for the carrier.

"It's all right. I've got her." I was already halfway to the door.

Grimaldi got there first, and held it open. I passed into the hallway with the baby carrier, and with Rafe behind me. At the end of the hall, Grimaldi moved in front to unlock the door into the lobby and held it while we passed through.

An older man was leaning on the reception counter, and when we came through the door, he straightened. He glanced at Grimaldi and gave me a quick up-and-down look, but it was just a second before he moved his attention beyond both of us to Rafe. The expression on his face was sneering. So was his voice. "Well, lookee who's here. That's a face I ain't seen in a long time."

Three

For a moment, nobody said anything.

I had never met the man before, although I assumed he was Tucker, still talking to the receptionist. Grimaldi's greeting clinched it. "Sergeant Tucker. I'll be with you in a moment."

Her voice was even, almost pleasant, but I've known her long enough to recognize the steely undertone. I also recognized the way she unobtrusively put herself between Tucker and Rafe, as if she were worried my husband was about to pounce on the sergeant.

She didn't have to worry. Not only is Rafe unlikely to attack a man twice his age—not without a lot more provocation than he'd been given—but his voice was perfectly pleasant, if with that same edge of steel as Grimaldi's, when he nodded politely. "Tucker."

Tucker smirked. "You gotten yourself in trouble again, boy?"

Grimaldi opened her mouth, and seemed to think better of what she'd been about to say. Instead she looked at Rafe, who replied, fairly nicely under the circumstances, "Every day."

Tucker switched his attention to Grimaldi. "Need any help, Chief?"

"No," Grimaldi said. "The Colliers were just leaving." She gave Rafe a nod and me a tight smile. Neither of us mentioned anything about seeing one another later. The details were already worked out, and I guess no one wanted to mention it in front of Tucker. "Come on back." She gestured for him to precede her into the sanctum.

He strutted across the lobby, and would have clipped Rafe in the upper arm with his shoulder had my husband not moved out of the way. I could see his eyes fire for a second as he did it, but the flicker died down immediately.

The door closed behind Grimaldi and Tucker, and he turned to me. "Let's go."

I nodded. I had questions, but they could wait until we were in the car. No sense in talking in front of the girl cop on duty at the desk. She'd probably report whatever we said back to Tucker.

By the time I had her car seat clicked into the back of the Volvo, Carrie was starting to make noises, and as I slipped into the passenger seat, I told Rafe, "Let's go to the mansion. She's going to be hungry when she wakes up, and I can feed her in peace and quiet."

I couldn't go around flashing my boobs in public, especially here in Maury County, without it getting back to my mother. Who'd have something to say about it.

Rafe nodded. The car was already running, and he reversed out of the parking space and headed for the entrance to the parking lot.

"Mother might be there, too," I added, although I wasn't sure whether that was an inducement or the opposite. I wasn't even sure why I mentioned it.

When I first got involved with Rafe, Mother had been dead set against it. On a list of eligible bachelors she could imagine her youngest daughter getting involved with, Rafe would be very close to the bottom, if not off the page altogether.

And that's the way it had been up until the day I was supposed to marry him but didn't, since someone had kidnapped the groom while I'd been sleeping. Rafe had come out of that ordeal with a patchwork of knife wounds across his chest and stomach, and one particularly nasty cut clear through one arm, where the psycho who was torturing him had kept him pinned to the table with a knife driven through his forearm and into the tabletop.

If I think too hard about it, it still has the power to make me feel queasy.

At any rate, Mother had seen him in the aftermath of that experience, and had seen him sideline the injuries and the pain to track down the man who had hurt him, and who had killed a handful of working girls, and who came close to killing Mother herself and Rafe's son David... and something had changed. Now he was pretty close to her favorite person. She thought the world of him, and while a year ago she would have taken every opportunity to tell me I could do better, now she was giving me the impression that nothing I did was good enough for him.

Rafe's lips curved. "I like your mama."

"She likes you, too," I said.

He shot me a look. "Never thought you'd see the day, huh?"

I shook my head. "I'm glad she changed her mind, but in all honesty, I wouldn't have been surprised if she'd held a grudge for years. And speaking of grudges and years..."

Rafe made a noise that was halfway between a snort and a laugh. "Caught that, did you?"

"It was hard to miss," I said. "I guess Sergeant Tucker was someone you used to run into when you were younger?"

Back in the days when he was the scourge of Sweetwater and Maury County.

"He arrested me in Dusty's Bar when I was eighteen," Rafe said.

Ah.

It was a deceptively simple statement, but one that held a

whole lot of information for anyone who knew a little about his background.

The summer Rafe was eighteen and just out of high school, LaDonna Collier had been involved with a man named Billy Scruggs. And one day that summer, Billy had taken his fists to LaDonna, probably not for the first time. The difference was that this time, when Rafe had come home for a visit and found her beaten and bloody, he'd gone to Dusty's Bar in Columbia to confront Billy, and had ended up putting the older man in the hospital.

He hadn't come through it unscathed himself, either. Billy had been a big guy, still in reasonable shape for his age, and had inflicted some damage on Rafe, too, in the process of fighting him off. But there was no question who had started the fight, and the outcome was that Rafe was arrested and charged with assault and battery, and sentenced to five years in Riverbend Correctional Facility.

Where the TBI found him, and organized his release into their care.

"Sergeant Tucker arrested you after the fight with Billy?"

Rafe nodded. "He wasn't a sergeant then. Wasn't the first time we'd run into each other, neither."

I wasn't surprised. Rafe's teenage years had been one long string of drinking and fighting and joyriding and being talked to by the police. I had thought the law enforcement encounters had been mostly limited to run-ins with Sheriff Satterfield in Sweetwater, but I guess the Columbia PD had been involved, too, from time to time.

"I'm going to guess Sergeant Tucker isn't familiar with your exploits since he arrested you," I said.

"Guess not." He maneuvered the Volvo south on the Columbia Highway.

"Grimaldi might set him straight." If Rafe's name came up

in the conversation Tucker and Grimaldi were probably in the middle of right now, and I had to assume that it would.

Or maybe not. If Tucker didn't bring it up, maybe Grimaldi wouldn't. I guess it depended on whether Tucker could resist the opportunity to put in his two cents worth or not.

Did the cops at the Columbia PD know that their new chief of police wanted to hire Rafe? Or hadn't that news gotten around yet?

I could make a good guess that Tucker wouldn't be in favor. Patrick Nolan, on the other hand—my sister Darcy's boyfriend—and his partner, Officer Lupe Vasquez, had no problems with Rafe. I guess it came down to the people who remembered him from before, and those who didn't.

"Dunno that that'd make a difference," Rafe said, and he could be right about that. It had taken Sheriff Satterfield a while to come around, even after he knew what Rafe had been doing all those years. They were on better terms now—the sheriff had even apologized for some of his earlier behavior—but it had taken Rafe proving himself in person, and not just the knowledge of his exploits on behalf of the TBI, before the sheriff changed his tune. Likely it would be the same with anyone else who remembered Rafe from the old days.

"I'm sure this didn't make it any more likely that you'll take Grimaldi's offer," I said, as we zoomed south toward Sweetwater. Beulah's Meat'n Three was just coming up on the left, the *OPEN* sign cheerfully lit in the window, and the parking lot full of cars.

Rafe shot me a look. "I don't want the job. I don't wanna come back here, where everybody thinks they know me and nobody's gonna let go of the past."

Well, that was plain enough, anyway.

"But I gotta have a job. You and Carrie depend on me. I gotta be able to take care of you."

"You can take care of us in Nashville," I said. "There are jobs you can get there. They probably won't pay as well as this," the salary Grimaldi had mentioned was more than adequate compared to what Rafe could make in some menial job in Nashville, "but we'd be OK."

I twisted in the seat to look at him, to make sure he could see my face. "I just want to be with you. And I want you to be happy. If being here would make you miserable, I don't want to be here."

Rafe nodded.

"But now you have the details. And you can talk to Grimaldi more tonight. And when we go home tomorrow morning," back to Nashville, "at least you'll know exactly what you're turning down."

Rafe nodded.

"And if this isn't what you want," and after running into Tucker and getting a small taste of his attitude and what might be coming down the pike if Rafe did decide to move back here and go to work for Grimaldi, it would be hard to blame him, "we'll figure something else out."

Rafe nodded.

We drove in silence a minute.

"The SWAT team?" I said.

His lips curved. "Don't you think it'd be kinda fun?"

"For you, maybe. Not so much for me."

He gave me a quick look. "I don't imagine the situations they get into are all that dangerous, darlin'. Not down here."

"You'd rather be on the SWAT team than be a detective?" The driveway to the mansion was coming up on the right, and I pointed.

Rafe nodded. "Less chance I'll run into anybody I know. Or at least less chance they'll recognize me."

"I think you'd be a pretty good investigator." And Grimaldi

obviously did, too.

"I'm pretty good with weapons and tactics, too," Rafe said, turning the Volvo into the driveway and up toward the house.

There'd be no argument from me on that score. "If being on the SWAT team is what it would take to get you here, I think both Grimaldi and I would put you on the SWAT team. That doesn't mean we both wouldn't prefer something else. But it's up to you, ultimately."

He nodded as he pulled the car to a stop at the bottom of the staircase leading up to the front door. "We can talk about it later."

"You don't want Mother's input?"

"No," Rafe said. "I know what your mama's gonna say."

So did I. "I'll get the baby," I said, opening my door. "You get the stuff."

Rafe nodded. I swung my legs out just as the front door opened to the sound of joyous barking, and a gray bullet shot down the steps to greet us.

Back in the fall, when we'd been in Sweetwater for the Skinner investigations, I had found a dog. Or she had found me. Or maybe it was mutual.

Pearl had lived with Robbie Skinner, chained up under his trailer in the hills near the Devil's Backbone. Rafe and I had found her the morning we found Robbie. He'd been dead, Pearl hadn't, and a few days later, I'd brought her back to the mansion. It was Mother who had named her, after a Chihuahua she had as a child.

The current Pearl was no Chihuahua. She was a stocky, big-headed, square-jawed pitbull mix with a lot of teeth and what would look like a terrifying canine grin to anyone who didn't know and love her.

Robbie had trained her to do dog fighting. We were hoping that love and care and enough food and treats would turn her back into the sweet and devoted pet she'd been destined to be from the beginning.

And with a few minor setbacks, things were working out pretty well. She was still fiercely protective, and suspicious of anyone she didn't know, but she loved Mother with slobbering devotion, and when it came time for me and Rafe to go back to Nashville—this was before we had Carrie—Pearl had chosen to stay here. Now, I guess, she was moving with Mother to Sheriff Satterfield's house.

Or maybe not. It hadn't occurred to me to ask whether the sheriff was taking on Pearl as well as Mother. If he wasn't, she might have to come back to Nashville with us. And might have to stay there, unless Rafe decided to come here.

But that was a question for later. Now she was bounding down the staircase barking a greeting, her tongue flapping. Behind her, Mother stepped into the doorway and shaded her eyes against the midday sun.

After a moment, she smiled. "Rafael! It's good to see you. And you brought the baby. Hello, Savannah."

You'll notice the order of importance there. I smiled back. "Hello, Mother. We drove down so Rafe could talk to Tamara Grimaldi. And now I need a place to nurse the baby."

Carrie had woken up when I hauled the car seat out of the Volvo, and was gearing up to start screaming for sustenance. "Shhhh," I told her. "We're here. Just another minute."

Pearl came bounding around the car. She had gone to greet Rafe first, maybe because he looks the most threatening. Unlike Mother, Pearl actually prefers me to my husband. And he must have convinced her that he was no threat, because now she came to see me. She wagged her stubby tail ecstatically, making the entire back half of her body wiggle.

"Hello, sweetheart," I told her, and made her wag harder.

And then she noticed Carrie, and stuck her head into the

baby carrier.

For a second my heart stopped. I love Pearl, but I do worry about her and things that are smaller than she is. I bought her a stuffed toy once, and she reduced it to shreds in a few seconds.

Rafe made a move toward us, too, but it turned out to be unnecessary. Pearl sniffed Carrie delicately, and withdrew her head. Once she was clear of the carrier, she gave another bark.

Carrie scrunched up her face and let out a wail, and Pearl started dancing around, barking harder.

Mother clapped her hands to get Pearl's attention. "Biscuit, Pearl! Biscuit!"

And Pearl, her love of Mother only eclipsed by her love of biscuits, went bounding back up the stairs and through the open door.

"I'll take care of her," Mother said and turned away. I could hear the clicking of her heels fade away across the foyer and down the hall toward the kitchen.

Rafe slammed the door on his side of the car and came around to my side, with Carrie's diaper bag over one shoulder, her bouncy seat under the other arm, and the big bag with her extra changes of clothes, extra blankets, extra diapers, extra bottles and pacifiers and all the other things a baby needs, in his hand. "I'll get the crib tonight. Ready?"

I nodded, and headed up the stairs with Carrie while he followed with the rest of her stuff.

Inside, he dumped it all on the floor of the foyer and shut the door behind us. January in Tennessee is often no big deal, but this week, at least, it was too cold to leave the door open. There was snow in the forecast for next week.

From the kitchen, we could hear Mother admonish Pearl to sit like a good girl, and the scrabbling of Pearl's nails as she obeyed.

"Good girl," Mother said, and then there was the crunching

of a dog biscuit.

Mother's heels came clicking back up the hallway toward us. "You didn't tell me you were coming."

"It was spur of the moment," I said, in the middle of unhooking my squalling child from the car seat holding her captive. "Rafe lost his job."

Mother's eyes widened, and she turned to him. "After everything you've done for them?"

For once, Mother and I were in complete accord. "Can you believe it?" I said, handing Carrie off to Rafe for a second so I could shrug out of my coat before taking her back. "I have to feed the baby. I'm going to go sit in the parlor."

Mother nodded. "Come with me, Rafael. I have coffee." She tucked her hand through his arm. A year ago she would have chosen to fall on her posterior rather than let him touch her, so it was nice to see the change. Perhaps a little less nice that she towed him down the hallway away from me, but I can't have coffee anyway at the moment, and it was nice of them to drink theirs where I wouldn't be tempted.

"Bring me a glass of something," I told his back, and he nodded, but without turning around. I watched for a second more, just because the view was nice, and then I took Carrie into the parlor, where I sat down on great-great-aunt Ida's peach velvet loveseat and lifted my shirt. Carrie rooted like a piglet before she latched on, and I leaned back against the back of the sofa and closed my eyes.

Footsteps a few minutes later was Rafe, bringing me a glass of orange juice. When I opened my eyes, he was standing next to the coffee table with that same expression he often gets when he watches Carrie nurse: half amused, half amazed, and somewhere between turned on and tender.

I smiled back at him. "Mother being nice to you?"

"Very." He put the orange juice on the table, careful to nestle a coaster underneath the glass first. "She just spent a long time telling me how brainless all of the TBI must be for letting me go."

"Hard to argue with that."

He nodded. "Need anything else?"

I shook my head. "Go back to Mother. Let her tell you how wonderful you are. I'll be there when Carrie's finished."

He took himself off down the hallway, but not before he'd given the baby and what she was doing another of those special looks.

I closed my eyes again.

By the time Carrie had concluded her business and I made my way down the hallway to the kitchen, Mother and Rafe seemed to have concluded theirs, too. At least the one that involved the many failings of the TBI. They were discussing Pearl.

"Bob doesn't mind if I bring her," Mother was saying, "although there's no question she likes me better than Bob."

Rafe nodded. "She likes Savannah better'n me, too. No surprise, when Robbie didn't treat her right."

"She's welcome there," Mother said, "but I don't think Bob's feelings would be hurt if she didn't make the move with me."

"We can take her to Nashville with us," I said from the doorway, and they both turned and looked at me.

There was a second before Mother said, "Nashville? But…"

She stopped before saying anything else, but it was too late. What she hadn't said was obvious.

"We're still thinking," I said. "That's why we're here, to talk to Tamara Grimaldi about what it would be like if Rafe went to work for the Columbia PD."

Mother nodded. And waited.

"She offered him a job in criminal investigations. He'd rather be on the SWAT team."

Mother turned to look at him. His lips curved.

"Grimaldi said she'd rather have him on the SWAT team than not have him at all." I wandered into the kitchen and over to the island with the baby in the crook of one arm and the juice glass in the other. "I'd be fine with either. The idea of SWAT is a little scary, but in a quiet place like this, I'm sure the SWAT team doesn't end up doing anything very dangerous."

Mother shook her head, and watched as Rafe reached out to take the baby from me. "Hello, beautiful," he told her before putting her up on his shoulder and keeping here there with one big hand that covered her from butt to the back of her head. Carrie squeaked, and Pearl's ears twitched.

"Would being part of the," Mother paused delicately, as if putting it in quotes, "SWAT team make it more difficult for you to spend time with Savannah and Caroline?"

Rafe shrugged. "No law enforcement's nine-to-five. When somebody gets killed, you work until you solve the case. When somebody starts shooting up a concert, you go to work, even if it's midnight on a Saturday."

And being an investigator instead of on the SWAT team would make no difference to whether he'd get dragged out of bed at night.

"I just want you to be happy," I told him. "Do whatever would make you want to get up in the morning and go to work."

His mouth curved. I flushed, since I knew exactly what he was thinking. Mother cleared her throat delicately, carefully not looking at either of us. "How about some lunch?"

Rafe chuckled. "Sure. I can always eat."

I nodded. I'm sure I looked hungry, too.

Four

Halfway through lunch my phone rang, and I glanced at the display and excused myself. By now we had moved the bouncy seat into the kitchen and put Carrie in it—up on the counter, away from Pearl—and Rafe was digging into a roast beef sandwich Mother had made for him. She was nibbling daintily on a smaller one herself, with a ruff of lettuce and a wafer-thin circle of red onion peeking out the side.

When I put down my own sandwich—also decorated with lettuce and onion—they both looked at me. "Alexandra Puckett," I said. "I'll be back in a minute."

It's rude to take a personal phone call in front of other people. Especially a personal phone call from someone one of the people present doesn't know.

"The young pregnant girl?" Mother asked as I walked away.

Rafe nodded. And that was all I saw before I ducked into the hallway and put the phone to my ear. "What's going on?"

"Jamal told me Rafe got fired," Alexandra said, which was getting straight to the point. "Are you OK?"

"Oh." If I'd thought about it, I should have realized that she'd hear the news. "Yes, we're fine. In Sweetwater right now, actually. Having lunch with Mother."

And since I didn't know whether Rafe had told Jamal and the others about the job offer from Grimaldi before—or after—all this went down, I didn't mention it. "What about you? Aren't you in school?"

"Lunch," Alexandra said. "And I gotta go back to class soon. Will you be back by Saturday? Can we meet for lunch?"

I supposed we could. Rafe and I weren't doing anything else. Rafe would probably spend the day helping Clayton and José load up their belongings before waving them off in two different directions.

I had thought that maybe Jamal would have invited Alexandra to accompany him to our house Friday night, but it seemed not. And since he hadn't, I wasn't about to bring it up.

"Sure," I said instead. "I can do lunch."

"Wanna meet at the FinBar?" It was a sports bar just down the street from the real estate office where I'd been hanging my shingle for the past couple of years, and we'd met there before.

"That works." We settled on a time—high noon—and I wandered back into the kitchen and put the phone on the island before picking up my sandwich again.

"Everything all right?" Mother asked.

I swallowed. "Of course. She'd heard about what happened. We're having lunch together on Saturday." I glanced at Rafe. "I figured you'd probably be spending the day getting Clayton and José ready to go."

He nodded, his mouth full of roast beef.

"How long are you staying in Sweetwater?" Mother wanted to know, wiping the tips of her fingers on a napkin.

I told her we'd be here until tomorrow morning. "If that's OK with you. We're having dinner with Grimaldi tonight. Somewhere that isn't the police department." Somewhere it might be easier to talk more freely.

"Of course, darling," Mother said, with a glance at Rafe. "You're always welcome here."

Good to know. Especially when, for a long time, that hadn't been the case.

"You're having dinner with the sheriff, I assume?"

Mother nodded. "Perhaps we'll see you there."

"Unlikely," I said, since Mother's go-to restaurant for dinner with the sheriff is the Wayside Inn. "We're going to Beulah's." Where Mother wouldn't want to be caught dead, amid all that fat and fryer grease. Not to mention the less than upscale clientele.

"Oh." She gave a gentle shudder. I glanced at Rafe, whose eyes were lit with amusement.

"Beulah's is more my speed," he told her. "And it's easier for Tammy to get to."

Grimaldi's rental was in Columbia, north of us, while the Wayside Inn—which really was a wayside inn some two hundred years ago—was south of Sweetwater, on the way to Pulaski.

Mother looked taken aback. Not by the fact that he preferred Beulah's to the Wayside Inn. That probably didn't come as a shock, even if she wasn't predisposed to understanding it. "You call Detective Grimaldi—Chief Grimaldi—Tammy?"

"Not to her face," I said, while Rafe smirked. "Even Dix... I mean, even her friends call her Tamara." And I've always called her Detective, although now I supposed I'd have to stop doing that.

Mother nodded, but not without a worried little wrinkle between her brows. Maybe it was the mention of my brother. Although with Grimaldi here in Maury County now, I had no idea how long Mother could turn a blind eye to what was going on.

Not that I had much knowledge about what was going on. Grimaldi and Dix had become friendly after my sister-in-law was murdered a year and some months ago. It happened in Nashville, so Grimaldi caught the case. Or grabbed it, once she realized that Sheila was related to me.

But of course Dix wasn't in any kind of position to jump into another relationship then, so while I started to see them together occasionally, I had no real clear idea of what their relationship was. Furthermore, I had absolutely no idea how much Mother knew, or suspected, about any of it. She knew Grimaldi and I were friends. She knew Grimaldi and Rafe were friendly. But I had no clue whether she knew that Grimaldi and Dix were involved.

If she didn't, I guessed she was in for a rude awakening.

All the more reason to stick around, or to move here, to be on hand for the big reveal. It had the potential to be almost as entertaining as when Mother realized I was serious about Rafe.

Which hadn't been all that entertaining at the time, admittedly. Not from my perspective. Although, since he and I had laid a lot of the groundwork, hopefully Dix would have an easier time introducing Grimaldi to the family than I had, when I fell in love with Rafe.

And that was if I hadn't totally misconstrued their relationship, of course. But seeing that Grimaldi had given up what seemed to have been a good job that she enjoyed in Nashville, so she could come to Columbia and be closer to Dix, I didn't think I had.

"You've known her a while," Mother said, which sounded like the beginning of a fishing expedition.

I nodded. "Since the day we found Brenda Puckett's body in Mrs. Jenkins's house. A year and a half ago now."

"She thought I did it," Rafe added, with a smirk.

"Only until she figured out who you were, and what you were up to." And it hadn't taken her long. "I was the one who spent several months worrying about having fallen in love with a criminal."

Mother clicked her tongue disapprovingly. "Savannah, dear..."

"He knows," I said. "Anyway, yes. We've known Grimaldi a while."

Mother pleated a corner of her napkin. "Bob seems quite impressed with her abilities."

He must be, to recommend her for the job. And at her age, too.

"She was a very good detective," I said. At least I'd always thought so. "And the city council must have been impressed, too, since they agreed to hire her."

Mother nodded. "I suppose she realizes that she'll have some challenges down here, that maybe she isn't used to from being in Nashville?"

Challenges? Such as there being no 24-hour drugstore, or the wine merchant was closed on Sundays? Or the fact that the murder rate dropped by roughly 98% as soon as she crossed the county line from Davidson to Maury?

And yes, I know there's a county between Davidson and Maury, too. Williamson County. The crime rate isn't high there either.

And then I realized what Mother was referring to. I have no idea how, with the way she was talking around the issue, but I got it.

"Oh. Yes, I'm sure she realizes that she'll have to deal with people like Sergeant Tucker." People who thought they knew more than they did. Or at least more than she did.

Mother's brows rose. They're very elegant brows. Everything about my mother is elegant. "Sergeant Tucker?"

"He was waiting for Grimaldi when we came out of her office," I said. "He recognized Rafe. Turns out he arrested him once. I'm sure he's told Grimaldi all about it."

"Prob'ly still talking," Rafe murmured, with a look at the kitchen clock.

I glanced over at him, and felt a corner of my mouth twitch.

"I'm sure he has plenty to say."

Mother looked from me to him and back. "Is this man going to be a problem for you, Rafael?"

"Not as far as Grimaldi's concerned," I said. "She knows all about Rafe already."

"Or at least whatever Tucker's likely to be able to tell her," my husband added. It was probably less than Grimaldi already knew. Certainly less than I knew.

"Well, that's what I'm talking about," Mother said. "Not this man Tucker specifically, but people like him. People—older men—who think they know more because they've lived their lives in this little town, and she's an outsider, and a woman, and younger, and they think they can push her around."

I never would have suspected my mother of such feminist views. Even if, in this case, they were misplaced. Kind, but misplaced. "I wouldn't worry about it," I told her.

"Tammy don't intimidate easy," Rafe added. "And she don't take crap from nobody. As I'm sure Tucker's finding out."

"Will he make trouble for you?" After a second, Mother added, "If you go to work there?"

"He can try." The corners of Rafe's mouth lifted. "I don't intimidate easy, neither."

No, he didn't. Although it occurred to me, as probably it should have occurred to me before, that maybe Grimaldi wanted Rafe here not only because she likes him—and me—and was sorry to leave us behind in Nashville, but because going into a new department full of people like Tucker, she might have anticipated the problem Mother was worried about, and had thought that Rafe would be a good someone to have her back should she need it.

Her staff would come to respect her whether they wanted to or not—or I suspected they'd find themselves taking early retirement—but while she got situated, and dealt with what might be a lot of pushback, she might want to have someone on her side she could rely on to do the job the way she wanted it done, without any backtalk.

I didn't mention it, since I didn't want it to influence Rafe's decision. If he wanted to come to work here, it would have to be because he wanted to, and not because Grimaldi could use the support. But it was something for me to keep in mind, if nothing else.

"What are the two of you planning to do this afternoon?" Mother asked, as she got to her feet and started to clean up after lunch. Rafe made to get to his feet, too, to help her, and she put her hand on his shoulder to keep him there. "No, stay. I've got this."

Yet another reminder of how much things had changed.

"I should prob'ly go see my grandma," Rafe said, with a look at me.

I nodded. "We can't come down here and not do that. And if we're going into town anyway, we should probably stop by the law office and see Dix and Darcy and Jonathan, too. And Catherine, if she's there."

"Charlotte's back," Mother told me, in the process of loading roast beef and horseradish and ruffled lettuce back into the refrigerator.

"Charlotte?" My best friend during high school. She had moved to, of all places, Charlotte, and had married a cosmetic surgeon, and had a couple of kids. "You mean she's home for the holidays, right?"

The holidays were over, granted. But Charlotte's parents, the Albertsons, still lived in town. And Charlotte's kids weren't old enough to be in school yet, I thought, so getting them back for that wouldn't be an issue.

Mother shook her head. "I got the impression she's back to stay."

"What about Richard?"

"I didn't get the impression Richard was with her," Mother said primly.

My eyes widened. More. "Charlotte left Richard?"

The last time I'd seen her had been at my wedding. We hadn't had a lot of time to talk. The time before that had been during our ten year high school reunion in May, when we'd talked a lot, but mostly about the fact that I was living in sin with Rafe and had gotten myself knocked up by him. Charlotte couldn't understand how the girl I'd been could have done such a thing, and I'd had an impossible time explaining to her that I wasn't the girl I'd been anymore.

While there might have been subtle indications that the honeymoon was over—theirs, after four or five years of marriage—I'd gotten absolutely no impression that Charlotte was thinking of leaving Richard. "Are you sure it isn't just an extended visit? Maybe one of her parents is ill."

"If so, I haven't heard about it," Mother said, and closed the fridge door with a decisive flick of the wrist. "Although it's certainly possible. If you go and see her, you'll find out."

I would, and then I could tell Mother. Which was the implication here. While Mother would strenuously object if I called it gossiping, she's just as interested in what the neighbors are doing as any small town housewife.

"Fine by me," Rafe said with a shrug. "Less'n you think she'd be more likely to spill if I wasn't there."

That was also possible. "We'll figure it out when we get there. But you may have to make an excuse to give us thirty minutes alone, if she doesn't seem inclined to talk while you're there."

Rafe nodded, scooting off the chair at the island. "Ready?"

I guess I was.

"You can leave the baby with me," Mother offered, "unless

you think your grandmother or Charlotte would like to see her."

That actually sounded nice, and it was also nice that Mother wanted to spend time with her granddaughter. However — "I'm sure Audrey and Mrs. J would like to see her. Charlotte may not care."

Mother nodded.

"If we move here, you'll get plenty of opportunities to babysit, though."

"I'll get her," Rafe said, and headed in the direction of the baby and bouncy seat, but not before he'd stopped next to Mother and bent to drop a kiss on her cheek. "Thanks for lunch."

He moved on. Mother just stood there for a second before she caught me looking and flushed delicately. I smiled. After a moment, she smiled back.

"We'll be back later," I said, as Rafe came toward me with Carrie cradled against his chest and the bouncy seat dangling from one hand.

He passed the baby to me. "I'll carry the stuff upstairs before we go."

I nodded. It would give me a chance to use the restroom. "Here." I handed the baby on to Mother. "Hold her for a minute."

I followed Rafe down the hallway and up the stairs. "I'm just going to stop in across the hall."

"You can call it the bathroom," he told me over his shoulder. "I don't mind."

Of course not. Being in my mother's house tended to bring out old habits. "You need to go before we leave?"

"It couldn't hurt." He passed into our bedroom, the room I'd slept in growing up, with our stuff, while I walked through the door across the hallway.

When I came out, he was waiting. "I'll be right down."

Mother was waiting in the foyer, and I plucked Carrie out of her arms and turned to the car seat. "She's beautiful," Mother said.

I might be a touch biased, but I think so, too. She has Rafe's coloring—the golden skin and dark curls, with thick, sooty lashes and perfect little brows—but her eyes are blue, and showing no inclination to turn. I was told at the hospital that they might, that a lot of babies are born with blue eyes that turn brown later, and given her coloring, I shouldn't be surprised if they did… but so far, they've stayed blue. I'm hoping they'll continue to do so, since it would be nice to see a little of myself in my daughter, too. Otherwise, she's all Rafe.

"Thank you." I got her settled and strapped in. She blinked up at me with those long, thick lashes. "She looks like Rafe."

"She has your eyes," Mother said, and looked up as the man in question came down the stairs. "All ready?"

He nodded. "We'll be back later. We don't have to be at Beulah's till six-thirty." He stuck one arm and then the other through the sleeves of the leather jacket I held out, and grabbed the car seat with the baby.

"Have a good time," Mother told us, and shut the door against the cold when we were through and out. We clicked the baby carrier into the back seat of the car, and with Rafe behind the wheel, headed down the driveway and south.

The Martin Mansion sits on a little knoll north of town, outside Sweetwater proper. After you pass some more recent houses—recent as in nineteen-fifties and -sixties—you get to the city limits, and once you're past the Oak Street Cemetery, the older neighborhoods start to crop up, full of Victorian houses and Craftsman bungalows and little cottages, all built in the first half of the twentieth century.

Audrey lives there, in a little Folk Victorian she inherited from her parents. These days, Mrs. Jenkins occupies the second bedroom. My Aunt Regina and Uncle Sid live nearby. And the Albertsons have a house on the next street over, where Charlotte grew up.

"Where d'you wanna go first?" Rafe wanted to know, as we approached town. "Audrey's at the store, prob'ly."

Probably. She runs Audrey's on the Square, the only designer boutique in the county, and maybe all of Middle Tennessee, outside of Nashville and Franklin. Mother does all her shopping there. And it was a weekday, so chances were the store would be open. Mrs. J might be there too, or she might be home by herself.

"How's your grandmother doing these days? Is she well enough to be home by herself, or does Audrey have to take her to work with her?"

Mrs. Jenkins has dementia, or something of that nature. Half the time, she has no idea who Rafe is. Or rather, she doesn't know that he's Rafe, and thinks he's his father Tyrell instead. During those times, she thinks I'm LaDonna, Rafe's mother. It's all very convoluted. Since Rafe added his son David to the mix—David is almost fourteen—things have gotten even more confusing.

While she lived on her own in Nashville, she'd wander off occasionally, and get lost. Rafe hired a nurse for a while, but when she got killed—long story—Mrs. Jenkins ended up in a home. For her own safety, pretty much, since Rafe wasn't around to make sure nothing happened to her, and he and I weren't together yet. And once we were, Mrs. Jenkins was happy where she was, so we left her there.

But that situation came to a head before the holidays, and since then Mrs. J has been living in Sweetwater with Audrey, the daughter of her long-lost sister Oneida.

Another long story.

"She seems like she's doing all right," Rafe said. "I told

Audrey to call me if there was a problem, and she hasn't."

"So you have no idea whether your grandmother would be at the store with Audrey or home by herself?"

He shook his head.

"Why don't we just stop and check? If she's at home, we can visit with her for a while, and then go knock on the Albertsons' door. If she isn't there, we'll go see Charlotte and then see both Audrey and Mrs. J at the store." And after that, stick our heads through the doors at Martin & McCall to say hi to Darcy, Dix, and Jonathan. And maybe Catherine.

"Works for me," Rafe said. "This way?"

I nodded, and watched the old houses go by as he drove slowly down the picket-fence-lined street toward Audrey's little Victorian.

There was no answer there, though, so Mrs. Jenkins must be at the boutique with Audrey. At least I hoped she was, and not wandering around somewhere on her own. We drove the couple of blocks to Charlotte's parents' house instead.

It's another Victorian, but big and white with two stories. Like a lot of the houses in the area, it was surrounded by a picket fence. Mr. Albertson, Charlotte's father, mustn't have had the time to take the Christmas decorations down yet, because there were still wreaths on the downstairs windows and a swag of greenery draping the porch railing.

Two small children in puffy winter coats—one pink, one navy—were running in circles on the dry grass, shrieking, while a figure in a brown fur coat sat huddled on the porch steps.

At first I thought it was Charlotte. They were her children, or so I assumed. She had two, a boy and a girl, and these looked like they were in the right age range.

But once the car stopped and I got out, I saw that it wasn't Charlotte at all, it was her mother. Mrs. Albertson looked exhausted, and not at all happy to see me. For a second it looked like she thought about disappearing up the steps and inside the house without greeting me, but if she did, she must have thought better of it. When I approached the gate, she got up and came to meet me. "Savannah." Her gaze moved past me to the Volvo, but there was nothing to see there—not yet, anyway—so she turned her attention back to me.

"Hi, Mrs. Albertson," I said politely. "Happy New Year."

"Likewise," Mrs. Albertson said, without making any effort to sound like she meant it.

I didn't get the impression she was trying to be rude, in case you wondered. It was more like she was too tired to care.

"My mother told me Charlotte's here. I wanted to stop by and say hi."

She'd started nodding when I mentioned Charlotte's name, and kept doing it after I stopped talking.

I looked past her at the house. "Is she inside?"

"She went to lunch," Mrs. Albertson said.

"Oh." And left her kids with her mother? "Who with?"

Mrs. Albertson shrugged. "I'll tell her you were here," she said, before her attention strayed beyond my shoulder again. Her eyes turned stony. From the reaction, and the noises behind me, I deduced that Rafe had opened his door and gotten out.

"Please do," I said lightly, since the last thing I wanted was any kind of unpleasantness. "We're only here until tomorrow morning. And we have dinner plans. But I could meet her for breakfast, maybe. If she wanted."

Mrs. Albertson nodded. "I'll tell her."

She glanced across my shoulder again. I thought about telling her she was safe, that he wasn't about to come around the car and attack—as if he's some kind of dangerous beast—but I figured she wouldn't get the joke. So I just thanked her and turned back to the car. Rafe gave her a polite nod—one she didn't acknowledge with anything but a long stare—and got back into the car. I took the couple of steps to the curb and did the same.

"That was weird," I said when we were moving again, away from Mrs. Albertson and her house and her shrieking grandchildren.

He shrugged. "Looked pretty normal to me."

"I don't mean the way she treated you." But yes, that was pretty normal, sadly. He'd seen a lot of that kind of thing growing up. *And will see more of it if he comes back here to live,* a little voice in the back of my head reminded me. I ignored it. For now. "She said Charlotte had gone out to lunch. And she looked exhausted."

"Maybe something's wrong," Rafe said, turning the Volvo around the next corner and making his way back to Oak Street and the town square.

"She looked like she was so tired she had no idea what she was doing. She started nodding and didn't seem like she was able to stop again. I hope Mr. Albertson isn't ill, and that's why Charlotte's home."

"Wouldn't your mama know if somebody's ill?"

I would have thought so—there isn't much that goes on in Sweetwater that my mother misses—but… "She didn't mention it earlier," I said. "Maybe Charlotte will call me and I can ask."

Rafe nodded, as we pulled onto the square and started looking for a parking space.

Five

The Sweetwater town square looks just like the town square in a hundred other little Southern towns. There's a statue in the middle, of some long-forgotten Civil War hero—a conflict usually referred to as The War Against Northern Aggression in these parts—and then cobblestones and four walls of small, one-story, turn-of-the-last-century commercial buildings lining the square on four sides, with parking in front. We found an empty slot a few spaces down from Audrey's boutique, and Rafe pulled the Volvo in there, between a pickup truck and what I recognized as my sister Darcy's Honda.

"I'll get the baby," I said, since she was on my side of the car. That way, when I'm driving, I'm able to look sideways into the back, and see her.

Rafe nodded. "Audrey's first?"

Fine by me. I hauled the car seat—and Carrie—out of the back of the Volvo and headed for the entrance to the boutique.

A little bell tinkled above the door when we walked in, and a few seconds later, Audrey came loping toward us.

She's been my mother's best friend since Mother came to Sweetwater as a young bride thirty-some years ago. And very nice of Audrey, too, seeing as Mother had married the love of Audrey's life. Despite that, Audrey befriended Mother and they've been inseparable ever since.

Except for the month or two this fall, when all this came out and Mother needed some time to process it all. But they're back to being friends now, and Audrey looked delighted to see us.

"Savannah! And Rafe!" She zeroed in on the car seat. "And you brought the baby!"

"I know we were just here," I said, since we had in fact been in Sweetwater just over a week ago, for Mother's usual Christmas Eve shindig and dinner the following day. "Rafe came down to talk to Tamara Grimaldi."

Audrey was busy peering into the car seat. "She's precious! And she's getting so big!"

Not that much bigger than she'd been a week ago, surely?

"We stopped by the house," I said, while Audrey reached out a long finger tipped with red, to tickle Carrie's cheek. "Your house, I mean. We thought Mrs. Jenkins might be there."

Audrey shook her head and straightened. "She's in the back. Working on a coloring book."

She gestured us to follow.

She and my mother look totally different. Mother's a little shorter than me, soft and pretty, with blue eyes and blond hair that she keeps blond by regular visits to the spa. She dresses in soft silk blouses and expensive-looking skirts and slacks.

Audrey, meanwhile, is close to six feet tall in her heels, and there's nothing soft about her. Or not about the way she looks, at any rate. She has black hair in a sharp wedge to her chin, and cheekbones for days, and today she was dressed in severe black and white, with a pair of fire engine red, patent leather shoes with platform soles on her feet. The four inch heels did nothing to slow her down as she legged it toward the back of the store.

Mrs. Jenkins was indeed sitting at a desk in the small back room, with a box of colored pencils and a coloring book in front of her. When Audrey came in, she looked up, and then she caught sight of us, and her mouth split in a wide, toothless smile. "Baby!"

She was talking to Rafe, not Carrie. He smiled back, and brushed past me to walk over and go down on one knee next to her chair, where she could put her wrinkled hand on his cheek and head and reassure herself that he was real, and here.

"Have you been to see your mother?" Audrey asked me, while Rafe and his grandmother were getting reacquainted. It was too soon to tell whether she knew who he was, or whether she thought he was Tyrell, but she was happy to see him, anyway, so that was something. One of these days, she might not realize she knows him at all, but that day wasn't today.

I nodded. "We drove down this morning, and stopped in Columbia so Rafe could talk to Tamara Grimaldi. Then we drove to the mansion and had lunch with Mother. Now we're here." I glanced at her. "Why do you ask? Is something going on?"

If anything was, I hadn't noticed it. Mother had behaved just as she always does.

But Audrey shook her head. "Just making sure. If you'd come here first, her feelings would have been hurt."

"It's nice of you to worry about that." Especially since Mother's actions after the big reveal about Dad and Audrey this fall hadn't been tender of Audrey's feelings at all.

"She's my best friend," Audrey said simply, as if none of that had ever happened. "And she's so happy about little Caroline."

She directed another look into the carrier, where Carrie had noticed a brightly colored stuffed elephant hanging from the handle of her car seat and was trying to reach it. Her hand-eye coordination wasn't all that yet, so it took effort, but eventually she managed to hit it and make it swing.

"She's smiling!" Audrey said.

She did look like she was smiling. But so many times I'd thought she was smiling, and been told it was just gas, that I was afraid to believe it. "You think?"

"Clear as day," Audrey proclaimed. "She's gorgeous,

Savannah." She glanced at Rafe, still kneeling next to his grandmother's chair, and added, "The two of you make beautiful babies."

She'd hear no argument from me.

Rafe turned to wave at me, and I brought myself and the baby carrier closer, so Mrs. J could see Carrie. She greeted me too with a toothless smile and a, "Hi, baby!" before she devoted her attention to the real baby.

I stepped away and turned back to Audrey, lowering my voice. "How is she doing?"

"Well enough," Audrey said. "I take her with me when I go to work in the morning. I'm afraid, if I leave her at the house alone, she'll get confused and wander off. She hasn't yet, but I haven't given her much opportunity to, either."

I nodded.

"But we're doing well. We're talking a lot about my mother, and what it was like when they were growing up. Things Mom never wanted to talk about."

No wonder, seeing as Audrey's mother had spent her entire adult life passing as white. Audrey knew she wasn't, of course. And Audrey's father. But no one else. And I imagined, to make the deception work, Oneida probably thought about, and talked about, her past as little as possible, even to the people closest to her.

"Mother told me Charlotte's in Sweetwater," I said, changing the subject. "Do you have any idea what's going on? Mother said she thought it wasn't a visit, but that Charlotte's here to stay. With both her kids."

"Have you spoken to her?"

I shook my head. "We drove by on our way from your house to here, and Mrs. Albertson was out in the yard with both the kids. But Charlotte wasn't there. Her mother said she'd gone to lunch. So I have no idea. Did she leave her husband?"

Audrey shrugged. "People are saying that she did. That that's why she's back here without him. But unless she's told someone that, I don't know how they can know."

I didn't, either. "I left a message with her mother to have Charlotte call me. If she does, I guess I'll find out."

"How long are you staying?"

I told her just until tomorrow morning. "We're meeting Grimaldi for dinner at Beulah's Meat'n Three. Then we'll spend the night with Mother and drive up tomorrow morning." I lowered my voice. "Rafe lost his job."

Audrey looked shocked.

"It didn't have anything to do with the job offer from Grimaldi. She said that if she'd known the TBI was thinking of letting him go, she'd have told him. Wendell didn't know, either. He resigned, too, when he found out."

"Good for him," Audrey said robustly.

I nodded. I think it was rather nice of Wendell, to be honest. He'd had a career at the TBI before Rafe come along, so neither of us would have blamed him for staying. "We came down to talk to Grimaldi about the job offer. Rafe wasn't really interested for as long as he had a job, but now that he doesn't, we should at least investigate it." Even if he wasn't really that interested now either.

"Is it something he can imagine doing?" Audrey wanted to know, with a glance at him. He had taken Carrie out of the car seat and given her to Mrs. Jenkins, who was holding on to her and beaming. "He didn't have an easy time growing up here. It's hard to imagine that he'll want to come back."

"He doesn't. Not really. Although he's willing to." I hesitated a second before I added, "I think it's a little different now, maybe. His grandmother's here, and you're here, and Darcy. He has family he didn't know he had. And then there's my family. Even Mother has finally accepted him. There are ties here. Not all bad ones. And Todd's getting married, so Rafe doesn't have to worry about him hanging around and trying to change my mind anymore…"

Audrey nodded. "For what it's worth, I'd love to have you both back in Sweetwater. And I know Aunt Tondalia would, too."

"We'll have to see what he decides," I said, and then turned my head as the bell above the door tinkled. "Sounds like you have a customer."

Audrey nodded. "Excuse me."

She legged it out of the back room and into the shop. I heard her voice, all solicitous charm. "Hello. Can I—?" And then it changed. "Oh. Charlotte."

I glanced at the threesome over by the desk. Mrs. J was holding the baby, and Carrie seemed just fine, blinking up at her great-grandmother. Rafe was right next to them both, making sure nothing went wrong. I could duck out for a minute.

I left an, "I'll be back," hanging in the air behind me as I pushed through the curtain into the boutique behind Audrey.

She and Charlotte were standing near the front door, and at first Charlotte didn't notice me. "I was wondering whether, perhaps, you needed some help…" she was saying, and then she stopped when she saw me coming. A flush crept up in her cheeks. "Savannah. I didn't realize you were here."

And if she had realized it, she wouldn't have stopped by. Or at least that was the very distinct impression I got.

"I'm just down for the day," I said, advancing. "I didn't expect to see you, either. Although Mother said you were in town. We stopped by your house on our way here."

"We?" Charlotte glanced over my shoulder toward the back of the store.

"Rafe's in the back with Caroline and Mrs. Jenkins. Visiting."

Charlotte nodded. "I heard she had moved to town. And that you're related." She glanced at Audrey, and quickly away.

"My aunt," Audrey said. "On my Mother's side."

There was an awkward few seconds while nobody spoke. "So how are you?" I asked brightly. "I haven't seen you in a while." Since the wedding, more specifically. June. "I don't think you were here yet when we came down for Mother's shindig on Christmas Eve."

Charlotte shook her head. "We didn't leave North Carolina until the day after Christmas."

And by then Rafe and I were heading back to Nashville.

"Is everything OK?" I asked.

Charlotte gave a sort of jerky shrug. "Nothing I haven't suspected for a while."

Ah. It had a familiar ring to it. But since Richard's infidelity — or whatever, but probably infidelity—wasn't something I felt like we needed to discuss in front of Audrey, I just said, "We're only here for the day. We're driving back to Nashville tomorrow morning. And we have plans for dinner. But if you wanted to grab some breakfast before we head out in the morning, we could talk."

"That's OK," Charlotte said, in a tone of voice that added, *"Not on your life."* "I don't want to keep you. I'm sure Rafe has to get back to work."

He didn't. But since I didn't feel like getting into that again — and since I was OK with giving her the easy out—I said, "Give me a call sometime, then. I'm only an hour away. And we may be spending more time in Sweetwater in the future, anyway."

Charlotte nodded. She gave a longing glace over her shoulder at the door to the outside. "I should go."

She hadn't finished asking Audrey whatever it was she'd come here to ask—for a job, it sounded like—but I didn't point it out. "Good to see you."

"You, too," Charlotte said, without meeting my eyes.

I didn't think it was personal. And for once, I wasn't inclined to see it as a rejection of Rafe, either. Charlotte had worked through that, or so I thought. No, this time I'm pretty sure it was just embarrassment and not wanting to talk to me about what was going wrong in her own marriage. Something had to be, if she was here and Richard was still in North Carolina.

But it was none of my business unless she wanted to tell me about it, so I just nodded. "See you around, then."

Charlotte nodded back, and slipped through the door and out. The chimes tinkled one final time, and then quieted.

"That was strange," Audrey commented.

No question. "Sounds like she's left her husband and is looking for a job."

Audrey nodded. "There's not enough work here for anyone but me. This business isn't exactly a money-making venture. I do it because it's fun, and because it serves a need, and because I can keep it in the black, mostly, from month to month. If that ever changes, I'll close up shop. But I'm not looking for employees."

I imagined most businesses around here weren't. That's usually the way it is in small towns. Charlotte might find it hard to get a foothold, after ten years away.

And so might I, for that matter. Although maybe my real estate career would get a boost from being back here, where everyone knew me. Unless I'd negated any clout the Martin name had ever had by marrying the last of the Colliers, and it was likely I had.

Oh, well. I could always write that bodice-ripper romance I'd been toying with in my head for the past year and a half.

I turned on my heel. "I'm going to go back and check on Rafe and Mrs. Jenkins."

"Right behind you," Audrey said, and we headed back to

the office.

We took our leave another twenty minutes or so later, after Mrs. Jenkins had had her fill of both Rafe and Carrie. She went back to coloring while Rafe carried the car seat with Carrie through the store and back into the nippy winter afternoon. Audrey closed the door behind us with a wave.

I looked around. "I guess we should probably say hi to Darcy and Dix while we're here. And Jonathan and Catherine, if they're there."

"No reason not to," Rafe agreed. The law offices of Martin and McCall are literally within spitting distance of Audrey's boutique, just on the other side of the Café on the Square.

As we walked the couple of yards, I looked around for Charlotte, but didn't see her. "Did you hear what was going on outside the curtain while you were back there with Mrs. J?"

"Charlotte came in," Rafe said, "looking for a job."

I nodded. "She must be back in Sweetwater to stay. Maybe Richard cheated on her, and she left."

"Or maybe Charlotte cheated and Richard kicked her out," Rafe answered.

I stared at him.

He arched a brow. "Didn't think about that, did you?"

I hadn't. I had jumped to the conclusion that it was Richard's fault. It's my default setting. When a marriage breaks up, it's the husband's fault. "You think she'd do that?"

He shrugged. "I dunno, darlin'. Didn't have much to do with her when we were kids. I have no idea whether she's the type to do something like that or not."

I wouldn't have thought so. But in thinking about it, I realized I didn't really know one way or the other anymore.

I had sensed tension back in May, during the class reunion. I'd gotten the impression that Charlotte wasn't happy with herself, with the way she looked—and after ten years and two kids, she couldn't expect to fit into her cheerleader uniform anymore, but maybe she did, anyway—and I'd also formed the idea that Richard was pressuring her to change. He was a cosmetic surgeon, so it seemed like something he'd do. Try to turn his wife into some work of art he was responsible for. But that could all be just supposition on my part. I didn't really know.

If Richard was making Charlotte feel inadequate, she might have sought approval somewhere else. And I knew just what that felt like. Not that I'd cheated. It had been two years between the time I divorced Bradley and when I took up with Rafe. But being with someone who liked me the way I was, and who didn't try to change me, and who loved me in spite of all those imperfections I'd always thought I had to hide, was a powerful aphrodisiac. If Charlotte's marriage was unhappy and her husband was a jerk, she might have ended up looking for love somewhere else, too.

"I told her to call me," I said, as we reached the door to the law office. "If she does, I guess I'll find out what happened then."

"Don't hold your breath," Rafe advised, and he was probably right. If I held my breath waiting for Charlotte to call, I had a feeling I'd suffocate before the phone rang.

Darcy was manning—or womanning—the desk in the lobby inside Martin & McCall. She'd been doing that for a couple of years before we even knew we were related. Now that I knew, I could see a little of Audrey in her face—the high cheekbones, the shape of the jaw—but the severe bone structure was less dramatic in Darcy's younger face. If I looked closely, I could also see hints of my dad, and of Catherine and Aunt Regina, who both take after the Martins.

She looked up with a polite smile, that turned welcoming when she saw us. "Savannah. And Rafe. And you brought the baby!"

Everyone was so delighted to see Carrie again, it was as if we'd been gone months instead of days. Darcy left the desk and came around to coo at the baby, as leggy as her mother in a tight gray skirt and crisp blue blouse.

"Dix is in his office," she told me over her shoulder as she bent over Carrie. "You can go back. I'll keep the baby if you want."

"We didn't come here specifically to see Dix," I began, but Rafe had already put the carrier on the floor and moved in that direction. Maybe he had something he wanted to talk to my brother about.

I shrugged. "I'll catch up."

He nodded and kept going. I waited until the door from the lobby to the back of he building had closed behind him before I turned back to Darcy. "He lost his job."

She sat back on her heels to stare at me. "At the TBI? That's awful."

It was. "At least he has options. Grimaldi offered him a job with the Columbia PD over Christmas, remember? Effective whenever he wanted, after she'd taken over the job of police chief down here. We came down to talk to her about it."

"Is he going to take it?" Darcy wanted to know, getting to her feet again and moving back behind the desk.

"He's not sure." I turned along with her as she moved. "We figured this way, at least, he'd know exactly what she was offering." And what he was turning down.

"And what exactly is she offering?" Darcy asked.

I perched a hip on the edge of the desk. There was a waiting area with a couple of chairs on the other side of the room, but while it's a small room, it was too far away for comfortable conversation. "She originally wanted him to be a detective. Investigator. She was thinking criminal investigations rather than narcotics."

Darcy nodded.

"But then Rafe decided he'd rather join the SWAT team."

Darcy's brows arched. "The SWAT team?"

"Special Weapons and Tactics. The guys in black who come over in their armored car when something especially bad is going on. You remember the SWAT team that came to my house in Nashville that day we were up there, when we found the dead gang banger."

Darcy nodded, and a shadow crossed her face. She had fainted at the sight of the dead gang banger, and Rafe had had to carry her out of the room. It probably wasn't a happy memory. I'd had the same thing happen to me when I saw my first dead body—including being carried by Rafe—so it wasn't like I had any room to criticize.

"I think he's afraid being an investigator wouldn't be as much fun as driving fast and shooting at people," I said. "And he'd look good in the uniform."

Darcy's lips curved and she nodded. "Yes, he would."

"I guess we'll see what happens. There's a chance the TBI might change their minds, I think. His immediate supervisor—the guy above Wendell—said he'd see if there was anything he could do. If not, I'd rather have Rafe on the SWAT team, and happy, than doing something he doesn't enjoy."

Darcy nodded. "Patrick's trained for SWAT, if they need backup. Maybe Rafe could do both, too."

Maybe. "How's Nolan?" I asked.

"You saw him at Christmas, didn't you?"

I had. And he'd looked the same as the last time I'd seen him. "You two doing OK?"

"Fine," Darcy said. "We've only been dating a few months,

you know. It isn't all that serious yet."

Although the 'yet' made it sound like it had the potential to become more so.

But she mustn't have wanted to talk about it, because she changed the subject. "Your friend Charlotte was just here."

"She stopped in at Audrey's, too," I nodded. "Looking for a job. What—?" And then it hit me. "Oh, no."

Darcy nodded. "She spent most of her time talking to Dix. In his office. But after she left, he told me she wanted him to give her my job."

My eyes widened. "She asked for your job?" Not only was that fairly rude, but also very forward of Charlotte.

"Maybe not in so many words," Darcy admitted, "but Dix said he had to explain to her about the relationship," that Darcy wasn't just an employee, but his sister, "before she'd stop talking about it."

"I guess her parents must have neglected to tell her about that." The big reveal had taken place since the last time Charlotte had been here, or at least since the last time I personally had seen her. And I hadn't felt the need to mention it to her long distance. It wasn't like we talked that often anymore, anyway.

"I'm not sure word's gotten around," Darcy said. "None of us who are involved feel a need to talk about it, I think. Everyone who matters, knows. And it's not like the rest of the county needs the details."

I guess not. Both Mother and Audrey would probably be happier to have a few of the finer points stay quiet.

"I should go back and see Dix," I said. By now, whatever Rafe had wanted to talk to him about—if anything—had probably been covered, too.

Darcy nodded. "I'll keep the baby."

By all means. "Speaking of... I think Audrey could use a grandbaby of her own. You may want to keep that in mind as you date Nolan. Neither one of you is getting any younger, you know."

And God, could I sound any more like my mother?

"Yes'm," Darcy said, as a dimple appeared and disappeared in her cheek.

I shook my head. "I don't know where that came from. And it's none of my business, anyway. Forget I said it. Please. I'll be back in a few minutes."

"Take your time," Darcy said and turned her attention to Carrie.

Six

Dix and Rafe had indeed finished whatever Rafe had wanted to talk to Dix about, if anything. When I got back to Dix's office, they were discussing dinner.

Unless that *was* what Rafe had wanted to talk to Dix about.

"Six-thirty at Beulah's. You're welcome to come, but it'll prob'ly be a lot of shop talk." Shop being the business of law enforcement, I assumed.

"I'll pass," Dix said. "I'd have to bring the girls, and I'm not sure they ought to hear that conversation."

I wasn't either. Although— "Couldn't you ask Catherine to take them for the night?"

"I did that on Saturday," Dix said. "Not like I can impose on them every night."

No. And tomorrow was a school day, anyway. Abigail and Hannah should probably stay home and do their homework.

"Well, we'll miss you," I said, perching on the arm of Rafe's chair.

Dix looked around. "Where's the baby?"

"I left her with Darcy. She volunteered."

Dix nodded.

"She also told me that Charlotte stopped by. Angling for her job."

The tips of Dix's ears turned a little pink. Like Mother and me, he's fair skinned and blushes easily. "I had to explain that

Darcy isn't just the receptionist, but our sister. She hadn't heard the news."

"I was kind of surprised that her parents hadn't told her," I admitted, "but Darcy said she didn't think word had gotten out around town."

"Prob'ly just a matter of time," Rafe muttered.

I smiled at him. "You may be right." He'd certainly never had much luck hiding anything as a teenager. On the other hand, Audrey had managed to hide Darcy's existence, and Oneida had managed to hide her racial background, both of them for decades, so maybe it wasn't impossible.

"Rafe says you're thinking about moving back here," Dix said, with a glance at him. "You sure you want to deal with life in Sweetwater again, Sis? You got out."

The look on Rafe's face said that he agreed.

"I'm fine with staying gone," I said. "It's up to Rafe. If he wants to work for Grimaldi, we'll come back. If he doesn't, we'll find something to do in Nashville."

Dix nodded. "I'm sure Tamara would appreciate having you. It won't be easy for her to take over the Columbia police department after Chief Carter. It wouldn't be easy for a woman to do that in this town anyway, in spite of her experience and the fact that Sheriff Satterfield approves of her."

I shook my head. No, indeed. There are still some misogynistic attitudes lurking, and as I had surmised after meeting Sergeant Tucker, there were probably a few of the old guard who would try to patronize her and maybe not take her seriously because she was A) female, B) young, and C) not from around here.

The fact that she was a highly experienced and respected homicide detective from Nashville would do nothing to change that.

"But then there's how Carter left," Dix added, "and how far

into the department that kind of behavior stretched."

That kind of behavior…?

Between you and me, former chief of police Carter had been slightly insane. That wasn't the official description, of course, but I'm sure there's one that means the same thing. How else would you describe a police chief who commits crimes so he can solve them and look good?

There'd also been some talk—some of it from me—about how maybe Carter was a bit too chummy with Beulah Odom's sister-in-law and niece, and how he might have helped them cover up Beulah's murder. Which was what had led to the conversation with Patrick Nolan I mentioned earlier, about whether Detective Jarvis was ethical or not.

Was there some question that Carter hadn't been doing what he was doing alone? Or that that type of behavior from other members of the department was still going on? Were there, in fact, more bad cops in Carter's—or what had been Carter's—command, beyond Carter himself?

It would explain why Sheriff Satterfield had pushed for Grimaldi to take the job. And why the city council had voted to offer it to her, in spite of her being female, and young, and not from around here.

It would also explain what she wanted Rafe for. Not just someone she could trust to have her back and be in her corner, but someone who'd help her figure things out, with no loyalty to anyone or anything in the existing police department, except Grimaldi herself.

And it certainly explained why Dix didn't want to bring his daughters to dinner, if that was the kind of conversation we'd be having.

"Did you know about this?" I asked Rafe a bit later, after we'd finished making small talk with Dix, and with Jonathan, who also stuck his head in to say hello. We were back in the

Volvo headed toward the mansion and Mother, and I added, to clarify my first question, "That there was an ulterior motive for Grimaldi getting, and taking, the job here?"

And an ulterior motive for the job she'd offered him, as well.

He shook his head. "Not to say know. I wondered."

I hadn't. I'd just assumed that Grimaldi wanted the job because it was close to Dix and she wanted to give their relationship a chance. It hadn't had much of one while he was a single father with a law practice in Sweetwater, and she was a homicide detective with a job she enjoyed in Nashville.

"The sheriff offered me the job first," Rafe added, "remember?"

Now that he mentioned it, I did remember. It hadn't been a serious suggestion, or at least I hadn't thought so at the time, but Bob Satterfield had floated the idea that maybe Rafe wanted to become interim chief of police for Columbia after Carter was hauled off in handcuffs. It had been a pretty crazy idea, and Rafe had turned it down flat. I'd mostly figured that the sheriff was joking, or making some sort of half-joking good-will gesture with no expectation that Rafe would actually say yes.

But now the suggestion made more sense, and so did the sheriff approaching Grimaldi when Rafe said no.

"Did you realize what he wanted? Back then, I mean."

Rafe shook his head. "I didn't think about it enough to figure that out. And he didn't say nothing about it. But it makes sense now."

It did. And put a different complexion on Grimaldi's job offer, too.

Rafe nodded when I said so. But before he could answer, his phone rang, and he dug it out of his pocket instead. And pushed the speaker button. "Collier."

"Rafe," a male voice said. It could have been my imagination, but I thought it sounded strained. "Doug Brennan.

Any chance you could stop by sometime this afternoon?"

"No," Rafe said. "My wife and I took the baby down to her family in Sweetwater."

"Oh." Brennan deflated. "When are you coming back? Not until after the weekend?"

It was Thursday afternoon, and under other circumstances, we might have made a weekend of it. But we had the pizza party with Wendell and the boys to host tomorrow night.

"In the morning," Rafe said.

Brennan sounded marginally happier. "Could you stop by when you get into town? Just tell them in the lobby that you want to see me, and I'll leave word for them to send you up."

"Sure thing." Rafe dropped the phone into the console between the seats. In the back Carrie snoozed, not at all bothered by the noise.

"That didn't sound like good news," I said, as the Oak Street Cemetery went by outside the window.

Rafe shrugged. "Can't be nothing too bad, or he woulda said something."

Maybe. "It didn't sound like he convinced anyone to let you keep your job, anyway." Or find him another one.

Rafe shook his head. "Guess we'll find out tomorrow." He turned into the driveway to the mansion. I deduced the subject was closed for now.

Grimaldi was already there when we walked into Beulah's Meat'n Three at six-thirty sharp, seated in a booth in the rear with her back to the wall.

Beulah's is a small cinderblock building with all the charm of a cargo container. But it has a loyal clientele who seems to appreciate the plastic tablecloths and cheap food, so it's always busy. Or at least that's the way it had always been when Beulah Odom ran it. Now that it was open again, after several months of Yvonne McCoy haggling with the Otis Odoms over the will, I was pleased to see that the patrons were back, in droves, and that everything still looked the same as it had before.

Yvonne greeted us at the door, with a wink for Rafe, a "Hello, princess!" for me, and a descent into the baby carrier to gush over Carrie. "She's gorgeous!"

"We think so," I said modestly.

"Looks like her daddy." She winked at Rafe, who grinned back. Since I'd told my mother the same thing earlier, there wasn't anything I could say about this slight insult to my own looks.

Yvonne looked around. "We're pretty full up. But if you can wait a couple minutes…"

"We're meeting someone," Rafe told her. "She's in the back."

Yvonne glanced that way. "The new police chief? You in trouble already, handsome? That didn't take long."

"She's an old friend," I said, before Yvonne could get any actual ideas and start spreading them around. "We'll just head on back."

Yvonne nodded. "Good to see you, princess." She turned to Rafe. "And it's always good to see you!"

He gave her what I knew was a melting grin, even if I couldn't see it because I'd started walking. "You too, sugar."

"You're incorrigible," I told him a few seconds later, when we'd reached Grimaldi's table. He scooted in next to her, which let me put the baby carrier on the seat next to me. Beulah's is narrow enough that I couldn't really leave it in the aisle, and it had the added benefit that Rafe, too, could put his back to the wall.

Grimaldi arched her brows, and glanced in Yvonne's direction. "Old friends?"

"Old bedmates," I said. "One-night-stand in high school."

"That's a long time ago."

The corner of Rafe's mouth turned up. "What can I say? I'm unforgettable."

While that was certainly true, I rolled my eyes and addressed Grimaldi. "We saw Dix this afternoon. And he gave us a slightly clearer picture of what's going on."

Her expression didn't change. But she also didn't ask me to explain, so I figured what Dix hadn't exactly said, and what we'd surmised from it, was pretty close to correct.

"I gotta couple questions," Rafe added.

Grimaldi nodded.

"I don't imagine this changes a whole lot of what we talked about earlier."

She shook her head.

"Is there an expiration date on the job you offered me?"

"You mean, do you have to decide by a certain time? No. I'll take you anytime I can get you. But sooner would be better."

Rafe nodded. "I meant at the end of it."

"No," Grimaldi said again. "I'm the chief of police. It's official. I can hire whomever I want." And fire whomever she wanted, I assumed. "If I hire you, you work for the Columbia PD, not me. If I stop being the chief of police, you'd still have a job. If you wanted one."

"Do you…" I thought about what I wanted to say, and how I wanted to say it, before I continued, just in case someone at a nearby table was close enough to hear the conversation, "Is there a chance you won't be staying for long?"

"I have a contract for a year," Grimaldi said. "It's shorter than usual, but under the circumstances—" She proceeded to outline the circumstances, minus what I figured was the most important one. "With me being younger than usual, and not from around here, I figure the city council thought there was a chance things might not work out, so they wanted to give me an easy out if I needed one. If I decide, at the end of the first year, that I want to stay, and I've done the job to their satisfaction, there's no reason why they wouldn't extend the contract."

"They said that?"

She nodded.

I opened my mouth to ask something else, but before I could, a waitress appeared next to the table, order pad in hand and gum snapping. "What can I getya to eat?"

I hadn't looked at the menu, nor had any of the others. But we'd all been here enough to know that they had the basic fare. I asked for a salad, Rafe for a burger with fries, and Grimaldi for the meatloaf special with green beans and mashed potatoes. The waitress withdrew and we got back to business.

"Any idea yet what you're dealing with?" Rafe wanted to know.

Grimaldi shook her head. "I've only been here three days. It's going to take longer than that."

He shifted his weight on the red Naugahyde. The booths have been here for going on half a century, longer than either he or I have been alive, and between you and me, aren't the most comfortable seating. "I imagine Tucker told you all the reasons you shouldn't hire me."

"I didn't tell him I was hoping to," Grimaldi said, "but yes. He has some preconceived notions about you that he wanted to share with me."

The waitress approached with my iced tea in one hand, the coffee pot in the other, and the handles of two mugs looped through her fingers. We sat in silence while she deposited the tea and mugs on the table, filled them with coffee, and wandered off again, telling us over her shoulder, "The food'll be right up."

"They ain't so much preconceived," Rafe said when she was out of range. "He arrested me once. And hassled me plenty before that."

Grimaldi nodded. "So he said."

"Do you know what happened back then?" I wanted to know. "With Rafe and Billy Scruggs?"

"I know enough," Grimaldi said. "And what I didn't know, Tucker filled in."

Probably not with any degree of accuracy. I opened my mouth to say so, but Rafe shook his head. "Leave it."

Fine. I picked up my tea and took a sip instead. Meanwhile, Rafe turned back to Grimaldi. "I imagine he wouldn't be best pleased to work with me."

"I imagine not," Grimaldi agreed. "But I wasn't planning to put you in narcotics anyway."

"That what Tucker's doing?"

"For a while now. I guess he wasn't doing that back when you knew him?"

"He was just a patrol officer," Rafe said. "And on my case a lot."

Grimaldi nodded. "If I'd been a patrol officer when you were a teenager, I'd have been on your case, too."

And now she wanted to hire him. Funny how that had worked out.

"I guess you were a law-abiding teenager?" I asked.

Grimaldi glanced at me. "For the most part. After my mother passed, I acted out a little."

Not surprising, I guess. Fourteen is a tough age for a young girl to lose her mother.

Not that there's ever a good time. "You grew up in Ohio, right? Columbus? How did you end up here?"

She opened her mouth, and I added, "In Nashville, I mean. I know how you ended up in Sweetwater."

"My college roommate was from Nashville," Grimaldi said. "She talked about it a lot. And I wanted to work in a city on the I-65 corridor."

Interstate 65? "Why?"

She shifted on the bench seat. Glanced beyond me to the restaurant and then back to my face. "I grew up in Columbus, Indiana. It's a small city, forty thousand people or so, south of Indianapolis. Similar in size to Columbia. Nowhere near the size of Columbus, Ohio."

"On I-65." Or so I assumed. Not just because she'd mentioned the I-65 corridor, but because Interstate 65 runs from Alabama up through Nashville, Louisville, and Indianapolis almost all the way to Chicago.

Grimaldi nodded. "My mother's body was found at a truck stop off I-65 just at the Kentucky/Tennessee border."

A truck stop? I opened my mouth and closed it again.

Six months ago or so, Grimaldi and I had visited a truck stop off I-65 in Nashville. It was the day after what should have been my wedding day, after Rafe didn't show up to get married, and we were trying to figure out where the dead body in my bed had come from. The quest had taken us to the truck stop off Trinity Lane in north-east Nashville, where we'd made the acquaintance of some of the lot lizards working the truck stop.

"Um…" I said. "Your mother wasn't…?" Was she?

Grimaldi shook her head. "She worked the night shift at a motel near the interstate. One morning, she didn't come home. They found her a day later a couple of state lines away."

That would be a case for the FBI, then, and not local law enforcement. "Did they never find out what happened to her?"

"It was obvious what happened," Grimaldi said. "She was picked up by somebody, raped and strangled, and dumped by the side of the road. But no, no one was ever arrested for it."

"How come you didn't join the FBI?" Rafe wanted to know. "It'd be their case, wouldn't it?"

"I wanted to work along I-65," Grimaldi said. "There have been at least a dozen women found dead along I-65, from Mobile to Gary, in the past twenty years."

My eyes widened. "And no one's been arrested for any of the murders?"

She shook her head. "I thought, if I kept an ear out, I might learn something new. Something that might help." After a second she added, "You didn't come here to talk about this, though."

No. Although it was interesting. But I surmised that she was the one who didn't want to talk about it anymore, and who could blame her?

"So now you're here. Not very far from I-65 still."

She nodded. "But with more recent crimes to worry about."

Indeed. "Brennan called me," Rafe said, just as the waitress approached with the platters of food. "I'm gonna have to go back and talk to him tomorrow."

"Will he offer you your job back?" Grimaldi nodded her thanks to the waitress for the plate of meatloaf that descended.

Rafe waited until his burger and my salad had also been deposited on the table and the waitress had withdrawn before he answered. "No idea. He didn't say on the phone. Just asked if I could stop by and see him tomorrow."

"Today," I added. "This afternoon. It was only after Rafe told him we aren't in Nashville, that he changed it until tomorrow."

Grimaldi picked up her fork. "D'you think he's worked something out and is planning to keep you on? Or offer you a different job?"

"He already did that," Rafe said, and detailed Brennan's suggestions from yesterday. "Unless he's come up with something better, I don't figure you need to worry about it."

Grimaldi nodded, plunging her fork into the green beans. "I'd like to have you here." She glanced at me. "Both of you, but for the department side of things, mainly your husband."

I nodded.

"This isn't going to be an easy takeover no matter how you slice it," Grimaldi said. "There are plenty like Tucker, who don't like me because I'm a woman, and younger than they are. By a lot of years. And I'm not local. I fully expect some pushback from that type, for any or all those reasons. There are people in the department who—probably very sincerely—thought they deserved a shot at the chief's position when Carter left. And instead they got me, and now they've got to be polite to me—because I'm rank—and obey my orders. That's going to stick in some craws. And beyond that, there are the other concerns."

The ones we wouldn't mention by name or definition. But the employees and activities Grimaldi was here to root out, if they existed.

"None of it's going to be much fun. And I'd like somebody around I can trust. So I don't have to rely only on my own observations and instincts." She toasted Rafe with a green bean on the tines of her fork. "You've got good instincts. And we've worked together before. I know I can trust you."

"I think there are probably a few other people you can trust, too, you know," I said. "Patrick Nolan is dating Darcy. He's probably trustworthy. And his partner, Lupe Vasquez. I've dealt with her a few times—Rafe has, too—and she seems like she's a good cop as well as a decent human being."

"I'm sure most of them are decent human beings," Grimaldi said. "Some of them might even be good people but bad cops. And it isn't always easy to see the difference."

Maybe not.

She turned to Rafe, who told her, "Lemme see what Brennan wants. If it ain't a nice promotion with a big, red bow on it—and I don't figure it is—you got yourself a deal."

Grimaldi nodded. "I appreciate it."

"Don't mention it," Rafe said. And grinned. Evilly. "If it gets me the chance to slam the cell door behind Tucker, it'll all be worth it."

"Just make sure he's guilty first," Grimaldi said.

Seven

We made it to Nashville in the late morning on Friday, and Rafe dropped me and Carrie at the house. "I'll just take the bike up to the TBI and see what Brennan wants."

"Take the Volvo," I said. Not only was it cold, but— "You can go and buy beer for tonight on your way home. Hard to do that on the bike." And I had no particular need to go with him on that errand. Nor any particular expertise when it came to picking out beers.

Not that they were likely to be fancy beers. We'd probably end up with a few six packs of something like Budweiser or Corona, instead of a hip collection of local craft beers. Rafe isn't fancy, and I didn't think any of the others were, either.

So he helped me inside with Carrie and all her assorted stuff, and then he got back in the Volvo and took off up the road toward Trinity Lane and the TBI.

I fed Carrie, and burped her, and changed her diaper, and gave her tummy time on a blanket on the floor, and time on her back, all while I watched her intently, because that's what you do when you have a six-week-old baby.

When she went down for a nap I spent some time moving around the downstairs tidying up, since we'd have people over tonight. And they aren't any more likely to care about the dust on the mantel than they are about the beer they drink, but I'm enough my mother's daughter that I care about presenting my home in the best light. So I dusted, and straightened, and pulled out the vacuum to get the dust bunnies out of the corners. I was down on my hands and knees straightening the fringe on the old Persian rug in the front parlor when I heard a car pull up outside.

I assumed it was Rafe coming back, and I was busy, so I didn't go to greet him at the door. Instead, I was still on the floor when the doorbell rang, busily making sure every strand of fringe was going in the right direction.

When I looked over my shoulder, a head was staring at me through the window in the top of the door, looking sort of disconnected from the rest of its body, which I assumed was also outside.

I got to my feet with what dignity I could muster, and made my way to the door. Where I kept the security chain on when I opened the door a crack. It's never a bad idea to be careful. "Can I help you?"

"I'm looking for Rafael Collier," the man outside said. His voice was a bit gruff, but otherwise polite enough. And he pulled a wallet out of the inside pocket of his jacket and opened it for a second, flashing a badge.

"Oh." This must be Mr. Brennan, who maybe hadn't had the patience to wait until Rafe got there, but had come looking for him instead. "He went to the TBI building. Maybe forty minutes ago. If you hurry, you might be able to catch him." He'd probably stopped in to talk to Wendell and any of the boys who were inhouse, too, before he went to buy the beer.

The guy hesitated. I thought he might say something else, but after a second he just nodded and turned away.

"You're welcome," I told his back, and watched as he walked down the steps and got into the vehicle parked behind Rafe's Harley-Davidson. It wasn't an official TBI vehicle—they're white with the TBI logo on the door—but maybe the higher ups at the TBI drove their own cars to work. This was a fairly nice, late model Toyota SUV of the sporty type, with big, beefy tires.

Rafe rolled in sometime in the middle of the afternoon with the trunk full of beer, all of which went into the fridge to stay cold for later.

"So did Brennan find you?" I asked after he'd unloaded everything and was sitting at the kitchen table eating a sandwich. I'd done my best, but it couldn't match my mother's elegant concoction from yesterday with its little ruffle of lettuce and paper thin onion. Rafe didn't seem to mind. He was happily scarfing down turkey and Swiss on whole wheat.

And shook his head at my question. "Whaddaya mean, did he find me?"

"He showed up here thirty or forty minutes after you left." After a second I added, "At least I assumed it was Brennan."

Rafe swallowed. "Small, skinny guy in his forties? Thinning hair and glasses?"

Not at all. "Must have been someone else. This guy was tall, almost as tall as you, and beefy. He did have thinning hair, but no glasses."

"What did he want?" Rafe asked and took another bite of the sandwich.

"You. At least that's what he said. That he was looking for Rafael Collier."

Rafe shrugged. "If it was important, I'm sure he'll be back."

Probably so. "So Brennan wasn't there?"

Rafe shook his head. "Didn't come to work today, they said. He did leave word that they were supposed to send me up, but since he hadn't shown up, they wouldn't let me in." He sounded deeply disgusted. "I tried calling him, but he didn't pick up."

So he'd gone up there, and we'd come all the way back from Sweetwater, for nothing.

"Maybe he meant that he wanted you to stop by his house?" I suggested. "Not the TBI."

"He shoulda said that, then." After a second he added, "You heard what he said yesterday. He didn't mention nothing about his house, did he?"

He hadn't. Not at all. And if he'd left word in the lobby to send Rafe up, that made it pretty clear he'd been talking about Rafe coming to see him at the TBI.

"I left a message saying I'd been there, and to call me again when he got it. Guess I'll just wait to hear from him."

There wasn't much else he could do. "I straightened up," I said, looking around.

He nodded. "I saw. You didn't have to do that, darlin'. Nobody's gonna care if there's dust in the corners."

"I'd care."

His mouth quirked. "Your mama'd care. You only care 'cause you think your mama would."

Guilty as charged. You can take the girl out of Sweetwater, but you can't take Sweetwater—entirely—out of the girl.

"Anything else we need to do before they get here?"

"No," Rafe said and stood up. He took his plate to the sink. "I'll call in the pizza thirty minutes before they get here. That way it oughta be here right after they show up."

I nodded.

"Other'n that, we have the whole afternoon to ourselves." He smiled. "Carrie asleep?"

"For now." But probably not for a whole lot longer. Even at six weeks, I'd noticed she slept a little less than she used to just a week or two ago.

"We better take advantage while we can," Rafe said. "Pretty soon she'll be walking, and the kitchen table'll be off limits till she's eighteen and off to college."

And at that point we might be too old to think sex in the

kitchen in the middle of the day was anything to get excited about.

"I'm up for it if you are," I said.

"Darlin'…" He advanced toward me, his eyes intent, "I'm always up for it."

I giggled, and then he scooped me up and deposited me on the table, and nudged my knees apart so he could step between my thighs, and then he leaned in and kissed me… and the rest, as they say, is history.

The doorbell rang again just before four. Rafe glanced at the clock and arched a brow. "Somebody's early."

I nodded. "Maybe one of the boys wants some extra time with you before the others get here." Clayton and José were leaving, after all, and Rafe was leaving the TBI, so it made sense.

"I'll get it." He uncoiled from the sofa and headed for the door.

"Mind the fringe!"

He gave me a jaundiced look over his shoulder, but stepped over the edge of the carpet rather than mess up my handiwork.

There are only a few feet from the sofa in the parlor to the front door, so I had a good view of what happened. Rafe glanced out through the window in the top of the door, and I saw his brows arch. When he swung the door open, I deduced he wasn't worried about who was outside, but it wasn't anyone he was happy to see, either. "Yeah?"

"Rafael Collier?" It was the same voice I'd heard earlier, except this time it was a whole lot less polite. I removed myself from the sofa and made my way toward the foyer, while the voice continued. "Grab your jacket. You're coming downtown for questioning."

There was a pause. "You arresting me?" Rafe asked. His voice was level, but I didn't think anyone could have mistaken the warning in it. "'Cause if you ain't prepared to put me in handcuffs right now—and you better make sure you have a damn good reason, and some solid evidence to back it up if you do—I ain't going nowhere."

By now I had reached the open door and stuck my head around it to peer out. "Hello again. You didn't tell me who you were earlier." Although if he wanted Rafe to come downtown for questioning, and not up to the TBI, he was probably MNPD. A former colleague of Grimaldi's. They have their offices in downtown.

"I showed you my badge," the gentleman said dismissively, like the tenth of a second he'd waved it under my nose was supposed to be long enough for me to make out his name and rank.

He turned his attention back to Rafe, but before he could say anything more, my husband told me, still in that same very smooth, very even tone, "This is Detective Goins, darlin'. He wants to talk to me about something."

"What might that be?" I asked.

Goins's eyes—small and muddy brown—glinted with resentment, but he said, "The death of Doug Brennan."

There was a beat. "Brennan's dead?" Rafe said. "Since when?"

"I'm the one asking the questions here," Goins answered. "Where were you last night between eight and midnight?"

"That when he died?"

Goins didn't answer, and Rafe added, "Not in Nashville. I was in Sweetwater, Tennessee, having dinner with the chief of police for Columbia, and then going home to my mother-in-law's house. She's sleeping with the sheriff of Maury County."

Goins looked at him like he wasn't quite sure whether he could believe it or not. And to be honest, it wasn't the kind of alibi most people serve up when they're asked.

I smiled apologetically. "It's true. I was there, too."

Goins gave me a dismissive look. Followed by a grunt. "Not like you wouldn't lie for him."

He had that right—I would absolutely lie for him—but in this case there was no need. That's not to say the suggestion, and the tone it was delivered in, wasn't offensive. "We were more than an hour away all night, Detective Goins. Feel free to call Chief Grimaldi in Columbia or Sheriff Satterfield in Sweetwater to verify. Or my mother. I'd be happy to give you the number."

"I wouldn't," Rafe said, "at least not till I know why I need an alibi. And why some detective with the MNPD is accusing my wife of lying. What happened to Brennan? And what's it gotta do with me?"

"Mr. Brennan met with an accident last night," Detective Goins said coldly. "Going home from work."

Rafe folded his arms across his chest—nice arms, very nice chest—and leaned a shoulder on the door jamb to listen. Cold air was seeping into the house, but I guess he didn't feel like inviting Goins inside to continue the conversation. "And you don't know if it was at eight or midnight?"

"He ran off the road a few miles from his house," Goins said. "The car wasn't discovered until this morning. When I spoke to his colleagues at the TBI about anyone who might have wanted to hurt him, your name came up."

Rafe's eyes narrowed, but he didn't speak. Goins smirked unpleasantly. "I understand he fired you recently?"

"They eliminated his position," I said. "It isn't quite the same thing."

Rafe shot me a look before he turned back to Goins. "What if he did?"

"Couldn't have been much fun," Goins said, in what was probably supposed to be an understanding tone, but which just came across as insinuating and oily. "Might be hard to find another job, what with your background and all."

I opened my mouth to tell him that Rafe already had a job offer, and that it had been in place a week or more before we had any idea that he'd be losing his job with the TBI. But then I thought better of it. This was Rafe's business. I should let him handle it.

He gave Goins a nod. "Might be. But killing Brennan wouldn't improve my chances."

"You might not have thought about that," Goins said. "Your type often acts first and thinks later." He sounded pleased.

"Oh, sure." Rafe did fake pleasant much better than Goins did. "The stupid type, I guess? Too dumb to realize that killing the man who fired me wouldn't get me another job, unless I wanted to spend another couple years making license plates?"

Goins was either extremely stupid in his own right, or he lacked the ability to recognize sarcasm when he heard it. "Exactly."

"I ain't that stupid," Rafe said. "And I wasn't in Nashville last night. I was nowhere near Brennan's house. I don't even know where he lives. Not like we were friends."

"Your wife said you went to the TBI to talk to him this morning." Goins glanced at me and then back at Rafe. "Why was that?"

"He wanted to see me," Rafe said. "He called yesterday afternoon. I couldn't make it, seeing as I was in Maury County yesterday. So I told him I'd stop by when I got back to town this morning."

Goins looked doubtful.

"If I knew he was dead," Rafe asked, "why'd I waste my time going to see him?"

Goins sounded triumphant. "To make it look like you didn't know?"

"Sure." Rafe shook his head. "I had no reason to want Doug

Brennan dead. It wasn't his choice to do away with my job. Doing away with him wouldn't get me the job back either way. And I wasn't nowhere near Nashville when he drove off the road."

"Why is that even something you investigate?" I wanted to know. "It sounds like an accident. You even called it an accident. Why are you here asking my husband questions about it?"

"That's for me to know," Goins said. And turned back to Rafe. "So you deny having anything to do with Doug Brennan's death?"

Rafe nodded. "And you can't prove I did. 'Cause I wasn't here."

"You could have compromised his brakes before you left town yesterday."

"I woulda had to be out early," Rafe said, "seeing as we left around eight-thirty. Brennan prob'ly wasn't even at the TBI yet."

"And we were together all morning," I added. Not that my saying so was likely to matter much to Goins. He'd already made it clear what he thought about my honesty. "Is that what happened?"

Goins didn't answer. Another thing that was for him to know and the rest of us not to question, I guess.

"Are you sure he didn't just drive off the road by accident? Maybe a car swerved over in the wrong lane and he had to dodge, or a deer ran across the road, or something. The headlights of an oncoming vehicle blinded him for a second or two. Or he just lost control of the car. It's winter. The roads can get icy."

Especially outside of town, and if Doug Brennan had run off the road and died, it sounded like it might have happened somewhere that wasn't exactly the urban core. Anyone running off the road in our neighborhood would have hit somebody's lawn furniture, or maybe a picket fence or mailbox first, but the chances of getting up enough speed so that something like that would be fatal, were slim to none. And there was no way the car wouldn't have been discovered until daylight the next morning. We get police drive-bys all the time around here, and regular people come and go all day and night, too. What happened to Doug Brennan sounded more like it had taken place in a suburban or even rural setting.

But Goins wasn't likely to give us any of the details. Wendell might know where Brennan lived, though. We could ask him when he got here.

"Anything else?" Rafe wanted to know. Goins looked like he'd bit into a lemon wedge. But since he wasn't willing to arrest Rafe on the evidence he thought he had, there wasn't much he could do except shake his head.

He couldn't resist a parting shot, though. "Don't leave town."

"That ain't how it works," Rafe said, and shut the door.

We watched Goins as he made his way down to the driveway.

"Is that true?" I asked Rafe. Outside, Goins hesitated at the bottom of the steps instead of making for the Toyota.

Rafe glanced at me. "What's that?"

"That he can't tell you not to leave town."

"Sure." He nodded. "It's a free country. I can go anywhere I want."

Outside on the driveway, Goins had made his way over to the Volvo and was walking around it, inspecting the fenders and lights. A total waste of time on his part, since the car had been in Sweetwater when Brennan went off the road. Not that I'd gotten the impression he'd believed me when I said so.

"Even if you're a suspect in a crime?" Not that he was. Since he had an alibi. "Or a person of interest, or whatever?"

"Yeah," Rafe said, as Goins left the Volvo to make the same inspection of the Harley. After a second he added, "Why?"

"No reason. Back when we discovered Brenda Puckett's body, Grimaldi told me not to leave town. I was going to Mother's birthday party in Sweetwater, so I had to negotiate with her."

Rafe smirked. "It works with some people. Not people who know better."

Of course. "I don't expect she told you that? Not to leave town?" When I got to Sweetwater, he'd also been there, cleaning out his mother's trailer in the Bog.

"Can't recall. But if she did, I woulda said no, ma'am, and left anyway." He shrugged, as Goins left the bike and headed for the Toyota. The detective directed one final displeased look at the house before he got in and turned the engine over. We watched as the Toyota maneuvered past both the Volvo and the Harley on its way toward the street. On Potsdam it made a right turn and was gone.

Rafe pushed off from the doorjamb and headed back to the parlor.

"Is this something we need to worry about?" I asked him, as I trailed behind.

He glanced at me over his shoulder. "Can't imagine why. We were in Sweetwater. We can prove it. And I had no reason to want Brennan dead."

"Was there no hint of this when you were at the TBI earlier?"

He shook his head. "Nobody said a word."

"That's a little weird."

"Wendell and the boys'll be here soon," Rafe said. "Maybe they know something we don't."

Maybe they did. Because I had a feeling this wouldn't be the last we heard of it.

Eight

Wendell showed up at six-thirty sharp. Before he'd even made it up the stairs, José's truck, with the Virgin Mary on the back window, turned into the driveway and headed for the house.

José is a short, Hispanic guy with an accented voice and biceps that almost rival Rafe's. The difference is that José is half a foot shorter and looks like a fireplug. He favors polo shirts, and keeps his sleeves rolled up almost to the shoulders, not because he's trying to show off—at least I don't think so—but because his biceps are so big that I doubt the fabric would stretch far enough.

Wendell, meanwhile, is African-American and in his fifties, and the closest thing Rafe's ever had to a father. His own dad died before he was born, and while he grew up with his mother and grandfather in the Bog, the trailer park on the south side of Sweetwater, Old Jim Collier wasn't any kind of father to a growing boy. He's the one who shot Tyrell Jenkins, for the crime of knocking up LaDonna, and he had no compulsions about taking his fists, or his belt or anything else that was handy, to both his daughter and his grandson. When he stumbled out the door one night when Rafe was twelve, and didn't come back in, neither Rafe nor LaDonna took the trouble to go look for him. He was found the next day, drowned in the Duck River.

But I digress. Wendell waited for José, and they walked in together. Clayton Norris, scrawny and white, with a skinhead buzz cut and tattoos up and down his arms, turned his Camaro up the driveway a few minutes later, and Jamal Atkins showed up at the same time as the pizzas. Jamal's black, almost as tall as Rafe, but with at least thirty pounds less muscle.

They descended on the pizzas like a horde of barbarians, and for a while, nothing was heard but chewing and swallowing and ribbing.

Rafe waited until the feeding frenzy had abated before he said, "I had cops on the door earlier."

Wendell shot him a look. Jamal swallowed the bite of pizza he'd taken and said, "What you do now?"

"It wasn't what I did," Rafe said, and added, "though he wanted to pin it on me. But it was something somebody else did. Y'all know Brennan's dead?"

There was a pause. The boys all looked at one another. "Our Brennan?" Jamal said.

Rafe nodded. "Detective named Goins came to the door and wanted to know where I was last night from eight to twelve."

"What happened to Brennan?"

"Apparently he ran off the road," I said, from where I was standing in the doorway holding the baby. "On his way home last night. A couple of miles from where he lived."

"Lives in Ridgetop," Wendell said. After a second he added, "Did."

Rafe glanced at him. "D'you know about this?"

Wendell shook his head. "I've been offsite today, working with the boys. None of us been at the TBI today."

So at least it wasn't a case of everyone else knowing what was going on and just not sharing it with Rafe. That thought had probably crossed his mind.

"Ridgetop is north of here," I said, "isn't it? Up toward the border to Kentucky?"

Wendell nodded. "He had a cabin up there. Drove in every

day."

And back out every night, I assumed. "Hilly?"

"Only been there a couple times," Wendell said, "but yeah. If he ran off the road, he coulda had a long drop."

"That's terrible." And sad to contemplate the idea that he might not have died right away, but might have stayed in his car, at the end of a long drop, dying slowly.

But no, that was probably just my imagination. He'd have had his phone with him, surely. If he'd been alive and aware, he would have used it to call for help.

"The detective share what happened?" Wendell asked Rafe.

My husband shook his head. "Suggested that maybe I'd 'compromised his brakes'," his tone made quotes around the words, "but when Savannah asked, he wouldn't say for sure that that's what happened. So something made Brennan drive off the road, but I'm not sure anybody knows what."

Or if they did, they weren't telling.

"I'll see what I can find out," Wendell said. "Somebody's gotta know something. And I still work at the TBI, so maybe they'll tell me."

Maybe. "Goins isn't likely to tell Rafe, anyway, so anything you can discover will be helpful."

Wendell looked from me to Rafe. "You got an alibi, don't you? You were in Columbia last night, right?"

Rafe nodded. "Not sure Goins believed me, though. And he made sure to let Savannah know he knew she'd lie if she had to."

I sniffed. Rafe grinned.

"I'm going to go call Grimaldi," I said. "Enjoy the pizza."

I took the baby with me down the hall. Behind me, the conversation continued. "What kinda car did Brennan drive?" Clayton wanted to know. He was the group's vehicular specialist, so if there was anything to know about it, Clayton would know.

I don't know what the answer was, though, as by then I'd made it down to the kitchen and out of range.

I put Carrie in the bouncy seat and sat at the table to pull out my phone. Grimaldi picked up after the first ring. "Ms…. Savannah."

"Quick question," I said, circumventing the whole issue of what to call her. "Are you somewhere with Dix?"

"No," Grimaldi said. "That's the quick question?"

"No. It's Friday. Why aren't you?"

"None of your business."

I didn't say anything, and after a moment she relented. "I'm going with him and the girls to the movies tomorrow. Was that the question?"

"No. I just wanted to make sure you had time to talk and I wasn't interrupting anything. What do you know about a detective named Goins?"

There was a beat of silence. "Rick Goins?"

"Stocky guy, early forties, looks like muscle gone to fat. Thinning hair, beady eyes."

"Sounds like Rick Goins," Grimaldi said. "Where did you come across him?"

"He came to the house, looking for Rafe."

Grimaldi sounded resigned. "What did your husband do now?"

I sniffed. "Nothing. He was in Sweetwater when this happened. Not that Goins seemed inclined to believe it."

"He has a suspicious nature," Grimaldi said. "When what happened, exactly?"

I told her what had happened.

"And Goins came to talk to your husband?"

"Brennan fired him," I said. "Or let him go, rather. Eliminated his position. It was Goins's contention that Rafe was upset about it, and too stupid to realize that killing Brennan wouldn't have gotten him his job back, but would instead have sent him back to Riverbend for a stretch of twenty-five to life."

"That must have gone over well," Grimaldi said dryly.

"Rafe was polite. Coldly polite. He refused to go downtown for questioning, and when Goins told him not to leave town, he told Goins it doesn't work that way."

Grimaldi didn't say anything. "You told me not to leave town after Brenda Puckett's murder," I said.

"Sometimes it works," Grimaldi answered, with no sign whatsoever of a guilty conscience.

Sure. "So what can you tell me about Goins? Is he as much of an idiot as he seems? Do I have to worry that he'll arrest Rafe even though Rafe spent last night in Sweetwater and can prove it?"

Grimaldi took a second to think about it. "He isn't the most imaginative cop," she said. "Very much by the book. Doesn't take many chances. Tends to leap to the obvious solution early on and then spends a lot of time making a case to prove it."

"And in this case, Rafe's the obvious solution."

There was no need for Grimaldi to confirm it, so she didn't. "Detective work isn't brain surgery," she said instead. "Ninety-nine percent of the time, the obvious suspect is guilty."

"Except this time." Grimaldi didn't answer, and I added, "Why does he have a suspicious nature? Just a result of the job, or some other reason?"

"I shouldn't be telling you this," Grimaldi said, and proceeded to tell me anyway. "Rick and I rubbed along all right, and would have gotten along better if I hadn't been a woman, and I didn't close a lot of cases."

"So he's a misogynist. And jealous."

"Not so much of me," Grimaldi said, "although you probably won't be doing yourself any favors by mentioning me."

Too late. "We already did. You're one of Rafe's alibis for last night. And while Goins might not like you much, I'm sure he'll trust you when it comes to being someone's alibi."

Grimaldi admitted, a bit grudgingly, that he probably would.

"So if not you, who's he jealous of?" Surely not Rafe, since I hadn't gotten the impression that Goins had ever laid eyes on him before.

"Remember Jaime?" Grimaldi said.

How could I forget? Homicide detective Jaime Mendoza, another of Grimaldi's colleagues in the MNPD. I'd met him for the first time on what should have been my wedding day, after Rafe didn't show up, last summer, and Mother had asked him—Mendoza—whether he wanted to marry me instead.

He's just the type Mother appreciates. Very handsome, very well dressed, extremely charming. He'd handled the question, and having to reject me, beautifully. Rafe and I had met him a few times since, too, and I could well understand why someone like Goins would be jealous of someone like Mendoza, who's not only drop-dead gorgeous, but very smart, and also quite a good cop.

"Not just that," Grimaldi said when I said so. "When Jaime cheated on his wife, it was with Goins's girlfriend. Who slept with Jaime because she knew it would drive Rick crazy."

"That's ugly."

Grimaldi agreed. "In Jaime's favor," she said, "I don't think he realized that that was the reason. But all that aside, Rick doesn't have a habit of arresting the wrong man. And he does close cases. It just takes him a bit of time to get there sometimes."

"So he'll be investigating Rafe for a while, while the real killer—if there is one—has time to cover his tracks. But when it comes right down to it, he isn't likely to arrest Rafe."

"Probably not," Grimaldi agreed.

That was good to know, anyway. Not that Rafe would be happy to sit around and wait while Goins came to that conclusion. "I don't suppose he's likely to share information."

"No," Grimaldi said. "Especially when your husband no longer works for the TBI and Rick thinks that's the reason for the murder."

That made sense. I thought for a moment. "You don't have access to that information, do you?"

"No," Grimaldi said again, firmly. "And I have cases of my own to deal with. And a department of officers, detectives, and support personnel I don't know if I can trust."

Right. "Just hold on until Rafe gets there. I'm pretty sure he'll decide to come lend a hand. But at this point you'll probably have to wait until this Brennan thing is figured out."

"I'm still getting situated," Grimaldi said. "I'll probably be spending the best part of next week getting to know my staff. Individual interviews and the like. But when he gets around to it, if he decides to, I can use him."

I told him I'd let him know, although I figured he already did.

"Keep me updated on what happens," Grimaldi said. "And if Rick calls to check your husband's alibi, I'll do what I can to set him straight."

"We'd appreciate that," I said. "Have a good time with Dix and the girls tomorrow. Enjoy the movie."

Grimaldi said she was sure she would. "It's an animated Disney feature about a princess. What's not to like?"

Let me count the ways.

Not that I particularly mind Disney princess movies. I've watched my share of them—more than my share—babysitting Abigail and Hannah. But Grimaldi is a whole lot less girly than I am, and would probably prefer the latest action thriller featuring The Rock or Bruce Willis or someone like that. Explosions and car chases and weapons discharging, not to mention fight scenes that weren't choreographed right. Rafe likes those, too, and likes to point out everything that's wrong with them.

Although in another couple of years, he'd be watching his own share of Disney princesses, as our own daughter grew up.

I glanced at her, where she was sitting in the bouncy seat watching her toes wiggle inside the pink one-piece with little Minnie Mice all over it, and tried to picture her in a couple of years, curled up next to her daddy on the sofa watching *Sleeping Beauty*. It was surprisingly easy. "I should go."

"Stay in touch," Grimaldi said and hung up. I did the same.

The boys and Wendell stayed until midnight. By then, I'd given up the fight and gone to bed. When Rafe climbed in next to me, I snuggled close and went back to sleep. For the little bit of time I had before Carrie woke up hungry, and I had to stagger into her room to feed her.

She had nursed herself to sleep and I had put her down in her crib, careful not to wake her, and was on my way back to my own room when I glanced out the window into the side yard and saw a shadow moving between the trees there.

It was shades of déjà vu. A couple of months ago, just before Carrie was born, this same thing had happened. It had been Mrs. Jenkins showing up in the middle of the night, in the front yard that time, with blood all over her, and just the memory of it sent a chill down my spine.

I scurried across the hallway, the bottoms of my feet cold on the hardwood floors, and hissed my husband's name." "Rafe!"

"Mmm?"

"Somebody's outside."

He went from asleep to awake in the span of a second, just

as always. "Who?"

"Can't tell. But something was moving around down in the side yard. Behind the gazebo."

He was already out of bed and pulling a pair of faded jeans up over nothing, tucking himself away efficiently and pulling up the zipper. "Stay here."

That's what he'd told me last time, too.

"Be careful," I said, as he headed for the stairs. "You don't even have a gun anymore."

"If this kinda shit's gonna happen, I'm gonna have to get one."

He didn't wait for me to speak, just headed down the stairs two steps at a time. I heard the front door open and close. I made my way back into Carrie's room and over to the window while he made his own way around the outside of the house a floor below. When I peered out, I could see him come around the corner, still shirtless and barefoot.

He stood for a second and looked around. My heart was knocking against my ribs, waiting for that hypothetical shot to come, but nothing happened. I peered beyond the gazebo, where I'd seen movement earlier, but there was nothing there now.

After a few moments, Rafe moved away from the corner of the house and into the grass. I watched as he wandered beyond the gazebo, between the dry bushes, until he turned back toward the house. He disappeared around the corner again. I stayed where I was, looking at the yard, just in case whoever had been down there would come out of hiding now that Rafe was gone.

But nothing happened, and a few seconds later I heard the front door open and close, followed by the deadbolt and the security chain. I left Carrie's room for the second time and waited for Rafe at the top of the stairs.

"Sorry," I told him when he started climbing. "Must have

been my imagination."

He shrugged, as if sending him outside at the beginning of January, barefoot and bare-chested, in the middle of the night, was no big deal. "I didn't see nobody. But that don't mean somebody wasn't there."

"What else would it mean? You looked, right? And nobody was there."

"Nobody was there now," Rafe said, reaching the top of the stairs and pausing in front of me. I could feel the chill from outside clinging to his body. The viper tattoo that curled around his upper arm flicked its little forked tongue out at me. "That don't mean somebody wasn't there earlier."

He dropped his hand to the button in his jeans. My eyes dropped with it, and he grinned. "I'm awake. How about you?"

I was awake, too. No question about it.

He flicked open the button and pulled down the zipper, but made no move to get out of the jeans. Instead he reached out and snagged me around the waist, and pulled me up against him. The fabric of the jeans was cold against my legs, but the heat of his chest and stomach was warm through my nightgown.

I ran my hands up over arms, across the viper, to his shoulders. Smooth, warm skin covering hard muscles. "I love you."

"Love you too, darlin'." His voice was easy as he turned me toward the bedroom. We did a sort of dance—shuffle, step, turn—through the door, and ended up at the foot of the bed. The corner of his mouth curled up. "Remember the first time we did this?"

"Not something I'd forget," I said. And not just because the sex had been good—or more than good; life-changing—but because everything else about the encounter had changed my life, too.

He bent to nuzzle my neck, just below my ear. "Sometimes I

can't believe it, you know?"

"Believe what?" My voice was breathless.

I could feel his lips curve. "That you're still here. I figured I'd wake up the next morning and you'd be gone."

"I did leave." Just not first thing in the morning. I'd wanted a repeat performance first. Or if I hadn't thought about it quite that clearly, I hadn't been ready to leave. I'd known, or thought I knew, that I should, but I hadn't wanted to.

"You came back."

Not to his bed. Not then. The next time we made love, it was in my bed, in the apartment I used to live in over on Main Street.

But we were back now. And married. And I wasn't going anywhere.

"I don't think you understand just how crazy about you I am," I told him.

"The sex, sure." He lifted his head to give me a grin. "I figured I could make you come back for that. But I thought for sure you'd wise up before you actually hitched yourself to me permanently."

"There's nowhere I'd rather be permanently," I said. "And nobody I'd rather be hitched to."

And on that note he tumbled me onto the bed and followed me down, and if someone was outside in the yard, skulking around, neither one of us gave them a second thought.

Nine

Rafe left in the morning to help first José and then Clayton load up and leave. I didn't tag along. Partly because I was meeting Alexandra for lunch, and partly because I figured he needed the time on his own, surrounded by his friends, to deal with this. His life was changing. He would never be working with either of these men again. His time with the TBI had come to an end. He and Wendell were done as a team. And as far as José and Clayton were concerned, he might never see them again. They were going into dangerous situations in other places, and nobody knew better than Rafe that every day could be the day when someone figured out what they were doing and ended them for it.

He didn't need me tagging along and trying to make light of anything. So I kissed him goodbye, and let him go off on his own to deal with things in his own way.

After he left, I straightened up from the debauchery of last night. All the empty pizza cartons went into the trash and the empty bottles into recycling.

We have bins for both outside by the fence. I put on my coat for the trip, and left Carrie inside for the minute or two I figured it would take me to cross the yard. Then I headed across the porch and down the steps and over the grass with a stack of greasy pizza boxes under one arm, and a bag full of empty beer bottles in the other hand.

Mrs. Jenkins's house—an 1880s three-story Victorian with a tower on one corner—sits on a pretty big lot for one of the oldest neighborhoods in the city. The original mansions in the area, the antebellums, had acreage and fields, of course. Same as the Martin Plantation in Sweetwater. But Mrs. J's house was one of the 'summer cottages' of the elite of the post-Civil War era. They had their big houses on the west side of downtown, and in the summers, they'd travel across the river, to Edgefield and East Nashville, to stay in their summer cottages. And those—most of them not what we'd call a cottage these days—were all lined up neatly on urban-sized lots.

All except for Mrs. J's house. It sits on a corner, and it has a lot of space on three sides. There's enough room for a second house, actually, but instead, in the place where a second house might be, there's a gazebo. And just before Thanksgiving, I'd discovered—or Mrs. J had shown me—the tunnel that runs from the basement of the house to the underside of the gazebo.

Carrie had been born a few days later, and I hadn't had any time since to look into the tunnel and how it came to be there.

It wasn't part of the Underground Railroad. I did know that much. Not only was the house built too late for that, but most of the Underground Railroad activity in Tennessee took place in the eastern part of the state.

At any rate, as I was making my way across the grass with my pizza boxes and empty bottles, the thought crossed my mind that for anyone who knew that it was there, the gazebo, and the tunnel below it, made for a dandy second entrance into the house.

Or at least as far as the basement. After I showed it to him back in November, Rafe had made sure to nail the entrance shut on the inside, just so no one could get in that way. We kept the basement door locked, too, just in case. And he'd also been out here in the yard and nailed the entrance to the tunnel shut in the gazebo floor.

And I didn't really think anyone was down there. I didn't think anyone knew about it, other than us and Mrs. Jenkins. Rafe had lived in the house for the best part of a year without knowing that the tunnel existed, and I'd been there almost as long, so the chances of anyone else knowing about it were slim to none.

Nonetheless, after I'd put the pizza boxes in the trash and the beer bottles in recycling, I made my way across the dry grass, crunching under my feet in the cold weather, and up into the gazebo. Just to make sure that the entrance to the tunnel was still nailed shut, and that our nocturnal visitor last night hadn't made it into the tunnel and was either lying at the bottom of the shaft nursing two broken legs, or had dragged himself all the way down the tunnel to the house, and was even now scratching on the inside of the basement door with his fingernails.

Yes, I have a vivid imagination. You can blame it on my brother Dix and the ghost stories he used to tell me as a kid.

But no. The nailheads Rafe had pounded in a month ago were still bright and shiny, and the trap door didn't move when I dug my fingernails into it and tried to lift. So whoever had been hanging around our yard last night—unless it was just a neighbor cutting across the grass instead of walking up to the corner and around—he or she hadn't made it into the tunnel.

I wandered back and around the corner. Only to come face to face with Rick Goins, getting out of his Toyota at the bottom of the steps.

He stopped when he saw me, and an expression of dismay crossed his features. I pretended I didn't see it. "Detective Goins. What can I do for you?"

"Your husband around?" Goins asked.

I shook my head. "He left about an hour ago."

"Back to the TBI again?" He smirked.

"Not this time," I said, without volunteering any information about where he might have gone. I didn't know exactly where José lived, anyway. "I don't expect him back for a while. Can I take a message?"

Goins expanded. There's no other word for it. I guess the knowledge that Rafe wasn't around made him feel more comfortable. He moved his feet farther apart and squared his shoulders. "I thought you might have changed your mind about providing an alibi for him the other night."

Oh, really? "Don't be ridiculous," I said. "First of all, he's my husband. I wouldn't change my mind. But his alibi doesn't need any help from me. You can call my mother. You can call Sheriff Satterfield in Maury County. You can call Chief Grimaldi in Columbia."

"I already did," Goins said triumphantly.

"Then what are you doing here?"

"She said you finished dinner by eight o'clock. It's an hour's drive from Columbia to Nashville. Your husband could have gotten here in plenty of time to run Doug Brennan off the road."

"That's stupid," I said. "I was with him. We didn't drive to Nashville. We went back to the mansion and sat around for a while. We didn't go to bed until eleven. And he had no reason to want to get rid of Brennan. If you spoke to Grimaldi, I'm sure she told you that."

"Tamara isn't here," Goins said, with relish. "I am."

"You might still want to listen to her. She knows us both better than you do."

He had no answer to that, and I added, "You realize that while you insist on going down this path, after a man with no motive and a solid alibi, the real murderer is getting away with it?"

He had no response to that, either, and I continued, "That's if there is a real murderer. So far, it sounds like it might have been an accident. Do you have any evidence that it wasn't?"

He opened his mouth, but must have thought better of volunteering whatever he'd been about to say, because he closed it again.

"I thought so," I said.

He scowled. "Now, you listen here, missy—!"

I channeled Mother. And looked at him down the length of my nose. It's quite possible to do, even when the man you're looking at is half a foot taller than you. In this case I had indignation on my side, so that made it easy. "That's Mrs. Collier to you. And until you have some evidence that my husband has done something—which you won't get, because he wasn't anywhere near Ridgetop two nights ago—I'll thank you not to come around here again with your questions. Go do your job, and find the real murderer. If there is one."

I headed up the stairs to the porch.

"How do you know it happened in Ridgetop?" Goins asked from behind me.

I turned at the top of the stairs and looked down at him. "Seriously? You told us Brennan ran off the road near his home. He lives in Ridgetop. My husband worked under him for eleven years. My husband's boss worked under Brennan for even longer. People know where he lived."

Goins had no response to that.

"If you'll excuse me?" I said, and headed for the door. He didn't say anything to stop me, so I let myself in and closed and locked the door behind me. And watched through the window as Goins stood for a second and looked around, before he walked back to the Toyota and got in. As the car started moving down the driveway, I went to find my daughter.

The FinBar was hopping when Carrie and I got there at noon. And Alexandra was early, already sitting in a booth by the window munching on French fries. She saw us coming and waved, and I headed for her. "Good to see you. Goodness, you look about to burst."

She made a face as she dropped down on the seat again after giving me a hug. "I've gained twenty-five pounds. I'm eating like a pig."

She was a little rounder in the face, and a lot rounder in the stomach, than the last time I'd seen her. "Are you sure you're only six months along?" I shoved the car seat with Carrie into the booth and followed.

"Positive," Alexandra said and picked up another fry. "It's Jamal's baby. No question."

OK, then. I wriggled out of my coat and smiled at the waitress, who had appeared like magic once I sat down. "I'll have a sweet tea, please. And a Cobb salad." Might as well order, since Alexandra had gotten a head start.

"Me, too," Alexandra said, so I guess the plate of fries was just the appetizer.

I could remember being pregnant. I was hungry all the time, and got light-headed if I didn't eat regularly. I'd feel like Carrie was gnawing on my stomach lining. If Alexandra was dealing with those sensations, I didn't blame her at all for stuffing fries in her mouth.

"So how are you?" I asked. "Hungry all the time?"

She nodded. "I swear, I eat all day long."

"It takes a lot of fuel to make a baby. And a lot of sleep."

"Tell me about it." She rolled her eyes, heavily made up. She's always looked several years older than the seventeen I knew her to be. "I sleep like twelve hours every night."

I did, too, back when I'd been six months pregnant. "Look at it this way. You're saving up for after the baby's born. I'm up a couple of times every night now."

"Great," Alexandra said, in a voice that said the opposite.

She stuffed another fry in her mouth and added, around it, "I can't wait."

"Are you keeping the baby? If you're not, you can give that duty to someone else."

We'd talked about this on and off over the past five months. She was young. She was still in high school, at least until the summer. She was hoping to go to college next year. She wasn't really in a great position to become a mother.

And her baby's father was only a few years older than she was, and not really in a great position to be a parent, either. Not only was he young, around twenty or so, but he was going into undercover work. Of the kind where he could be gone for weeks and months at a time, when she'd have no idea where he was and what he was doing, and whether he'd make it back in one piece.

I'd had a little experience of that with Rafe's undercover career. Just for the last few months of it, before it all exploded in his face and blew his cover sky high. And it wasn't something I'd wish on anyone. Especially not a seventeen-year-old, new mother.

She put a hand on her stomach. "I think I am. Keeping it. I can't see myself carrying it for all this time and then giving it to somebody else."

I nodded. I could certainly relate to that. By the time I gave birth to Carrie, if anyone had suggested taking her away from me, I would have clawed their face off.

Different if you go into it with that idea, of course. But it didn't sound as if Alexandra had.

"Do you know what you're having?"

"The ultrasound was last month," Alexandra said. "The tech said she thought it was a boy. It's not for certain, though, but that's what she said."

She picked up another fry.

"Do you have a name picked out?"

Rafe and I had gone back and forth a little bit. I'd always been in favor of Caroline for a girl—after my few-times-great-grandmother, who had a baby with the groom while her husband was away fighting the Damn Yankees—but I'd wanted to make sure he didn't want something else. Like LaDonna, after his dead mother. If we'd had a boy, I would have pushed for William, who'd been the son of Caroline and the groom. Robert, after my late father, had been another possibility, but Catherine had already beaten me to that one, and anyway, we ended up with a girl.

"I thought maybe I'd call him Rafe," Alexandra said.

I choked, and then took a look at her face. "You're not serious."

She nodded, eyes wide. "I am. Jamal and I met at your wedding. It seems appropriate."

Sure. Name the poor kid after my husband, whose responsibility it was that twenty-year-old Jamal had knocked up seventeen-year-old Alexandra and ruined her life.

"If you're going to name him after someone," I said, "maybe you should go with Martin." And put the blame on me, where by rights it belonged. "Rafe is such a romance novel name, don't you think?" Probably the reason why 14-year-old LaDonna Collier had come up with it thirty-one years ago. "Are you sure you want to give your son something like that to live up to?"

Alexandra thought about it. "Maybe not."

Thank you, God.

"Jamal told me what happened," Alexandra said, with a look at me across the table. "That the TBI fired Rafe."

The waitress came and dropped off my iced tea, and I waited for her to leave and took a sip before I answered. "They didn't exactly fire him. I mean, he didn't do anything to get himself fired. They're just not giving him anyone else to train until they see how Jamal and his friends do."

After a second, and another sip of tea, I added, "I guess they're essentially just eliminating his job. And Wendell's."

Alexandra nodded. "Jamal's going to be working with a guy named Kirk. He's kind of bummed."

I would be bummed, too, if I'd thought I'd be working with Wendell and/or Rafe, and got someone named Kirk instead. "I'm sure it'll turn out OK. Rafe doesn't really know much about the gang culture. That's more an urban thing. He didn't grow up with it. And he's getting a little old to pull it off."

Dreadlocks, gold teeth, and saggy pants four months ago notwithstanding.

"Kirk is even older," Alexandra grumbled. "And not near as hot."

I arched my brows, and she added, "Sorry. But your husband's hot. You know he is."

Of course he was. But that didn't mean it was OK for her to notice. Or remark on it.

She snorted. "I'm seventeen. Not blind or stupid."

"Stick with boys your own age."

"I did," Alexandra said. And although that wasn't exactly true—Jamal was three or four years older, she'd been underage, and he should have known better—I had to give her the point. He was only three or four years older, not fourteen, like Rafe. And in Jamal's favor, she didn't tell him how old—or young—she was, so he hadn't known she was underage when he took her to bed.

Not that that's much of an excuse, but he isn't exactly seasoned himself, either.

"How are the two of you doing?"

She shrugged. "OK, I guess. He went with me to the ultrasound. He says he wants to be there for the baby. But he doesn't want to get married, and I don't, either."

"You're a bit too young to tie yourself down. Especially if the only reason is that you're pregnant. Give it some time. If you're meant to be together, it'll be obvious."

I'd gotten married the first time at twenty-three, and had learned pretty quickly that I'd had no idea what I was doing, or any clue what I'd been looking for in a mate. The relationship lasted less than two years before Bradley dumped me for his paralegal.

"Easy for you to say," Alexandra said. "You got Rafe."

Indeed I did. The second time around, I knew exactly what I wanted. Even if it took me a bit of time to admit—to myself and anyone else—that he was it.

The waitress approached with the salads, and whisked away the now-empty plate of fries. Alexandra fell on her salad like she was starving, and I lifted my fork and started picking at mine, too. "How's your father doing?"

"Fine," Alexandra said between bites. "Handling the baby-thing like a champ. And it's been a year since Maybelle went to prison, so he's mostly over that, too. Maybe starting to date again."

Good for him. "It's not that long since your mother died. It can take time to get over something like that."

Alexandra nodded and swallowed. "He's taking it slow. There's a woman at work he's had dinner with a couple of times. No more than that. She seems nice. Much nicer than Maybelle."

It wouldn't be hard to be nicer than Maybelle. But since we both already knew that, I didn't bother to point it out. "And Austin?"

Alexandra's younger brother, a classmate of Rafe's son David at Montgomery Bell Academy, was also doing well. We spent the rest of lunch making small talk about Carrie, and the baby Alexandra was expecting, and Steven and Austin and how she was doing in school—Harpeth Hall, the exclusive girlschool equivalent of MBA—and any other little thing that crossed our minds.

The check had arrived and I'd signed for it by the time Alexandra asked, "So what are you going to do now? You and Rafe? If he isn't working at the TBI anymore?"

"We're thinking of moving back to Sweetwater," I told her. And amended it. "At least for a while. Rafe has been offered a job with the Columbia PD."

That maybe wouldn't last forever, or beyond the first year, now that I knew what Grimaldi's appointment to the position was really about. Maybe we'd better not sell Mrs. Jenkins's house, in case we needed to go back to it.

Alexandra's eyes widened. "Move away? But..."

"It isn't far," I said. "Just over an hour."

She nodded. "I know. I've been there. But we won't be able to have lunch together anymore."

And if she got in trouble, she couldn't call me in the middle of the night, the way she'd done once before, and have me—and Rafe—show up to extricate her.

Although with a baby on the way, hopefully those days were behind her.

"It may not last long," I said. "Rafe isn't all that fond of Sweetwater. He didn't have a great upbringing there. We'll have to see how it goes."

"I don't like it," Alexandra said, sticking her bottom lip out.

"I'm sorry. But he just lost his job at the TBI. Beggars can't be choosers. The Columbia PD is offering a salary and benefits, and we do need money to live, just like everyone else."

"I get it. I'm just sad."

"I'll come up and see you," I said. "We'll still be friends. Jamal will still want to see Rafe, I'm sure. We won't be strangers."

Alexandra nodded, if reluctantly. "I'll miss you."

"I'll miss you, too," I told her. "But we really aren't going far. And it isn't settled yet. For now, Detective Goins is trying to prove that Rafe had something to do with Doug Brennan's accident, and is asking him not to leave town." Not that he could enforce that. "While that's going on, I don't think Rafe's going anywhere. I'll let you know what happens later. And even if we do end up leaving, I'll only be an hour away. You can call me anytime."

"Don't think I won't," Alexandra said, and, putting her hands on the table, levered herself to her feet and waddled toward the door. I grabbed the car seat with the baby and followed.

Ten

I wasn't paying a whole lot of attention as I drove up Potsdam Street toward Mrs. Jenkins's house. It wasn't until I'd actually turned the nose of the Volvo into the circular driveway, that I noticed the cars parked there.

Detective Goins's Toyota was back. So were a black and white squad car, and a white van with the MNPD logo and *Crime Scene Unit* in blue letters along the back. And not only that: a handful of CSI techs in white coveralls were moving slowly through the back and front yards, eyes on the ground.

I stopped the Volvo behind the van and got out, leaving Carrie asleep in the back seat. In deference to her sleeping, I didn't slam the car door, although I wanted to. Instead I closed it carefully before I stalked over to Detective Goins, who was standing—hands on his hips and belly bulging gently over the waistband of his Sansabelt slacks—surveying his minions. "What the hell—heck—is this?"

He smirked. "What does it look like?"

I looked around. Not that I needed to. "It looks like you're searching my home."

"We started with the yard," Goins said, pulling a folded sheet of paper out of his inside pocket, "since you weren't home."

"The yard is private property too, you know." I took the paper away from him and unfolded it. As expected, it was a search warrant. And it looked legal. Not that I'd know, but it had today's date on it, and a signature on the bottom.

I started to hand it back, and then changed my mind. "I'm just going to take a picture of this."

"Why?" Goins wanted to know.

I glanced at him. "So I can send it to my husband. So he knows what's going on." I laid the warrant on the hood of Goins's SUV, pulled out my phone, and snapped a couple of pictures. Then I sent them off to Rafe's phone before I gave Goins his warrant back. "Would you like to go inside now?"

"As soon as we're done with the yard," Goins said.

"Any chance you'll tell me what you're looking for?"

It had to be related to Doug Brennan's death somehow, but if the man had driven off the road, it wasn't like there was a murder weapon to be found.

"No," Goins said. And added, "We'll know it when we find it."

Sure. "Well, I'm going to take my daughter inside and put her to bed." And hope she stayed that way. Although that wasn't likely, if a herd of CSI techs started to crawl all over the house.

My phone dinged a return message, and I opened it. Yep, a response from Rafe. A short and succinct one. *WTF?*

He won't tell me what they're looking for, I texted back.

A few seconds passed, and then I got another message. *Ignore it. We didnt do nothing.*

No, we hadn't. Ignoring it was easier said than done, though. When someone, or a whole lot of someones, crawl all over your property and search through your things to try to find evidence to tie you to a murder you didn't commit, it feels like a violation even if you didn't do anything wrong. But I did my best. Just gave Goins a tight nod, and went to pull Carrie out of the Volvo.

I had the car door open when a hail went up from one of the

crime scene techs on the other side of the yard. I shaded my eyes and saw that she was standing beside the trash and recycling bins I had filled earlier this morning.

Well, it made sense they'd check those. If we wanted to throw something away, it would be in trash or recycling. In fact, we had thrown away lots of things in trash or recycling.

Now the empty beer bottles I'd dumped in the recycling bin this morning were all over the grass, looking for all the world like someone in our household had a real problem with alcohol. Goins would probably think Rafe did.

I glanced at Carrie—still asleep—and closed the door again, gently, before I made my way across the grass. "We had a party last night. It's not like we usually have this many empty bottles in recycling."

Rafe drinks beer, but not in excessive amounts, and I'm nursing, so I'm off anything with alcohol in it for the duration. Since I'd been off alcohol during the nine months I was pregnant, too, I was used to it by now.

"I put those in there this morning," I added. "Along with the pizza boxes in the trash can. We don't usually eat five pizzas by ourselves, either."

The crime scene tech gave me a look I interpreted as sympathetic, and Goins leered, as if he didn't believe a word of what I'd just said. "How about this?" He brandished something. "Did you put this in the bin this morning?"

It was a knife. A familiar one. "That's Rafe's," I said. "Or at least it looks like Rafe's. Was that in there?"

The crime scene tech—a woman in her forties—nodded.

"Hidden under the bottles," Goins added, with relish.

"You mean it was at the bottom of the bin." Which had had some cardboard in it when I dumped the bottles on top this morning. "That's not surprising, you know. The knife's heavier than the cardboard. It would have slid to the bottom." Or might have. It wasn't unreasonable to think it would. "That doesn't mean anyone tried to hide it."

"Why would your husband throw his knife away?"

"I have no idea," I said. "I don't know that it's his. It looks like his, but that doesn't mean it is. One knife looks very much like another." Just like one gun looks much like another. At least until you do a ballistics test on it. Which you can't do on a knife. "But if he threw it away, it must be because it's broken."

Goins flicked it open and looked at it. "Doesn't look broken to me."

"Then there's no reason he would have thrown it away. And are you sure you should be handling it quite so much? Even with gloves on? There could be fingerprints, right?"

He didn't say anything to that, although the crime scene tech's lips quirked as she dug a brown paper bag out of a pocket of her coveralls and offered it. I deduced she might not be any more fond of Goins than me.

The knife went into the bag. I said, "Unless there's a law against throwing away your own property, I don't see that this proves anything. Besides, unless Brennan was stabbed to death, why does it matter that Rafe threw away his knife?" If he had.

"That's for me to know," Goins said.

I rolled my eyes. "Right. And for me to find out. I'll be inside. With the baby."

I stalked back across the grass to the Volvo. This time, nothing happened to stop me from lifting Carrie out and moving toward the stairs with her. I'd only made it a few steps when both doors in the squad car opened.

"Oh." I smiled. And felt some of the tension leave my body. "It's you two. What are you doing here?"

"Just keepin' an eye on things," Office Lyle Spicer told me. He and his partner, George Truman, were the cops who had answered the 911 call that morning when Rafe and I had found

Brenda Puckett dead inside Mrs. J's house. We'd become friendly since then. They knew Rafe, and liked him, and seemed to like me well enough too, and although they didn't seem to have anything to do with the search, just the fact that they were here made me feel better.

Spicer, in his forties with ginger hair starting to go silver, and what's usually called a lived-in face, bent to look at Carrie. "What's your husband done now?" he asked.

"Nothing. He lost his job at the TBI. Then his boss—not Wendell, the guy above Wendell—drove his car off the road a couple of nights ago. We were in Sweetwater seeing my mother and having dinner with Grimaldi. Rafe was nowhere near Ridgetop. But Goins doesn't seem open to reason."

Spicer straightened. His expression said he wasn't surprised to hear it. "The detective called us. Although I guess I should call her 'the chief' now." His eyes twinkled.

I smiled back. "I guess so. She's doing well. I saw her on Thursday. She wants Rafe to come down there and work with her."

"He could do worse," Spicer said. Meanwhile, it was Truman's turn to look at Carrie. He's twenty years younger than his partner, half a decade younger than me, and has a tendency to blush if I flirt with him. Since I was a sedate, married woman with a baby now, I didn't try. Just gave him a smile, too.

"It's good to see you both. Do you want to come inside?"

Spicer shook his head. "We'd better stay out here as long as they're out here." His glance took in Goins and the CSI crew.

"They're coming in later. When they're finished here. Feel free to join them."

"I don't think there'll be much point," Truman said. "I think they found what they were looking for."

"The knife?"

He shrugged. There was a pair of good shoulders inside the

uniform jacket. "Is that what they found in the bin?"

I nodded. "It looked like Rafe's, but then a lot of knives look the same."

"You could ask him," Spicer said, and I supposed I could.

"When I put the baby down. I told him they were here. He might be on his way home." I wouldn't be surprised if he were. And I also wouldn't be surprised if he were somewhat pissed when he got here. Especially as this little exercise had taken him away from the task of helping José and Clayton, probably—or at least possibly—for the last time.

"We'll be out here if you need us," Spicer said and gave Truman a nudge. They made their way back into the squad car. I carried the car seat up the steps to the porch, put it down while I unlocked the door, and picked it up again to carry inside.

Once she was safely deposited on the table in the parlor—no sense in taking her out of the seat only to put her in her bed; she might as well finish sleeping where she was—I shrugged out of my coat and dug the phone back out of my purse. *They found a knife in the recycling bin. Looks like yours.*

It took a few seconds before the response came back. *I got mine.*

So it wasn't Rafe's knife, then. That was a relief, although it might be hard to prove. He might have had two—or more accurately, Goins might surmise he'd had two—or he could have taken the one he was carrying off someone just today. Wendell or one of the boys, as a logical for instance. They all had the same equipment. When they carried guns, they were all the same guns, too. Standard issue.

Want me to tell Goins that?

On my way, the response came back.

OK, then. So I could expect my husband to show up in the next fifteen or twenty minutes, after having pushed the Harley-Davidson to its limits on the way here from Antioch or wherever he'd been when he got my initial text. And he wouldn't be happy.

I settled into the sofa to wait, with the TV on a rerun of *Barnwood Builders*.

Before Rafe got there, though, the search moved inside. Goins opened the door, without so much as a knock, and waved the crime scene crew inside. "Check it top to bottom. Don't miss anything."

"How many stories?" someone asked. It wasn't the woman from earlier, so maybe the CSI crew had a boss, and she wasn't it.

Goins didn't know the answer, so I supplied it. "Three, plus the basement. The top floor is just a big ballroom. Bedrooms and bath on the second floor. Common rooms down here. Basement entrance in the kitchen."

They spread out. Goins remained standing in the hallway, rocking back and forth on the balls of his feet.

"Rafe's on his way," I told him. "He isn't happy. And he's got his knife."

Goins's eyes narrowed. "Is that a threat?"

I'd ended up with the same crime scene tech again, wandering around the parlor peering at things, and now she snorted. Softly, but I think Goins heard it, because he scowled at her.

"No," I said. "It's a public service announcement, telling you that my husband is carrying his knife and the one you found outside isn't his."

"That doesn't prove anything," Goins said. And of course it didn't. And anyway, I wasn't getting paid to argue with him. I turned my attention to the screen, while the CSI tech finished her circuit of the room and moved on the library next door.

It took her maybe ten minutes to make her way into the kitchen, and then I heard the basement door open. It squeaks. On purpose. It gives the house a sort of spooky feel, but in the event that someone were to make it through the gazebo floor and down the shaft and through the tunnel and into the basement, it also lets us know that someone's there. At least that was the rationale Rafe gave me when I asked him if he could oil the hinges.

There was squeaking from over my head, too, where someone was wandering around what used to be Mrs. Jenkins's lavender bedroom, stepping on the century-old floorboards. And from even farther away, noises from the top floor. There's nothing up there. Just a big, empty room that was used for dancing a long time ago. There's a view of the downtown skyline—or at least of the very tops of the taller buildings—from the southwest facing windows.

Closer to hand, steps stomped down the basement stairs. I wondered whether she'd notice the door into the tunnel—it's sort of hidden under the stairs—and sure enough… "There's a boarded-up door here."

I got to my feet and wandered into the kitchen. Goins was there before me, already rattling down the rickety stairs into the dank and cold basement. "It's the entrance to a tunnel that runs over to the gazebo," I directed down the stairs. "We boarded it up so no one can get in that way. Feel free to pry the nails out as long as you hammer them in again."

Nobody said anything, and I went back to the parlor and the TV. Carrie stayed asleep through it all.

It was a few minutes later that I heard the familiar growl of the Harley coming up the driveway. The sound cut off, and then I heard the slamming of a couple of car doors. Spicer and Truman must have exited the squad car to say hello to Rafe. Or maybe to stop him from barging through the door and pinning Goins to the wall by his throat.

I got up and peered through the window.

Yes, there they were, having what looked like a pleasant

enough conversation at the bottom of the stairs. The cops had both put themselves between Rafe and the staircase, but he couldn't be too upset, or he'd have mowed them both down—or moved them both aside—to get in here.

Instead, they were standing there shooting the breeze. Spicer and Truman were both smiling, and as I watched, the tension left Rafe's shoulders, too. His eyes turned from flat black to their usual dark brown, and eventually he smiled. The encounter ended with Spicer slapping him on the shoulder before he and Truman went back to the squad car and Rafe came up the stairs.

I met him at the door. "There are three CSI techs plus Goins. Two of them are upstairs. Goins and the third are in the basement."

Rafe's brow arched, but he didn't say anything.

"They found the door to the tunnel. I think they think we're hiding something back there."

"Then they'll be disappointed," Rafe said. "Scuse me, darlin'."

He headed past me down the hallway to the kitchen. I trailed behind, and stayed at the stop of the stairs when he started down. There was a sound of prying coming from below.

"You better make sure you nail that up again after you're done," Rafe informed them. His tone was friendly, but I don't think any thinking person could have missed the undertone. Goins's shadow, which was all I could see of him, straightened its shoulders.

"We have a warrant."

"I didn't say a word about your warrant," Rafe told him. "See this?"

There was a pause, then Goins's voice came back. "Are you threatening me?"

"Hell, no," Rafe said. "What I'm doing, is showing you my knife. That I've had in my pocket all day. All day yesterday, too.

And the day before that. So whatever you found in the bin outside didn't belong to me."

"You might have had two," Goins said.

Rafe's voice stayed friendly, yet distinctly unsettling. "No law against a man having more than one knife. But as it happens, I only have this one."

"How do I know one of your friends didn't give it to you this morning?" Goins wanted to know.

There was a beat. Then— "You don't. You could ask'em. But you're gonna have to hurry, since two of'em are on their way outta town."

"Fleeing!"

I don't know if Rafe rolled his eyes, but I was tempted to. "They're all four of'em gainfully employed by the TBI, Detective. Neither one's any happier about Brennan being dead than I am."

"There was someone in the yard last night," I said down the stairs. "I saw him, or her, when I woke up to feed the baby. It was a little after two, I think. By the time Rafe got down there, whoever it was was gone. But obviously that's who dropped the knife in the recycling bin."

"Likely story," Goins said, with a heavy dose of disbelief running through his voice. "Why would anyone want to drop their knife in your recycling bin?"

Let me count the ways… "He used it to rob someone two blocks over, and didn't want it on him in case the police caught up?"

"Was there a robbery two blocks over?" Goins asked.

"That'd be your job to figure out, Detective," Rafe said. "We're civilians."

"But there are often robberies around here," I added, still talking down the stairs. "You may have noticed that this is what they call a transitional neighborhood. For the most part, the criminal elements leave us alone, but this guy might not have known whose recycling bin it was he dropped his weapon into."

"Or he mighta thought the trash would get picked up before anybody found it," Rafe added. "No reason to think anybody'd be turning my property over this weekend, after all."

No reason at all.

"Or maybe that's the knife you used to cut Brennan's brake cables," Goins said triumphantly.

"You keep saying that," I told him. "But you still haven't told us for sure that that's what happened."

And didn't this time, either. The CSI tech must have gotten the door open, or maybe she came back from crawling the tunnel to the end and back. In either case, I heard her say, "Nothing."

"Let me in," Goins said.

I pictured him crawling down the dirt tunnel on hands and knees, and shook my head. Rafe must have had the same thought, because when he came up the stairs a few seconds later, he told me, "Ain't no talking to some people."

I shook my head. "I'm sorry you had to come back for this. I could have handled it on my own. It isn't like they're going to find anything, after all."

"They found a knife," Rafe said. He put his hand on my lower back and nudged me down the hallway toward the front door and the parlor. "This guy you saw in the middle of the night. Could it have been somebody putting a knife in the recycling bin?"

I glanced over at Carrie. She was still asleep. "Of course it could have. I only got a glimpse of him out the window. He might have been a she. That's how little I saw. But it was on the side of the house where the bins are."

Rafe nodded. "This is circumstantial evidence in any case. The knife was outside, not in the house. Anybody coulda put it there. And we were an hour away on Thursday night, nowhere near Brennan's house. It's nothing to worry about."

I wasn't really worried. But in deference to the fact that we had six cops, or three cops and three crime scene investigators, on the property, I lowered my voice. "Do you get the impression someone's trying to set you up?"

"Goins," said Rafe.

I shook my head. "Not Goins. He's just following the trail. Grimaldi said he didn't have much imagination. But somebody put that knife there. And there's too big of a coincidence that it wouldn't have something to do with Doug Brennan. Besides, how did Goins know to get a warrant and search the place? We've both told him we weren't in Nashville on Thursday night. He spoke to Grimaldi and she told him the same thing. There's a reason he keeps coming back to you for this." And it wasn't because Rafe looked guilty. Any idiot could see that he wasn't.

Except maybe the idiot that was Rick Goins.

"You know," I said, "we got very lucky with both Grimaldi and Jaime Mendoza. And for that matter with Spicer and Truman. It's probably just the law of averages that we should end up with someone like Goins sooner or later."

Rafe grunted, but he put his arm around me and dropped a kiss on the top of my head. "Makes me wanna go to Sweetwater and work for Tammy, if this is the way it's gonna be from now on."

"You and me both," I told him.

The MNPD cleared out by late afternoon, after finding nothing more incriminating than the knife in the recycling bin.

Judging by Goins's expression, he thought it was plenty incriminating, but as Rafe had said, the bin was outside in the yard. Anyone, literally anyone in the whole neighborhood, could have dropped the knife in there. Goins could have put it there himself, to have an excuse to execute his search warrant. I decided to ask Grimaldi whether that was something he'd do the next time I spoke to her. Since she was spending the day, or at least part of the day, with Dix and his daughters, it wasn't something I needed to know badly enough to interrupt them.

Spicer and Truman had confirmed that there was some question about whether Brennan's brake lines had been cut. The car had been pretty mangled, apparently, by the time it had been found, and the evidence had been inconclusive. There'd been damage to the brake lines, but no way to know whether it had been deliberately done before the accident, or whether the trip over the edge of the road and down what might have been a rocky embankment had done the trick.

Goins seemed inclined to believe that the brake lines had been cut. But whether that was because he'd found the knife and thought it was connected, or whether there was something to actually suggest that the brake lines had been tampered with, Spicer couldn't say. Since Goins also seemed determined to believe Rafe was guilty, in spite of copious evidence to the contrary, we probably couldn't trust his instinct about the brake lines in any case.

Spicer and Truman took off, too, with a cheery wave, and Rafe turned to me. "Alone at last."

And just in time for Carrie to wake up and want another feeding. I went into the house and watched him close and lock the front door. Down at the end of the driveway, the squad car carrying Spicer and Truman took a right out of the driveway and disappeared in the direction of downtown.

"It was nice to see them," I said.

"Nice of Tammy to ask 'em to keep an eye on things." He glanced past me into the parlor.

"Is that what happened? Spicer told me she'd called, but I didn't put two and two together."

He nodded. "Seems that way. You wanna take a drive?"

"I wouldn't mind taking a drive. But can we put it off an hour, maybe, so I can feed and change Carrie, and give her a little time on the floor before we put her back in the car seat? She's spent most of the day there."

"Sure," Rafe said, and sat down on the sofa. He reached for the remote. "Mind if I change this?"

"Not at all." I sat down next to him and turned my attention to the manly game of basketball that appeared on the screen in lieu of my decorating show.

Eleven

We set out just before four. Rafe had seen the end of the game. I had fed Carrie, and changed her diaper, and spent time with her, on the floor as well as the sofa. Rafe had held her for a while, too, which never failed to make me feel good inside. He'd missed all this with his first child. When David was born Rafe had been in prison, and he hadn't known about David's existence until just over a year ago. By now, David was thirteen, and while that had a charm of its own—they were more like brothers when they got together, than father and son—Rafe hadn't been a part of any of the growing up. The fact that he was here now, and got to experience every little thing our daughter did—not that she did much of anything yet—thrilled me.

But just before four, we put Carrie back in the car seat, put on our coats, and got back in the car. Rafe took the wheel, and it didn't surprise me at all when he started out going north on Potsdam. At Trinity Lane, we moved east to Ellington Parkway, and then headed north again—the antennae on top of the TBI building waved at us from a distance as we zoomed past—before merging with Interstate 65 going north.

"Do you know where you're going?" I asked.

He asked. "Wendell gave me directions."

OK, then. I settled back in the seat and let him drive.

Ridgetop is little town way up north in Davidson County, straddling the line to Robertson. It's very hilly. On cold winter days like now, when the schools are closed for inclement weather, it's often because the school buses can't make it up and down the steep and winding roads in this part of the county.

We stayed on the interstate past Rivergate, past Goodlettsville and Millersville, and then struck out north. Pretty soon there was nothing to see but trees and fields and the occasional driveway. We hadn't met another car since we'd left the interstate.

"It's easy to see how someone could drive off the road up here and not be found until the next morning. Especially at night."

It wasn't night now, but it was still deserted.

Rafe nodded. He was scanning left and right as he drove. In the backseat, Carrie hadn't gone back to sleep yet, but was looking around with big eyes.

"Do you know where it happened?"

He shook his head. "Wendell told me where to find Brennan's house. This is the straightest route there from the TBI. I'm looking to see if I can find where he went off the road."

"Be careful." We were cresting a hill, and at the top of it was a sign with squiggly lines and the words *Bridge Freezes Before Road*.

Rafe slowed down. On his own he probably wouldn't have bothered, but with me and Carrie in the car, he obviously didn't want to take any chances.

The road crested and then dropped on the other side. The car picked up speed again. Until Rafe put his foot on the brake.

The car objected, and we fishtailed for a second before he got the car back under control. "They weren't kidding," I said.

He shook his head, and pulled the car over on the side of the road. Just ahead, on the shoulder and down the hill to our right, was the evidence of a lot of activity. The gravel shoulder of the road was broken in several places, and there were the imprints of tire tracks in the dirt. Down through the field and woods next to us ran several pairs of tracks across the grass.

Rafe reached for his door handle. "I'll keep the engine running so you'll be warm."

"That's not necessary." I was wearing a coat, and the last thing I wanted was to run out of gas here, in the middle of nowhere. We still hadn't seen a soul since we left the interstate, and hadn't passed a gas station, either. It was rural up here. "We don't know how long you'll be gone. I'd rather not risk it."

He hesitated, but turned the key in the ignition. The engine fell silent. "Here." He handed the keys over. "I don't imagine it'll take long, but just in case."

I didn't ask in case of what, just took the keys. "Be careful."

"I don't imagine there's anything to worry about," Rafe said.

"I wasn't afraid that somebody would be down there with a shotgun." Although there have been cases of the murderer returning to the scene of the crime. If Brennan had been murdered, his murderer could decide to come back.

Or maybe he'd shot out one of Brennnan's tires with a high-powered rifle from a mile away, and that was why Doug Brennan had gone off the road. Maybe he was watching us right now.

But surely that was ridiculous. I shook it off. "Just make sure you don't fall and break your leg. I'm not sure I can haul you back up here again if you do."

He nodded. "I'll see you in a few minutes."

He got out and closed the car door. I locked myself and Carrie in, for good measure, since you never know. And then I watched Rafe drop over the edge of the road and head down across the grass to the trees in the distance.

Sitting here, it was easy to see what had happened. At least it seemed obvious to me. Brennan had crested the hill on his way home Thursday night. It had been late and dark. There were no street lights on this road, and no houses nearby that would have had their lights on. And the time of month was wrong for a full moon. So it had been dark. It was cold this time of year. The sign on the other side of the hill warned of ice.

He'd either crested the hill, and there'd been ice, and he'd gone off the road and across the grass into the trees. An accident.

Or he'd crested the hill and something had been there, like a deer or a rabbit or even just someone walking a dog. He'd swerved to avoid them, and had gone off the road. Also an accident. And probably one involving an animal rather than a human, since if there'd been a person involved, I would hope that he or she would have gone to check on Brennan, or at least would have called 911 for help for him. That hadn't been done, so chances were no one but Doug Brennan had been here.

Unless someone had been here, but had been up to no good, and he or she hadn't wanted it known that they were here. But it would take a pretty cold person to let someone else drive off the road and die without helping them, just to keep secret the fact that you'd been here. I like to think that most people are better than that.

By now Rafe had made his way down to the bottom of the steepest incline and was following the tire tracks toward the trees, looking left and right. I watched for a second, and then went back to my thoughts.

The third solution was that someone had cut Brennan's brake cables, hoping for an accident. That pointed to someone at the TBI, since that's where Brennan had been on Thursday.

Whoever cut the cables couldn't have known exactly when the brakes would go out, though. They might have gone out when Brennan was on his way out of the TBI parking lot, and that accident wouldn't have been fatal at all. Brennan would have hauled his car to the shop and discovered that the brakes had been tampered with. And surely the hypothetical tamperer wouldn't have wanted that.

If the accident had happened on Ellington Parkway, on the other hand, or on the interstate or up here, the results would have been much as expected. Which I assumed would have been the reason someone did it. To get rid of Brennan.

But again, he or she wouldn't have had any way to control where the accident happened unless he or she was actually here.

Rafe reached the trees and stopped.

I decided to look at the problem from a different angle. The angle of who'd want to get rid of Brennan.

I knew nothing about him, except what Rafe had told me. He was in his forties, with thinning hair and glasses, and sat at a desk. He was Wendell's supervisor, which meant he was someone who worked with undercover agents at the TBI. At a guess, he probably oversaw several of them and their handlers, and coordinated operations, and things like that.

I knew he lived out here, in Ridgetop, in what Wendell called a cabin. He hadn't mentioned a family, so maybe Brennan lived alone. A bachelor, someone who'd never been married, or maybe divorced or a widower.

Or gay. No reason he couldn't be gay.

If I'd wanted to get rid of someone like Brennan, I think I would have staged a home invasion at his cabin in the woods. Far away from everyone, and with no chance that anyone would stop by until someone got suspicious. That'd be easier than messing with his brake lines in a busy parking lot, and there'd be less chance that something would backfire.

Of course, it would also take killing him personally, and I could see why someone might want to shy away from that. Much easier to tamper with someone's car and then leave the results to fate. Your hands wouldn't be exactly clean then either, but at least they wouldn't be bloody.

But whoever did this—if anyone did it—might have wanted

to make it look like an accident. Hard to do that with a home invasion gone wrong. It hadn't taken Goins long at all to find the compromised brake cables, though. So this hadn't looked like an accident for long, either.

Unless the brake cables weren't actually compromised, and Goins was imagining things.

Rafe must have looked around enough, because when I glanced in his direction, he was on his way back.

So who'd want to get rid of Brennan?

To Goins, it made sense that Rafe did. And if I hadn't known my husband, and if he hadn't had an alibi and been more than an hour away on Thursday night, I could see why. There are people who have done worse than kill a supervisor after losing their job.

Had Brennan fired anyone else? Had they been cleaning house of other people too, at the beginning of the new year, or was it just Rafe who'd gotten the boot?

And why was someone trying to implicate Rafe? Whoever it was couldn't have known that we'd be in Sweetwater the night Brennan was killed. It had been a spur of the moment decision, and we hadn't told anyone we were leaving. We hadn't told anyone we'd be coming, either. Both Mother and Grimaldi had been taken by surprise. The Harley-Davidson had been parked outside the house on Potsdam while we were gone, so if anyone had driven by, they would have seen it. And might have assumed that if the bike was there, Rafe was there, too.

If we'd been home Thursday night, this frame-up might have looked very different. As it was, Goins was spending valuable time looking at Rafe anyway. And while he was doing that, someone else was getting away with murder.

Rafe climbed the last few feet up onto the road, and I unlocked the doors and waited until he'd gotten back into the driver's seat. "Who'd want Brennan dead?"

He shot me a look. "If I knew that, darlin', this wouldn't be near the problem it is."

Uh-oh. "I didn't realize it was a problem," I said. "I mean... not really. Goins is running around looking at you for a murder you didn't commit, that might not even be a murder. I know it's annoying, but I didn't really consider it a problem."

He held his hand out for the key, and I dropped it in his palm. His inserted it in the ignition before he answered. "It ain't a problem. Not really. I've just spent a lotta time getting talked to by cops for stuff I didn't do."

He had. And that made it easy to understand why this would bother him. Although— "A lot of stuff you did, too," I pointed out.

A corner of his mouth—the one I could see—curved. "You got a point."

The car pulled away from the shoulder and rolled off down the road. I contorted my neck to look into the back. Carrie had fallen asleep again. I lowered my voice a degree, just in case. "You're not really worried he'll arrest you, are you?"

Rafe shrugged. "Hard to see how he'd get a judge and jury to convict on so little evidence. But it'd be a hassle while it went on."

No question.

"To get back to what I asked you. I realize you don't know who might have wanted Brennan dead. Specifically. And that's if anyone wanted him dead, and this wasn't just an accident. Goins might be seeing a crime that isn't here."

Rafe nodded.

"But if someone wanted him dead. Who'd that be? Not specifically. But what sort of reason might someone have for wanting someone like Doug Brennan out of the way?"

"Any number of personal reasons," Rafe said, steering the car down the road. "He mighta cheated at cards. He mighta been sleeping with someone's wife. He mighta cut someone off on the road, and they followed him off the highway and forced him off the road."

That last one hadn't occurred to me earlier, but it made a certain kind of sense. There are all sorts of crazies out there. As for the others… "He wasn't married, I guess? Wendell didn't mention a wife. So at least we can eliminate a cheating wife who wanted him gone so she could marry her lover."

Rafe nodded. "He's divorced. Wife's remarried and lives somewhere like Boca Raton, or maybe Baton Rouge. Two kids. Neither of'em old enough to think of this."

"Money?"

"I'm sure he gets paid OK," Rafe said, and corrected it to, "Did. But nobody in law enforcement gets rich. Least not honestly."

Right. "Without having seen it, the property might be worth a few dollars, but probably not millions or anything like that. Not out here." Different if it had been in Williamson County. The south of us goes for more money than the north.

"His kids'd get it anyway," Rafe said, which was true. And property is a dime a dozen out here, so it didn't make sense that anyone would kill him for it. Unless they knew something I didn't. Oil or natural gas deposits or something like that. Or the rumor that someone was going to be building something big out this way, that would increase property values dramatically. I could make some inquiries at work as to whether that was likely.

"Guess that means you'll be going to the sales meeting Monday morning," Rafe said.

Every week, LB&A has a big sales meeting, during which we discuss closings, new listings, and anything else that's going on in the company and the real estate world at large that might affect us. I'd had no closings and had no new listings, but it wouldn't be strange at all for me to bring up the question of whether anything was going on, real estate wise, in Ridgetop.

"If you wouldn't mind taking Carrie for a couple of hours."

"Not like I got anything else to do," Rafe said with a shrug.

"Still thinking about the Grimaldi thing?"

He glanced over. "Thinking I might do it. Now that I understand the job better."

And not the part of the job that was on the books and understandable. The part that involved sniffing out whether any of his new colleagues were doing something they shouldn't be.

"But not while this is going on."

"It might work well to do it while this is going on. We know, and Grimaldi knows, that you had nothing to do with what happened to Brennan. But that little bit of official suspicion might help you down in Columbia." Might help him to look less squeaky clean to anyone who'd look at him with suspicion.

Not that there's anything very squeaky clean about my husband. And not that anyone who knew anything about his background would form that opinion, anyway.

But at any rate, it couldn't hurt.

He gave me a look that was roughly divided between amusement and appreciation. "I hadn't thought about that."

"Then you can think about it now. And maybe talk to Grimaldi about it, and see what she thinks."

Rafe nodded. "Maybe I'll do that. For now, we got a little B&E to do."

He turned the car off the road and onto a smaller road, or maybe just a long driveway, that would its way down into the woods.

"B&E?" I repeated.

He grinned. "You know what B&E means. Not like it's your first time breaking and entering."

It wasn't. Or wouldn't be. But it just might be my first time breaking into the home of a recently deceased murder victim.

If we got caught, this would look extremely bad. Especially to Detective Goins.

On the other hand, it was so quiet and deserted out here, that the chances of anyone seeing us were slim to none. Or so I hoped. Sincerely.

The driveway went on for a while. Several minutes. Finally we got out of the trees and found what I assumed was Brennan's house.

It was, as Wendell had said, a log cabin. Not the old kind that's been in the same spot forever, though. This was fairly new, built within the past twenty years, maybe, of gleaming golden logs, heavy with shellac, and a wraparound porch on what looked like all four sides. A huge stacked stone fireplace protruded through the porch roof on either side of the house. Behind it, the landscape fell away to a rolling view of fields and trees. It wasn't quite Gatlinburg—not high enough up for that— but if you were looking for a peaceful country setting with a view, you could do a lot worse.

And best of all, there were no other houses in sight. Not even in the far distance.

Rafe stopped the car and turned off the engine, and silence ensued. Water trickled somewhere out of sight, and the dry tree branches made crackling noises where they knocked against each other when the wind rustled through. Otherwise it was quiet. Very, very quiet.

"I think I'd be a little worried being out here by myself," I said, looking around.

Rafe nodded, and opened his door. "Let's go."

"Do you want me to bring Carrie?"

"I don't figure this'll take that long," Rafe said. "It's a small house. But yeah. Bring the seat and set it inside. I don't wanna leave her in the car. And I want you inside with me."

Fine by me. I unhooked the car seat from the base and

carried it onto the porch. Carrie stayed asleep, as if nothing was going on.

Rafe is quite adept with a set of lock picks—as well as with a couple of hair pins, or anything else he can find—and it took less than a minute before we were inside Doug Brennan's house. I held my breath when Rafe turned the knob and pushed the door open—what if Brennan had a security system? And what if someone had armed it?—but nothing happened.

Rafe shut the door behind us and looked around. "Nice place."

It was. Not big, but plenty large enough for one man.

The ceilings were vaulted, and bisected with beams. In the part of the cabin where we were standing, there was total open concept: I could look around and see a sofa and two chairs in front of the fireplace, a dining table with four chairs, and the kitchen, all from where I was standing. A door in the back wall either went to a bathroom, a laundry room, or some combination. Or maybe a coat closet.

A wall separated us from the other half of the house. When Rafe opened the nearest door, it went into what looked like a combination guest room and office. There was a daybed, but also a desk and chair, and a filing cabinet in the corner. An empty space on the desk looked like where a computer might have been sitting. Chances were the police had taken it, maybe to see whether there was something on it that would tell them who had killed Brennan, although I suppose it was possible that someone else had been here before us and had made off with it.

The filing cabinet was left, though, and there were papers scattered over the rest of the desk, too.

"Knock yourself out," I told Rafe, since I figured this would be what he'd be most interested in. "I'm going to take a look at the rest of the place."

He nodded. "Don't touch nothing."

I stuck my hands in my pockets. "What about you. Aren't you— Oh."

He'd already put on a pair of gloves. Probably while I was taking Carrie out of the Volvo. I hadn't even noticed it when he was finessing the lock.

He grinned. "Enjoy, darlin'."

"You, too," I said, and left him to his investigating while I took myself off to indulge my own love for other people's dwellings.

I've always enjoyed seeing how other people live. I appreciate architecture, too, and good design and all that. But the main reason I became a real estate agent, was because I like to go into other people's houses and look around. Not in the same detail that Rafe was currently doing—I wouldn't make a good crime scene tech—but I do enjoy seeing other people's spaces.

In this case, I got the impression that Doug Brennan—a man I'd never met—was someone who enjoyed his privacy (the house was in the middle of nowhere, with no neighbors in sight), but who also liked his comforts. This was definitely no off-the-grid dwelling. The living room furniture had looked comfortable, facing a TV that rivaled Rafe's, and he had a king size bed situated so he'd see the view first thing when he woke up in the morning. The comforter was a fluffy and masculine plaid, and the sheets a hundred percent cotton, navy blue. There were no curtains on the windows, and no alarm clock, so either Brennan used his phone for that, or he let the sun wake him when it rose. The room faced east and took advantage of the view out the back.

He used Ban deodorant and Head & Shoulders shampoo, moisturizing, on what little hair he had left. There were no fancy face creams or aftershaves in the attached bathroom, which was also masculine, with a large, tiled shower but no tub. There was no sign he entertained women in this space. The bedside table held no sex toys and no condoms. The only pictures were of himself and what I assumed were his children: a boy and girl in their mid- to late teens.

I wandered back out, after a last look at the view. And found Rafe standing in the middle of the office-slash-guest room, with his hands on his hips and a frustrated expression on his face. "Nothing?"

He shook his head. "I don't wanna take the time for a real thorough search. Don't wanna spend any more time here than we have to. So there could be something hidden somewhere, that I didn't find. But everything looks like it's just what it says it is. Stationary and checkbooks in the desk, old bills and bank statements in the filing cabinet."

I nodded. "Nothing out of the ordinary on the bank statements?" Once upon a time, when he and I had broken and entered somewhere else, we'd found bank statements going a long way toward solving another murder. It can happen.

But not this time. He shook his head again. "There could be a piece of paper in one of these files that has something about something else on it, that might be a clue why somebody'd want him dead, but I don't have the time to turn everything inside out looking for it. And chances are it ain't gonna be here anyhow."

I nodded.

He gave one last, frustrated look around before he headed for the door. "Let's get outta here."

"What type of thing were you looking for?" I wanted to know when we were back in the Volvo, with Carrie safely deposited in the back seat again, and on our way back toward the interstate and town.

"If I knew that—"

"Right. I get it. But you were looking for something. You

would have known it if you saw it." Kind of like Goins had told me about the knife in the bin. "What was it?"

"Something that would explain this," Rafe said, with frustration leaking through his voice. "Something that didn't belong. Something that somebody woulda killed for."

"So maybe he wasn't killed. Maybe it was just a tragic accident, and Goins is making it into something it's not."

Rafe shook his head. "I don't think so. He ain't stupid. Or not that stupid." He glanced at me. "Remember when Brennan called me on Thursday night and asked me to stop by?"

Of course I did. Not that I'd given it much thought since it happened.

"He sounded like something was going on. Something he wanted to talk to me about. If I'd been in Nashville Thursday afternoon, and I coulda met him, maybe he'd told me. And maybe this wouldna happened."

"It's not your fault," I said.

"I know that, darlin'. But I'm wondering if he didn't see something, or hear something, or realize something. And that something's what got him killed. And if he'd had the chance to tell me, maybe it wouldna happened."

Maybe. But there was no sense in thinking about it that way. "If he realized something during the day on Thursday," I said, "it wouldn't be here. He was on his way home when he died. If he had it with him, the police have it. But he wouldn't have had the chance to bring it home yet."

Rafe nodded.

"More likely it's at the TBI. Or just in his head. He might not have written it down anywhere."

"Safer when you don't write nothing down," Rafe said. "Nothing for nobody to find."

"Until you die, and then nobody knows what you discovered."

"Which woulda been the reason for getting rid of him," Rafe said, and shook his head. "If he left something at the TBI, somebody woulda found it by now. So chances are he just kept it in his head. And now it's gone."

"So what are we going to do?"

"Eat," Rafe said, and pulled the Volvo into the parking lot of a roadhouse with a flashing light in the window advertising *Beer – Food – Dessert* in blinking neon lights.

Twelve

There was family style dining at long tables, food cooked with lots of grease and served on pitted metal plates with rolls of paper towels instead of napkins, but it tasted good enough that I would have licked the plate had I not been worried about word getting back to my mother.

Not that there was any danger of that. This was a place Mother would never, ever set foot. I was a little worried myself, to be honest. Racism still lingers in some of the nooks and crannies here and there, and not everyone is comfortable with a mixed race couple. But I needn't have worried. People were as nice as could be. The waitress snuck glances at Rafe, who's definitely worth looking at, and gushed over Carrie, who was awake and on her best behavior.

After catfish and slabs of cherry pie with whipped cream out of a can, we staggered back out to the car and headed for home. By then it was after seven, and by the time we cruised down Potsdam Street toward Mrs. Jenkins's house, closer to eight.

"Should have left some lights on before we left," I muttered, as the house came into view, looking like something out of a scary movie.

"You just stay in the car," Rafe said. "I'll go open up. I can see pretty well in the dark."

He could. As I could attest to. However— "I didn't mean it that way. Just that it would have been convenient to have some light. The house looks kind of forbidding when all the lights are off."

Rafe nodded and turned the car into the driveway. The headlights lit up the gravel and the tree trunks, and beyond, the gazebo in the back yard. I peered in that direction, but could see no sign of life. "If we end up going to Sweetwater, what did you want to do with the house? I guess we should probably keep it, right, in case we don't end up staying?"

"For now," Rafe said, and pulled the Volvo to a stop behind the Harley-Davidson. He cut the lights and reached for the door. "Stay here."

"I told you I didn't mean it that way." I pushed open my own door, too, and swung my legs out. And barely had time to register what I was looking at before I heard a "Shit!" from the other side of the car, and then Rafe came sliding across the hood rather than taking the time to run around.

He took the steps to the porch two at a time. "Call 911."

I was already fumbling for my phone while scrambling up the steps after him. "Who is it? What happened?"

Rather than answering, Rafe shoved the key in the lock and pushed the door open. He reached around the door jamb and flipped the light switch at the same moment as the heavy front door slammed against the wall in the foyer from the momentum. And at that point it was only too obvious who and what had happened.

Or at least who. The what was a little less clear, aside from the obvious fact that it was bad.

"Oh, my God!" I took a step back, and almost fell of the edge of the stairs. "Malcolm! Is he alive?"

Rafe fell to his knees next to the body, and I heard another muttered, "Shit." But then the 911 operator picked up, and I got busy talking to her.

"We just came home, and there's a body on our front porch."

My teeth were chattering, and I had to focus on slowing down so I could continue. "Or maybe it's not a body. Maybe he's still alive. My husband's looking at him. He's been shot. Or maybe stabbed. Either way, there's a lot of blood."

A whole lot of blood. Malcolm's narrow chest was covered with it. It soaked the polo shirt he wore under his winter jacket, turning the multicolored logo of the gas station where he worked a uniform red, and it had stained the fleece inside the jacket and run onto the porch floor under him into a pool.

Hard to imagine that anyone could have lost that much blood and still be alive, but Rafe was fumbling his hands over Malcolm's chest, trying to compress the wounds, so maybe there was hope.

"We need an ambulance," I managed. "To 101 Potsdam Street in East Nashville. As fast as you can. Or I don't think he's going to make it."

Rafe shook his head. His face was grim.

"Anything I can do?" I asked, over the 911 operator's exhortations that I needed to stay on the line with her. I wasn't going anywhere, and my hands could be put to better use trying to keep Malcolm alive than holding the phone to my ear.

"No." Rafe didn't look up, just kept trying to staunch the bleeding. "He's either gonna bleed out or he's not. Depends on how fast they can get here. Nothing we can do but wait."

"Hopefully it won't be too long," I said. "Skyline Hospital isn't far." Rafe had gotten me there in eight minutes flat once. The ambulance could probably do even better. "And the nearest fire station is even closer than that."

He nodded. "I'm just gonna sit here and put some pressure on this."

"Need help?"

He shook his head. "Just pray. And you should probably get Carrie out of the car."

I probably should. She was starting to make noise.

I made my way back down the stairs. My knees were a little unsteady, but I got there. As I reached into the Volvo to haul the seat out, something caught my eye a few feet away. I hadn't noticed it earlier, in the dark, but now the porch light was glinting on it.

I left Carrie where she was for another moment and walked closer. "There's a knife over here." With blood on it. But there was probably no need to mention that.

"Don't touch it," Rafe said.

"I wasn't planning to." In the far distance, I could hear the sound of sirens. "It looks like yours."

There was a beat. "Mine's in my pocket."

"I didn't think it was anywhere else. Are you sure you don't want me to pick this one up and get rid of it?"

"Positive," Rafe said. "We haven't been here. We can prove it."

"We were breaking and entering into Doug Brennan's house!" And that wasn't the kind of alibi I wanted to share with Detective Goins.

"This happened after that," Rafe said, his hands still pressed to Malcolm's chest. They were bloody up to the wrists. "No more'n fifteen or twenty minutes ago. Or he'd be gone already."

We might have passed whoever did it on our way down to the house. And if we'd been fifteen or twenty minutes earlier, we'd have seen him. "We'll just tell them we drove out there for dinner, then."

"Just what I was planning to tell'em," Rafe said.

The sirens reached an earsplitting crescendo as the ambulance—from south of us, so the nearest fire station instead of the hospital—came into view. It shrieked into the driveway and came to a quivering stop behind the Volvo. I stepped aside as two paramedics burst from the car, bags in hand, and ran past me and up the stairs.

Rafe moved out of the way, and they got busy. Since they definitely didn't need my help now, and since I couldn't very well pick up the bloody knife and slip it into my pocket while they were watching, I went back to the Volvo and removed the car seat with the baby. By now she wasn't just making noises, she was full on wailing. I carried her up the stairs, across the porch, and into the house, making sure to keep her on the side of me that was away from the body.

Away from Malcolm, who—*please, God*—was still hanging on.

And I realize that Carrie was probably much too young to even register what was happening, let alone understand it. But the subconscious is weird, and I didn't want to be responsible for her being traumatized and having problems later in life.

Inside, I removed my coat, and removed Carrie from the seat, and—after a quick grope and sniff to make sure she wasn't in desperate need of a diaper change—did the one thing that I knew would calm us both down: sat down on the sofa and lifted my shirt and proceeded to feed the baby.

The door was still open, and I could feel the cold air on the back of my neck, although the back of the sofa protected most of me, and all of Carrie, from getting cold. And I didn't want to close the door and leave Rafe out there, so he'd have to twist the knob to get inside. I also didn't, in a weird way, want to cut myself off from what was going on. So I sat there, with my neck getting colder and colder, while the central heat kicked on to combat the chill and while the EMT's voices came to me less in words than in cadences.

After a few minutes, there were more sirens. Then the crunch of gravel, and the sound of heavy cop shoes on the porch. "What the hell happened here?" Lyle Spicer's voice said.

He and Truman must have either been in the area, or had

recognized our address when the call came over the radio, and had high-tailed it over here.

It must have been an official question, because Rafe explained that we'd come home from dinner and had found Malcolm on the porch. The lights had been off, and we hadn't noticed him until we'd stopped the car. At that point, Rafe had opened the door first, to get the light turned on, before he'd done what he could for Malcolm. "There's a knife—" he began, and Truman went to pick it up.

At that point, the paramedics must have done what they could for Malcolm, and loaded him into the ambulance to take to the hospital. He must still be hanging on, and they had hopefully attached him to a bag of blood, so he'd continue to hang on, because they squealed down the driveway—or more likely across the grass—with sirens screaming.

"C'mon inside," Rafe said in the silence that ensued. "It's cold out here. And I wanna wash my hands."

They came into the foyer. I twisted my head so I could nod at them over the back of the sofa. I managed a sort of grimace that might pass in low light, but it wasn't in me to smile graciously at the moment. Even Mother couldn't have faulted me for that.

"Savannah's feeding the baby," Rafe said; they both blushed, not just Truman, "so why don't we go back to the kitchen. I'll stop in at the bathroom on our way past."

That seemed to be acceptable, because all three of them stomped down the hallway. Nobody said anything about Rafe not washing his hands. I heard the water kick on in the small powder room off the hallway, and a few seconds later, the scraping of chair legs in the kitchen, as Spicer and Truman seated themselves.

Rafe came out a minute later, and the interview continued. "So y'all came home from dinner," Spicer said, "and found the young man on the porch. Any idea what he was doing there?"

I imagined Rafe shaking his head. "He lives two houses up. Works at the gas station on the corner of Dresden and Dickerson. Mighta wanted to ask a question. Mighta seen the activity earlier and wanted to know what was going on."

That would certainly make sense.

"Or he mighta wanted to tell us something. Somebody was in the yard last night. Somebody who maybe put that knife in the recycling bin. The knife that Goins found."

This time I imagined Spicer and Truman nodding.

"Malcolm works the late shift sometimes. He mighta been on his way home last night, and seen something. Maybe he came to tell us about it. Or maybe he saw somebody now. Somebody doing something he oughta not be doing. And maybe Malcolm went to confront him, and the guy stabbed him."

"What do you figure this somebody was doing," Spicer wanted to know, "that he didn't want anybody seeing?"

I imagined Rafe shrugging. "Coulda been anything. Trying to break in. Trying to steal the Harley. Trying to plant more evidence."

"You think somebody's trying to frame you for Doug Brennan's murder?"

"I think somebody's trying to do something," Rafe said. "I'm not even sure Brennan was murdered. But somebody seems bent on involving me in it. I wasn't even here that night. I was in Sweetwater, in Savannah's mama's house. But Goins don't seem like he wants to let go of the idea that I had something to do with it. And he didn't come up with that on his own. Somebody told him Brennan fired me. Somebody prob'ly made it sound a lot worse than it was. And somebody mighta had a good reason for that."

"Because he's the one who killed Brennan!" Truman said.

Rafe didn't respond to that, but I imagine he nodded. Or at

least shrugged. "Goins ain't gonna tell me nothing. Tammy's in Columbia, and I don't wanna ask Mendoza for a favor."

I hid a smile. I don't know why I bothered, since nobody but Carrie could see me. But no, while my husband and Jaime Mendoza get along just fine, Rafe isn't likely to ask Mendoza to go out of his way for him. He heard that Mother asked Mendoza to marry me while Rafe was missing, but while I don't think he's in any doubt as to how I feel about him—or how Mother feels about him at this point—there's no denying that Mendoza is both gorgeous and charming.

There was a pause after Rafe's statement. I figured Spicer and Truman were contemplating what Rafe was saying, or rather, what he hadn't said, in so many words.

"Whaddaya need?" Spicer said finally, signaling his willingness to at least consider it, even if he wasn't quite committed to doing whatever it was yet.

"I just need to know who Goins spoke to at the TBI, who put the bug in his ear that I mighta wanted Brennan dead. I don't have access there anymore. Wendell's still there, and Jamal Atkins, but Wendell's leaving too, and I ain't asking Jamal to stick his neck out for me. He needs that job."

There was another pause. I imagined the two officers glancing at each other, communicating silently. "We can find that out," Spicer said. And added, "You know Goins is on his way here."

"I figured he was." Rafe didn't sound worried about it.

I hadn't thought about it, to be honest, but if he wasn't worried, I guess I needn't be, either.

"He's gonna wanna know where you were when this all went down."

"We were having dinner," Rafe said, and raised his voice. "Hey, Savannah? You remember the name of the place?"

I told him the name of the place. "It's up on the north side of town. Millersville area."

"Before you get to Ridgetop," Spicer said blandly.

I could hear the grin in Rafe's voice. "That's right."

"If Goins goes out to Brennan's place, I don't imagine he'll see any sign that you've been there?"

"Course not," Rafe said.

"So you were having dinner. When did you get there, and when did you leave?"

Rafe told him the particulars, and no sooner had he stopped talking, than I heard the crunch of gravel outside. I raised my voice. "Someone's here."

"Prob'ly Goins," Rafe said. I heard the scrape of chair legs, and then he must have changed his mind, because he added, "Maybe one of you two'd better do the honors."

"I'll do it," I said. By now Carrie had finished eating and was leaning on my shoulder while I patted her back. My blouse was back in place and I was presentable enough to open the door. Which I proceeded to do.

It was indeed Goins's Toyota that had come to a stop behind the squad car, and Goins himself who was stomping his way up the driveway to the house, scowling at the empty space between the squad car and the Volvo, where the ambulance had been before it left.

"Sorry," I told him. "The ambulance was there, and the officers didn't move their car up after it left."

He switched the scowl to me. "What the hell happened here?"

It was the same thing Spicer had asked, but in a very different tone.

"You'd better go in the kitchen," I told him. "The officers are talking to my husband. Now that I've finished feeding the baby, I planned to join them."

His brows beetled. "You stay right here, missy. No

influencing each other's testimony."

I refrained from rolling my eyes. I also refrained from telling him that I could hear every word. "Fine. I'll just stay in the parlor."

He gave me a sort of regal nod before he bustled off down the hallway. I shut and locked the front door and went back to the sofa with my daughter.

"Well, well," Goins's voice said, "isn't this cozy?"

I couldn't imagine what was cozy about it. Rafe hadn't offered anyone a beer, that I could recall, so at most they were sitting around the kitchen table talking. There might have been a bowl of fruit there, but either way, it wasn't like they were engaged in any kind of festivity.

"Just taking statements, Detective," Spicer said blandly. Goins must have given him a look, because he added, "Witness statements. These folks aren't suspects. They're witnesses."

There was a moment of silence.

"Pull up a chair," Rafe said, in a tone that didn't invite to argument. "We're almost done."

I heard the scrape of chair legs, so Goins must have opted to sit rather than stand, but he couldn't keep from a bit of unpleasantness even so. "You're not in charge here. You don't decide when you're done."

"You're in my house," Rafe said, and probably included Spicer and Truman in the statement, too, "so yeah, I'm in charge, and I can decide when we're done. So far, I haven't minded talking to the officers. If you do anything to change that, I'll show y'all the door. And if you wanna talk to me after that, it'll be through my attorney."

Goins snorted. "You don't have an attorney."

I raised my voice. "Actually, my brother, my sister, and my brother-in-law are all attorneys. And my mother's boyfriend's son is the assistant district attorney for Maury County. We can come up with quite a few attorneys if we need one."

Not to mention that I'd had some legal training of my own. I'd dropped out of law school to marry Bradley Ferguson, but that didn't mean that lawyering wasn't in my blood. My father and grandfather had been lawyers, as well.

Goins didn't respond to that, but I imagine he scowled. Just as I imagined Rafe grinning. "Thanks, darlin'."

"Don't mention it," I said.

The discussion in the kitchen went on for a few more minutes, but Spicer and Truman had covered all the salient details. Anyone reasonable would have been satisfied.

Goins, of course, wasn't. Neither satisfied nor reasonable. He kept pushing on our alibi, asking over and over where we'd been, when we'd gotten there, when we'd finished eating, what we'd ordered. As if chicken fried steak versus hamburger and fries made any difference at this point. Rafe kept answering the same questions over and over, with his voice becoming less and less patient as time went on.

"Listen," he said eventually, "I ain't gonna change my alibi if you keep pushing at me. If you have a question about it, call the café and ask'em when we came and left, and what we ate. Ain't that many mixed race couples frequenting the place, and the waitress liked the baby. They'll remember us."

"We have the receipt," I added, still from the parlor. "It probably has a time stamp on it."

There was silence, and then some rustling. I imagined Rafe pulling out his wallet, and digging out the receipt, and handing it to Goins.

The detective grunted.

"If we're done here," Rafe said, "I'd like to get to the hospital to see how Malcolm's doing."

"Not quite yet." Goins tried to sound like he was in charge.

"Tell me again how you know the victim."

Rafe told him again how we knew Malcolm.

"And he works at the gas station on the corner of Dresden?"

"Last I saw him," Rafe said. "He was there when we filled up the car before we drove to Sweetwater on Thursday morning."

"Did you speak to him?"

"For a minute," Rafe said.

"About?"

"Good to see you, how'ya doing, thirty bucks on pump six 'cause the machine ain't working."

"Is that all?"

"What else would there be?"

"I thought," Goins said silkily, or with his best attempt at achieving silky, "that maybe you'd told him you were leaving, so the coast was clear for him to cut Doug Brennan's brake cables."

There was a second's silence. I imagined that Rafe was too flabbergasted to say anything. I was a bit flabbergasted myself, to be honest.

Goins continued. "He worked with cars. He'd probably know how to do it."

"He worked behind the counter at a gas station," Rafe said, and I could hear the anger lacing through his voice. "He had a lot more to do with ringing up candy bars and selling lottery tickets than he did cars. It ain't a shop. Just a convenience mart."

Goins didn't say anything to that, and after a moment Rafe added, his voice tight, "Lemme guess. Next, you're gonna tell me that after I talked him into cutting Brennan's brake cables, Malcolm came to me for payment this evening, or maybe he came to tell me he was gonna rat me out to the cops, so I tried to kill him to shut him up."

"You said it," Goins said, "I didn't."

Uh-oh. I got up from the sofa and headed toward the kitchen, still holding the baby.

"My wife and I went out to dinner," Rafe said. "We found him on the porch when we came back."

"And stabbed him," Goins said.

"No!" Rafe took a breath, and another. And continued, his voice calmer. "No. He'd already been stabbed when we got here."

"The paramedics said you had blood on your hands," Goins said. I arrived in the doorway in time to see him look at them.

I also saw them curl into fists. It was hard to blame Rafe. I would have been tempted to hit Goins, too.

"Damn straight I had blood on my hands! I spent the time between when we found him and when the ambulance came making sure the kid didn't bleed to death."

"You washed the blood away?"

"In the sink," Rafe said tightly, "before we sat down. You woulda had blood on your hands, too, if you'd found him like that. Or at least you woulda, if you'd tried to help."

"Nobody's disputing that it was Malcolm's blood," I added. They all turned to look at me. It seemed the conversation had been intense enough that neither of them had noticed my arrival. Not even Rafe, and he doesn't usually miss much.

Goins brows drew together. "I thought I told you to stay in the living room."

"Parlor," I said. "You're back here accusing my husband of things he didn't do. Things I know he didn't do, because I was here. Malcolm was on the porch when we arrived. Flat on his back, with a lot of blood everywhere. The knife was in the bushes at the bottom of the steps, where I assume whoever stabbed him threw it after they were finished."

Spicer nodded. He indicated the bag. Goins pulled it closer, opened it, and peered in. "Same as the other knife."

"They're all the same," Rafe said. He dragged his own knife out of his pocket and slapped it on the table. Resisting the temptation to drive the point into the wood to relieve some of his feelings, no doubt. "Standard issue. Everyone at the TBI has one. Or anyone at the TBI who needs a knife."

"Brennan?" Spicer asked.

Rafe shook his head. "Brennan did desk work. All he'd need a knife for, was peeling apples. But I've got one. Wendell's got one. Each of the boys've got one. Everyone else who does undercover work or fieldwork's got one. And you can go to the store and buy'em, too. Sally sells'em."

"Sally?" Goins echoed.

"A small, yellow bungalow on Franklin Road in the Berry Hill area," I said. "Sally sells knives and throwing stars and Mace and things like that. Detective Grimaldi knows her." And had sent me there for a couple of small lipstick cylinders with pepper spray and a small, serrated blade at one point. They were still in my purse, but I hadn't needed to use either of them in a while.

And it was probably better if I didn't mention them to Goins, who'd insist on taking the knife in for testing, just in case I had stabbed Malcolm with it.

He grunted and pushed away from the table. "I'm off to the hospital. Don't go anywhere."

"We've been over that," Rafe told him. "But for the time being, I ain't planning to leave town. And if you're going to the hospital, we might see you there."

"I'm putting the boy under guard," Goins warned. "You won't get another shot at him."

I saw temper flash in Rafe's eyes, but he didn't let it out. "Glad to hear it. Make sure your guard knows to keep an eye on anyone else who comes in to see him, too. It'd be a real shame to lose him before he can tell you who stabbed him."

"Wouldn't it?" Goins agreed, and brushed past me into the hallway. A second later we heard the front door open and then close again with a slam.

"Well, well," Rafe said. "Wasn't that fun?"

Thirteen

Malcolm had been taken to Skyline Hospital. As I already mentioned, it was the closest hospital to us, and although some of the others—notably Vanderbilt—have more experienced trauma units, I guess Malcolm's injuries weren't so bad that Skyline couldn't handle them once the paramedics had gotten him stable and had started blood transfusions.

Rafe had called Wendell, who still had a valid TBI ID, and Wendell met us there to make sure we got up to the room. Hospitals don't like to let just anybody in and out, especially in circumstances like these, and since he'd had to give up his own badge and ID, Rafe had to rely on the kindness of strangers—or in this case Wendell—to get where he wanted to go.

"Good reason to get yourself another badge," I told him, softly, as we were in the elevator on our way up to Malcolm's floor.

He didn't look at me, or give any other indication that he'd heard me, but he nodded.

As Goins had said, there was a uniformed cop on the door. He straightened up when we came walking down the hall, but when Wendell showed him the badge, he just nodded. And looked past Wendell to us.

"They're with me," Wendell said. The young man looked like perhaps he wanted to protest, but when Wendell nodded us through the door ahead of him, the cop didn't actually try to stop us.

Malcolm was inside, in a hospital bed, hooked up to a lot of tubes and beeping machines. There were several different solutions going into his arm, a clear liquid as well as more blood. He was gray under the brown, and his eyes looked sunken. His whole chest, or what I could see of it above the blankets, was covered in bandages.

His grandmother, a black woman who looked barely old enough to have grandchildren, and certainly none Malcolm's age, sat on a chair next to the bed. She looked exhausted, and I could see tracks on her cheeks where tears had run. She wasn't crying when we came in, but when she recognized us, her eyes filled again. "Thank the Lord you came home when you did, or my boy woulda died!"

She launched herself at Rafe, who caught her and held her for a moment before passing her on to me. He stepped closer to the bed. "How is he?"

"Holding on," Vera said, turning toward him while dashing the moisture off her cheeks with her hands. "He lost a lot of blood. And some of the wounds were deep. One of them nicked a lung. But they stitched everything up. And they say he's gonna be alright."

Rafe nodded, his eyes still on Malcolm. "The detective in charge is trying to convince himself I had something to do with this."

"That's stupid." Vera shook her head. "And if he asks me, I'll tell him that. We know you. You'd never hurt my boy."

At this point Wendell stepped forward and introduced himself, and they shook hands.

"Do you have any idea what he was doing at our house?" I asked. "We went out to dinner. When we came back, he was there. On the porch. Did he say anything about talking to Rafe?" Because chances were he hadn't been there to see me.

But Vera shook her head. "He came home late last night. Had the late shift at the gas station. I was in bed by the time he got home. And I had to go to work this morning, while he was still asleep, so I didn't talk to him. Didn't realize anything was going on until the hospital called."

No help in that, then. If Malcolm had seen anything on his way home last night—and it made sense that maybe he had, if he'd worked the last shift—he'd kept it to himself.

Unless he'd gone out this afternoon, as Rafe had suggested earlier, and had seen someone on our property then. And that someone had decided to get rid of a young man who could identify him.

We stayed for a few more minutes, but Malcolm didn't wake up, and wasn't expected to for a while yet. "I'm staying the night," Vera said. "I'll call you if anything changes."

Rafe nodded. "I can be here in ten minutes if you need me."

"Is there anything we can do for you?" I added. "Do you want dinner? Or a change of clothes?"

She shook her head. "Just make sure my place is secure. I don't remember if I locked up."

No problem. We assured her we'd take care of it, and then we headed back out. The young cop in the hallway watched us intently, but didn't say anything.

We walked out together, into the dark parking lot. "Thanks for coming," Rafe said. "Sorry to drag you out at night."

"Not the first time, is it? And probably won't be the last."

Since Rafe was no longer working for the TBI, and Wendell wouldn't be for very much longer, it could very well be the last time. But I opted not to say so.

"Why don't you come on back to the house for a bit," I suggested. "I mean, I know you were just there last night. And you may have things to do. But I don't think either Rafe or I are going to be able to sleep anytime soon."

And this way, the two of them could stop by Vera's house together, and I wouldn't have to worry about Rafe doing it alone.

That seemed acceptable to them both, so they took me home, where they made sure I was safely inside with the door locked behind me before they left.

I went upstairs and started the evening ritual for Carrie, who got a bath before bed, and got dressed in her little pink pajamas, before I fed her one last time and put her to sleep. Before I was even halfway through with all of that, the men were back.

"Need any help?" Rafe called up the stairs.

I told him I had it covered, and to take care of our guest. They broke out a couple of bottles of beer that had been left over from last night's festivities—a lifetime ago—and settled down to rehash the facts of the case. While I dried and dressed and fed Carrie, I listened to Rafe tell Wendell everything, including the details of our breaking into Brennan's house this afternoon, as well as the verbiage of his interview with Detective Goins this evening. By the time I had put Carrie down in her crib, already half asleep, they were discussing whether Goins really was as stupid as he seemed, or whether he was putting on an act, for some reason we hadn't figured out.

"Grimaldi says he really is that stupid," I said, as I curled up in the sofa next to Rafe. "Or rather, she didn't say he was stupid. That's my interpretation. She says he lacks imagination. He closes cases, but he tends to leap on the most obvious solution, and he wastes time trying to prove it. Until he can't, and then— and only then—does he go on to look at other options."

"So eventually he'll figure out I had nothing to do with this," Rafe said, "but by then whoever did it's had plenty of time to get rid of all the evidence."

I nodded. "Pretty much, yes."

"Great."

"And don't mention Mendoza to him. He has a hang-up about Mendoza."

Rafe, who has something of a hang-up about Mendoza, too, snorted. "So that's where we're at," he told Wendell. "Spicer and Truman said they'd figure out who Goins talked to at the TBI, who told him I'd have reason to want Brennan dead. Once we figure out who that is, somebody's gonna have to take a look at him. Or her. And it can't be me."

Wendell nodded. "I'll take care of it."

"You worked with Brennan a long time," I said. "You must have known him somewhat well. Or at least better than Rafe did. Who do you think would want to get rid of him? Or why?"

"He wasn't dirty," Wendell said, "I can tell you that. Like Detective Grimaldi said about Goins, Brennan didn't have much imagination. He didn't think well on his feet. Worked by the book, and it could take some effort to convince him something needed doing, especially if it didn't fall squarely inside the lines."

I nodded.

"But he put the safety of his operatives above the job. When something went wrong, he shouldered the blame for it, even when it wasn't his doing. He was in charge, so he took the responsibility. It was Brennan who pushed for hiring Rafe after his cover was blown last year."

"I thought that was you," I said.

He nodded. "Course. But I couldn't do it without Brennan's say-so. He's the one who went to the brass and made the case. He's the one who pushed it through."

"So he wasn't dirty. He worked by the book, and had integrity. He cared about the people who worked under him. But he didn't have much imagination. And if someone was doing something they shouldn't be doing, not in Brennan's chain of command, but somewhere else, he might not notice."

"Might not," Wendell agreed.

"And if he did notice?"

"He'd tell someone," Wendell said, with a glance at Rafe.

My husband nodded. "I'm thinking he mighta tried to tell me. That maybe that's what he wanted to talk to me about on Thursday afternoon."

"But if he wanted to talk to you and not one of his superiors…" I said.

They both nodded. "The problem mighta been up the chain."

"He must have tipped someone off," I said. "Somehow, someone figured out that he knew something they didn't want him to know, and they killed him."

"You know the brass at the TBI better'n I do," Rafe told Wendell. "Who're we talking about here?"

Wendell shook his head. "Could be anyone of a handful of people. If we take the tier under Brennan out—I don't think he woulda worried about blowing the whistle on any of us—there's Foster. He's Brennan's opposite number in narcotics. Has a group of undercover agents under him, too, the way Brennan had us."

Rafe nodded. "Lotta money to be made in narcotics, if you don't mind skirting the line."

That was a fairly cynical assessment, but likely true.

"You must know Foster," I told Wendell. "Is that something he'd do?"

"I wouldna thought so," Wendell said, "but I ain't eliminating nobody just 'cause of how I feel about'em."

Good policy.

"Above Foster and Brennan, there's McLaughlin. He's got the whole undercover division under him, but he's also got the rest of narcotics and organized crime. There are supervisors on that side, too. Hammond, Grant, and Pavlova. Pavlova's female."

"Does that matter?" I wanted to know. Women can be just as evil as men, and while I wouldn't have the first idea how to cut someone's brake cables, I had a feeling that Grimaldi, for instance, would have no problem whatsoever. Knowledge of the underside of cars isn't a purely male thing.

"No, darlin'." Rafe smiled at me. "He's just thinking that Pavlova being female mighta been another reason why Brennan didn't go to the brass right away."

Ah. "So there are plenty of suspects. With anyone in narcotics or organized crime maybe a bit more likely than the others, since those might be easier fields in which to skim."

"If somebody was skimming," Rafe said. "It could be something else. Maybe Pavlova's sleeping with McLaughlin. Or with Foster or Grant or Hammond. Hell, maybe Grant and Hammond are lovers."

"Surely that's no reason to kill someone. Having an affair isn't illegal."

"But could be enough to lose someone their job," Rafe said. "You never know what might be enough for someone to commit murder."

It wasn't the first time I'd heard that sentiment. I nodded. "You're right, of course. But until we know more, there's probably nothing more we can do."

Wendell shook his head. "I'll take a look around tomorrow, with this in mind. See what I can pick up. If Spicer and Truman get back to you with a name, let me know."

Rafe said he would, and Wendell headed for the door. "Be careful going home," Rafe told him. "Whoever's doing this seems like he's quick on the trigger. Terminating people before he knows if it's necessary. Make sure you get home and inside in one piece."

"You're welcome to stay the night," I offered, since it was

getting late, and since I could see Rafe's point. "You can go to the TBI from here tomorrow morning."

Wendell gave me a look, and then gave Rafe one. "You trying to teach me my business, boy? I was handling myself just fine while you were in diapers."

Rafe grinned. "Yessir." He walked out with Wendell, and stood on the porch while Wendell walked down the steps to his black Town Car and got inside. Nobody shot at either of them. The Town Car took off, and Rafe came back inside and set the security on the door. And turned to me.

He held out his arms and I walked into them. "It's been a helluva day, huh?" His chest rumbled against my ear.

I nodded. "I feel like I've lived a couple of weeks, at least, just today."

"You ready for bed? It ain't that late, but I could use some time on my back."

"You got it," I said, and took his hand and pulled him after me up the stairs. If he wanted to be on his back, I'd give it to him.

I guess our visitor felt he had left enough knives on our property, or maybe what he'd had to do to Malcolm had scared him off, because when I peered out the window each time I was up with Carrie overnight, the yard lay quiet and deserted. Nothing bothered us until the next morning, when Rafe's phone rang just after seven.

Since he had no job to go to and nothing in particular to do—and it was Sunday, anyway—my husband was still in bed. He reached for the phone and put it to his ear, his voice husky and sexy with sleep. "Yeah?"

Whoever was on the other end quacked.

"On my way," Rafe said, and dropped the phone back on the bedside table at the same time as he rolled out of bed, all in one beautiful, economical movement. And then he noticed me looking at him, and grinned. "Morning, darlin'."

"Good morning to you, too," I said, and lowered my eyes from his face farther down his body.

The grin widened. "Normally I'd take you up on that. But I gotta get to the hospital. Malcolm's awake."

I forgot all about morning sex. Or maybe not all, but at least I understood the need for him to get going. "Oh, good. Do you want me to come?"

He shook his head, already pulling on his jeans, covering all that gorgeousness with denim and, a second later, the same shirt he'd had on yesterday. "Stay here with the baby. Keep the door locked."

"Shouldn't you at least brush your teeth?" I said, when he headed for the door.

"I intend to, darlin'." He disappeared into the bathroom. I heard the water kick on, as well as the flushing of the toilet. Two minutes later he was back. "I'll let you know how it goes."

He came over to kiss me goodbye, his own breath minty fresh. It didn't seem to bother him that mine wasn't.

I didn't manage to catch my breath again until he was out the door and all the way downstairs. And by then I didn't want to call after him, since Carrie wasn't awake and clamoring for food yet, and the last thing I wanted to do was wake her. So I snuggled back under the blankets to get what extra rest I could. Downstairs, the door opened and shut, and I heard the key in the lock, and a few seconds later, the growl of the Harley. It disappeared down the driveway, the sound fading in the distance, and I closed my eyes again.

It didn't last long, of course. By the time Rafe came back, less than an hour later, I was up and dressed, and had fed the baby, and changed her, and was sitting on the floor with her. When I heard the Harley pull up outside, I picked her up and headed down the stairs to hear the latest.

Rafe looked fairly upbeat, so Malcolm must be doing all right.

He nodded when I said so. "Holding his own. More stable than he was last night. His chances are better every hour."

He tossed the leather jacket over the back of the sofa and reached for the baby. I handed her over, and watched him cradle her and smile down at her. "Hi there, pretty girl."

She gurgled, almost as if she were talking back to him, and I laughed. "She's going to be a daddy's girl. I can already tell."

He headed for the sofa, still cradling her. "Were you?" he asked over his shoulder.

I followed. "Not sure I was anything in particular. I loved my dad, but we weren't especially close. No more than Catherine and my dad. He was more of the traditional type, I guess, so he spent more time with Dix than he did with his daughters. Catherine and I were Mother's domain."

Rafe nodded.

"Catherine put up with less than I did. She always had a stronger personality than me, and she was less interested in clothes and hair and things like that. The stuff Mother lived for. I was a typical girl, Catherine a little less so."

"You rebelled in your own time," Rafe said. "It mighta took you longer, but when you finally did it, you blew Catherine out of the water."

No question. There had been consternation when Catherine brought Jonathan home—a Boston Brahmin from New England, who wanted to marry into our genteel Southern clan—but it was nothing compared to the fuss that had ensued when I'd gotten involved with Rafe.

So yes, he was right. It might have taken me more time than Catherine, but when I rebelled, I'd done a much better job of it.

I sat down in one of the chairs opposite the sofa and leaned forward, elbows on my knees. "Were you able to talk to Malcolm?"

"I tried," Rafe said, still cooing at Carrie and tickling her chin with his finger. "He's still out of it, and don't remember much of what happened. We had to tell him what he was doing there."

"That's too bad."

He nodded. "The doc said the memories'll come back. Prob'ly. He might never remember everything, but he'll remember more. But it's gonna take time. I told him I'd stop by again later."

"Can I come, too?"

"Sure, darlin'." He kept smiling down at his daughter, and talking to me without looking at me. "Goins was there, too. Somebody musta told him that Malcolm was awake. Maybe the cop outside the door—a different guy than last night—or maybe somebody on staff. But he showed up fifteen minutes after me, and chewed out the cop in the hallway for letting me in, and then told me to leave. I figured I'd better."

"That was probably best," I agreed. And added, "That must have been frustrating."

"Tell me about it. I know the man's just doing his job, but the fact that he can't see reason's becoming a problem."

"You could talk to somebody."

He shot me a look. "Who're they gonna believe? One of their own detectives? Or me? A former criminal who just got fired from the TBI and is a suspect in my boss's murder?"

"You're not," I said. And amended it to, "Not really. Not by anyone sane."

"Goins is sane. Just slow on the uptake. And the MNPD are gonna stand by him, not me. There's nothing I can do."

Frustration wound heavily through his voice.

"Maybe Spicer or Truman will come through with the name of whoever Goins spoke to at the TBI," I said, "and then you and

Wendell can go to work investigating him."

"Wendell can. I can't step onto TBI property without getting in trouble, either."

"So you can go to the guy's house and look around." I smiled. "If Wendell keeps him—or her, in case it's Pavlova—busy at the TBI tomorrow, you can snoop. You know how much you like to snoop."

He smiled reluctantly. "You're talking to me like I'm four years old."

"Just doing my part," I said, since I could certainly understand that the situation was frustrating for him. I wasn't really worried that Goins would end up trying to arrest him. There was no real evidence against him, and Grimaldi had said that Goins usually came to the right conclusion eventually, even if it took him time. But while this was going on, Rafe's hands were tied. He couldn't really go to Columbia and start work for Grimaldi, not while he was a suspect—officially, at least—in a murder in Nashville. And without his own badge, he couldn't do much to investigate what had happened to Brennan, either. Not officially.

I wondered whether whoever had done this—and I was coming around to thinking that someone had done it, that Brennan hadn't just driven off the road on his own in a tragic accident—had taken that into account, or whether it was just a nice side benefit.

"I don't imagine it was the main goal," Rafe said when I asked. "I ain't important enough for that. If this woulda happened to Brennan without me getting fired first—"

"Laid off," I interjected.

He nodded, "—it ain't like I woulda gotten the job of figuring out what'd happened. The MNPD woulda prob'ly gotten it then too, since there'd be a conflict of interest with us investigating our own."

That made sense. "So someone wanted Brennan dead, and saw your leaving as a way to pin it on you. Or at least throw some suspicion on you and off himself."

Rafe nodded.

"Or this all came to a head after you lost your job. Brennan went to talk to whoever he planned to talk to after he spoke to you on Wednesday, and something happened during the course of that conversation to make him suspicious that someone was doing something they shouldn't be. Then that same someone caught on that Brennan was suspicious and decided to terminate him and make use of the fact that he'd just let you go to try to hide his own actions. But it was all decided on the spur of the moment on Thursday."

"Something like that," Rafe agreed.

"So who would Brennan talk to about you, if he wanted to try to get you your job back?"

"McLaughlin," Rafe said, smiling at Carrie. "Brennan's boss. But it don't have to be McLaughlin. He coulda decided to talk to one of the other supervisors to see if there was a spot for me on their crews. Like Foster."

Who was in charge of undercover narcotics, if I recalled what Wendell had said correctly.

"If your cover is blown in undercover organized crime, and in gangs—and we know that Jamal's friends figured out who you were last fall, since a couple of them showed up here at Mrs. Jenkins's house—your cover's probably blown for undercover narcotics, too. All undercover work. Don't you think?"

"Maybe," Rafe said.

"So Foster might be less likely than the other three. How well do you know Pavlova?"

"Enough to recognize her on the street," Rafe said.

"Not a former conquest?"

He chuckled. "No, darlin'. Christina Pavlova is twenty years older than me and not the kinda woman you flirt with. She don't appreciate my type."

His type? "What do you mean? She doesn't like men?" Or was he suggesting that Pavlova was racist?

"Gay," Rafe said, "and with no sense of humor. Lives and breathes the honor of the TBI. Works strictly by the book. Totally against riffraff like me—and Clayton and Jamal; José was OK—being on the payroll."

So maybe not a racist then, since if that had been a problem, she'd likely have approved of Clayton—criminal record notwithstanding—and disapproved of José.

"She probably isn't likely to be involved in anything illegal, then. Not something that would reflect badly on the TBI."

"Less'n she just puts on a good show," Rafe said. "At home she could be wearing satin and drinking champagne."

Possible. We probably shouldn't take her off the list.

"This is frustrating. I don't know any of these people or what they'd do."

"We're just gonna have to wait for Spicer and Truman to come through," Rafe said, "with whoever Goins talked to."

"But even then we don't know that that person is who we'd have to investigate. Say he spoke to McLaughlin. That would make sense, right? McLaughlin was Brennan's boss. And say McLaughlin told him that you'd just lost your job and were upset about it. That doesn't mean McLaughlin is guilty. He could have heard that from someone else, who wanted him to think you were upset, and he was just telling Goins what he thought was the truth."

Rafe nodded. He'd probably thought about it himself. "How about some breakfast?"

"I could eat," I said.

"Me, too." He stood up and handed over the baby. "Eggs and bacon?"

"Are you cooking?"

"I thought I might," Rafe said.

"Then whatever you want to make is fine." I should probably have something healthy like oatmeal instead of something fattening like eggs and bacon, but who was I to complain about whatever was put in front of me?

Besides, eggs and bacon sounded better than oatmeal.

"Eggs and bacon," Rafe said, and headed down the hallway toward the kitchen.

Fourteen

The eggs and bacon were tasty, and the domestic interlude lovely. Being married was wonderful. I hadn't thought so when I was married to Bradley, but then Rafe was a totally different person than Bradley had been. And while he might scare me into fits sometimes, with the risks he took and the possibility that he might not come back to me, I'd sooner deal with that than a cheater and big, giant jerk.

After breakfast—I loaded the dishes in the dishwasher since he'd done the cooking—we put Carrie and her stroller in the car, and drove to the park, where we took an actual, honest-to-goodness Sunday walk in the cold.

Carrie fell asleep, of course, and once we were back inside the Volvo, with the heat going, Rafe suggested we take a drive.

I gave him a sideways look. "Is this going to be a drive like yesterday, where we end up breaking into someone's house?"

He chuckled. "Not on a Sunday morning."

"Then sure. I'll take a drive."

"We'll get some lunch at the end of it," Rafe said and put the car in gear.

The first leg of the drive went from Shelby Park in East Nashville out east to Hermitage on the interstate. Rafe took off down toward the lake, which lay like a sheet of ice under the weak January sun. A few minutes later, he drove through the gates of a subdivision full of brick houses. Cookie-cutter houses, in three different styles and three different types of brick, but ultimately just the three similar floor plans and facades on every house.

"Does someone we know live here?" I asked, looking around.

"Hammond. Head of narcotics." He pointed to a red brick McMansion with Christmas lights still in the windows and a wreath on the door. As well as a couple of kid-sized bikes in a heap on the grass.

"Family man," I said, looking around. From the cozy look of the place, Hammond wasn't someone I would have expected to be working with narcotics. "Nice place. Family friendly."

"He's got a wife and a couple small kids," Rafe confirmed. He glanced at me. "That don't mean he ain't breaking the law. Sometimes, a wife and kids can be incentive to commit a crime, just as much as they can be incentive not to."

He had a point. "I guess he stays on the list."

"For now," Rafe said. "I don't see nothing here that would take him off. Do you?"

I didn't. Not unless having a nice house with a family inside meant anything, and Rafe clearly thought it didn't. He lowered his foot on the gas, and the Volvo rolled forward. In the mirror, I saw the door to the Hammonds' house open, and a pretty, blond woman usher two small children out.

No, we couldn't take him off the list. A man with a family might do anything he had to, to keep them safe and happy. Even break the law he'd sworn to uphold.

"Here's where Wendell lives," Rafe said fifteen minutes later. We'd crossed back over the interstate, away from the lake, and gone into Hermitage proper. Now we were idling outside a row of townhouses in a small community just off Lebanon Pike.

"He lives alone?" The place didn't look big. "No family for Wendell?"

"He has a daughter," Rafe said. "I think he's been married once. But she doesn't live around here."

So just Wendell in residence. "This is the townhouse he wants to sell, so he can buy the shack on the river?"

Rafe nodded. "He's serious about that. Or mostly serious. I don't think he wants a shack. But he does wanna sell and buy something more private for when he's retired."

I looked around. "This probably wouldn't be too hard to sell. It's not new, but it's well maintained. It looks like nice people live here. All the cars are in good shape. None of them are especially pricey, but they all look relatively new and well taken care of."

"Run some numbers," Rafe said, and moved his foot off the brake. The car rolled forward, past Wendell's townhouse and toward the exit turn that would take us back on Lebanon Road.

I glanced at him. "You didn't take me here because you think Wendell has anything to do with what's going on, did you?"

I mean, surely not. Rafe loved Wendell. They'd worked together for more than a dozen years.

Although… Brennan could have contacted Wendell with what he'd found out, especially when Rafe wasn't available until the next day. And he hadn't.

Although maybe Wendell hadn't been there, either. And Rafe had worked with Wendell for so long. They'd worked so closely together over the past year, training the boys. Rafe would have noticed if Wendell was up to something.

And what could he be up to anyway? It wasn't as if Clayton, Jamal, or José provided any kind of opportunity to make money. Not at the moment, at any rate.

Rafe shook his head. "It was on the way. I figured we'd drive by."

The car left the subdivision and merged with traffic on Lebanon Road again. "Where to now?" I asked, since we were headed east, out of town, instead of west toward downtown and home.

"Mount Juliet," Rafe said, picking up speed. "Pavlova has a spread out there."

A spread? "That sounds like it might take some money."

"Might," Rafe agreed and lowered his foot on the gas.

It took another fifteen minutes until we were out of Metro Nashville and into Wilson County, and another five before we were cruising down the winding country road where Christina Pavlova's spread was located. "I think it's gotta be this," Rafe said.

I peered out the windshield, at a quantity of fence surrounding a big field. "A farm?" Two horses with blankets across their backs were nibbling straw from a bale, while, behind the fence on the other side of the driveway, what looked like a herd of dogs were running along the fence, barking at the car.

When I tried counting, there turned out to be only six or seven, but that's enough when they're all making noise at the same time, running and jumping over each other, frothing at the mouth. Even the small terrier looked rabid, and it wasn't much bigger than Carrie.

"I think she rescues animals," Rafe said. "At least that's what I've heard. Old horses from the glue factory, stray dogs from the street or the kill shelter."

"That makes her sound like a nice person." Anyone who rescues homeless animals can't be bad.

"Nice people kill people, too," Rafe said. "And I imagine it costs money."

It probably did. Animals have to eat, and need veterinary care. When you have a lot of animals—and these eight or nine that we'd seen probably weren't all of them—it can add up. So Christina Pavlova might have excellent reasons for skimming money here and there. She might also be one of those people who thinks that animals are better than people, which would make her decision to kill Doug Brennan seem eminently reasonable. In her eyes.

"McLaughlin lives down in Brentwood," Rafe said, moving the car forward. "Big, fancy house in a subdivision. Similar setup to Hammond, but twice the space, and at least twice the price tag."

"So he lives high."

"He's higher up the food chain, so it could be within his means, but yeah. He's got an expensive house in an expensive part of town. Wife and a couple of kids. Teenagers, or maybe in college by now. College tuition can wear on a budget."

It could. "Are we going down there?"

Rafe shook his head. "I've seen it before. Don't seem worth the drive. And we wouldn't be able to get inside the subdivision, anyway."

"One of the fancy, gated ones?"

He nodded.

If he'd seen it before, then no, it wasn't worth driving all the way down there. Not if we wouldn't even be able to get inside the subdivision to see it. And I've seen my own share of fancy McMansions, so I could imagine what this one would be like without actually seeing it.

"So we've visited Hammond and Pavlova, and we won't be stopping by McLaughlin. Who's left?"

"Foster and Grant," Rafe said. "Foster lives in The Nations."

So clear on the other side of downtown. It would take us at least thirty, maybe forty minutes to get there from here. But he lived closer to the TBI than either Pavlova or Hammond.

"What's his reason for wanting Brennan dead?"

"Don't know that he has one," Rafe said. "He's single. Might have a girlfriend, but ain't married that I know of. Could be divorced. But he likes women. That always takes cash."

Especially if you wanted to impress the women you like.

"He drives a Mercedes," Rafe added. "And he just moved into a new house. So he's been throwing money around. And he's got Brennan's job, but in narcotics. With several handlers and undercover agents under him."

"So he'd have plenty of opportunity to run some sort of scam on the side. Lots of money to be made in narcotics."

"Like I said," Rafe nodded.

That took care of Foster, then. He sounded like a real possibility. Not only did he have means and opportunity, but he lived alone, so there was no one to ask questions if he disappeared in the middle of the night—to leave an incriminating knife in our recycling bin, say. Some of the guys with wives and/or children might not find that as easy to accomplish.

Then again, they worked for the TBI. Their significant others might not find it strange that they came and went at odd hours sometimes. I'd certainly had to get used to that with Rafe. "And Grant?"

"Lives over by us," Rafe said. We'd reached the interstate, and now he merged with traffic headed west toward town. "In the nicer parts of East Nashville, over by the park. We shoulda driven by when we were over there."

"That isn't a cheap area, either." And had become less so as time had passed.

"Convenient drive to the TBI, though."

It was.

"I don't know much about him other than that. We've never had any dealings. He runs the support department. Does a lot of research and logistics and stuff like that."

Research and logistics? "So he has access to everything everyone's doing?"

"Prob'ly," Rafe said with a shrug. "I never paid him much

mind. I don't write the reports. Or didn't till a year ago. I'd tell Wendell what was going on or what I needed, and he'd write it up and file it. Or make sure I got whatever it was. I couldn't spend my time doing that."

No, it wouldn't have been good if any of the people he was planning to put in prison came across him compiling official-looking reports on what he was doing.

"I think he's gay," Rafe added, still on the subject of Grant. "But not real open about it. He's never hit on me or nothing. But I catch him looking sometimes."

"That might not be because he's gay," I pointed out. "It might just be because you're good-looking. Maybe he wishes he looked like you."

A corner of his mouth curled up. "I've seen that look before, darlin'. And that ain't it."

Fine. He should know, after all. He'd been the recipient of plenty of those looks. Every time Tim, my broker, sees him, he practically drools. "If he thinks you're hot, do you think he'd set you up for murder?"

"No reason why not," Rafe said.

"Before you and I got involved, I thought you were hot. And I didn't want Grimaldi to arrest you."

"She wasn't gonna do that anyway."

She wasn't, no. She'd known about his undercover work several months before I did.

"Anyway," I said, "it sounds like we should take a look at Grant. And it'll be easy, since he lives close to home."

Rafe nodded. "Foster first, though. We'll hit Grant on our way back."

Fine by me. I settled into the seat for the drive.

The Nations is a semi-industrial area on the west side of town, not too far from the Women's Prison and for that matter

Riverbend Penitentiary, where Rafe had spent some time. It's situated between Interstate 40 and Centennial Boulevard, and the neighborhood name makes no sense. All the streets are either numbered from 45th up to about 60th or so, or they're named after states. California, Louisiana, New York.

No countries, and no Indian nations.

The street address Rafe had for Foster turned out to belong to a brand new three-story super-modern house with a garage on the bottom floor and a rooftop deck from which you could probably see all the way to downtown. It looked familiar, and I squinted at it. "I know that house."

Rafe arched a brow at me.

"I'm serious," I said. "It was one of Tim's listings. I remember he talked about it at one of the sales meetings. It was right around the time when the whole debacle with Jolynn and Todd went down, though, so I didn't pay a lot of attention. And since he fired me right around then, I didn't end up sitting an open house here. I think I was supposed to. But I didn't happen."

Rafe turned his attention back to the house.

"It wasn't cheap," I added. "I do know that much. I think Tim said it would be the highest sale in The Nations, if he could get close to list price."

"Did he?"

"I'm sure he did. I can check when I go into the office tomorrow. That, and whether there's anything going on with real estate in Ridgetop that we need to know."

Rafe nodded. "It's a nice place, anyway."

It did look like a nice place, if you liked flashy new construction in mostly industrial areas. I don't. I grew up in the Martin Mansion, which was built between 1839 and 1841, and now I'm in Mrs. Jenkins's house, from the 1880s. I like old woodwork and drafty fireplaces and not-quite-straight floors.

Old houses have personalities that brand new houses don't have, and will probably never have, because there was no way James Foster's house would still be standing a hundred and fifty, or a hundred and eighty, years from now. They don't build houses like they used to.

We lingered in front of the driveway for a moment. "That's a lot of house for a single guy." And a lot of money on a law enforcement salary. "Can I assume this guy's at the top of the list?" Spending money he might not have, working with undercover agents in narcotics, with easy access to all sorts of things, and living alone?

"For now," Rafe said, and lowered his foot on the gas. "Let's go see Grant."

"Carrie's probably going to wake up soon and want to eat."

"I could eat," Rafe said.

So could I. With the walk and then all the driving we'd been doing, it was past lunch. "We can stop somewhere if you want. Or go home and make something there. Since you're out of work at this point, maybe we should save our pennies."

"It'll work out," Rafe said, but since he didn't specify somewhere he wanted to eat, I figured we'd be going home.

It's about fifteen minutes to get from The Nations over to East Nashville. It was about twenty before we were cruising up Holly Street toward Larry Grant's house.

Rafe hadn't been kidding when he called it the nicer part of East Nashville. Out where we live, it's still a little like the Wild West. Guns go off occasionally, and there's more than the normal amount of crime, and more than half the houses are still run-down and in need of some TLC.

Not so over on this side of Gallatin Road. It's pretty much all renovated and yuppiefied, and has been taken over by people with a lot of money and good taste. There are craft breweries and fancy restaurants where you used to find downtrodden meat'n threes, and everything's so slick and shiny a lot of the personality's been taken out of it.

Grant lived in an old house, but it was easy to see that it had been renovated to within an inch of its life at some point not too long ago. The original wood lapsiding had been replaced with cementboard, and painted a subdued and elegant gray that wouldn't have been in the palette of the original builder. Craftsman bungalows were originally painted in warm, natural colors, with lots of wood trim. On Grant's house, the siding was a cold gray, and the woodwork had been painted white. It looked crisp and modern, but the old-house lover in me mourned what it had probably looked like when it was new.

There was no sign of life. There hadn't been at Foster's house, either, but he'd had an attached garage on the first floor of his house. If he was home, his car would be there.

Here, there was no garage and no off-street parking, and the space at the curb in front of the house was empty.

"Looks like he's out," I said, unnecessarily.

Rafe nodded. "Stay here."

He reached for his door handle. I twisted in my seat. "What are you going to do?"

"Just knock on the door," Rafe said. "And take a look through the windows. If he ain't here anyway, not like he'll know."

"I doubt you'll see anything incriminating through the windows." But if he wanted to go up on the porch and knock, I wasn't going to stop him. If Grant was home, Rafe would get a bit of a surprise—and Grant a bit of a thrill—and Rafe would have to think fast about an excuse for what he wanted, but if Grant wasn't here, it couldn't hurt to take a peek through the windows.

So he left the car running and headed up the walkway to the porch, where he knocked a couple of times. There was no answer, so Rafe moved sideways to the window on the right of the front door.

A Craftsman bungalow tends to be symmetrical. Or if they aren't all symmetrical, at least this one was. Door in the middle of the front wall, with sidelights, and a double window on either side. Rafe went to the one I thought must belong to the living room and peered through the window. After a moment he crossed to the window on the other side of the porch and peered in there, too. Then he came back down the walkway, across the sidewalk, and got back into the car.

"He wasn't home."

"I figured," I said. "Any signs of a guilty conscience through the windows?"

He grinned. "No. And no signs he's living above his means, either. The furniture's nice, but nothing special. And though he's got a big TV, it ain't no bigger than the one your brother's got."

"So if he's getting money from something nefarious, he isn't spending it on his house."

Rafe shook his head and pulled the car away from the curb. "So far, this has been wasted effort."

"I hope you didn't think we'd find a sign above one of their houses saying 'It was me, I killed Doug Brennan.'"

He didn't answer, and I added, "I don't think it was wasted. I got to spend a couple of hours with you. That's always nice. And we took a look at all of them, except McLaughlin. Of the four we've seen, I'm leaning toward Pavlova or Foster. Hammond's setup made him look like a decent family man, and there's nothing ostentatious about Grant's place. It's expensive—everything in this neighborhood's expensive—but he doesn't look like he's living above his means. But Pavlova rescues animals, and that can probably get expensive. And it's the sort of cause where a murder or two might not matter, if she's passionate enough about it. If Brennan found out that she was skimming, and threatened to pull the plug, and it would mean that she'd have no more money for more animals, she might kill him. And feel justified."

Rafe nodded.

"And Foster's living high on the hog, and he's probably spending everything he's making on maintaining his lifestyle. As you've told me often, you don't get rich going into law enforcement. And he's living like he's rich."

"Makes sense," Rafe said, even if he sounded dissatisfied.

"Something about it you don't like?"

He shook his head. "Just frustrated by the whole thing, I guess."

Hard to blame him for that. I was, too. "Goins will figure it out sooner or later. He'll stop thinking you had something to do with it, and then we can go to Sweetwater and you can work for Grimaldi and help her figure out whatever's going on in the Columbia PD."

"We can hope," Rafe said, and turned the car off Holly Street and onto South Eleventh for the trip home.

Fifteen

We headed back to the hospital around five. By then, we'd had lunch, and Carrie had taken a nap, and we'd even heard from Lyle Spicer, with the information that according to the official report, Detective Goins had spoken to Supervisory Agent Ben McLaughlin on Friday morning, after Doug Brennan's body had been found.

"No surprise there," Rafe said after he hung up the phone with Spicer. "McLaughlin's head of the department. And Brennan's boss. It makes sense that Goins would talk to him."

I supposed it did. "Why would he try to make you look bad to Goins?"

"I dunno that he did," Rafe said. "On Tuesday, when he gave me the news—"

"McLaughlin was the one who fired you?" Not Brennan?

"Nobody fired me," Rafe said. "The brass decided not to reup the training program for this year. McLaughlin got the job of telling me, since he's in charge of the department. And I don't think I behaved in a way that woulda made anybody think I was gonna kill somebody. But I'm sure McLaughlin could tell I was disappointed. Still, it woulda made more sense for me to kill him or one of the higher-ups if I was gonna kill somebody. Brennan was trying to get me my job back. I had no reason to kill him."

Right. "So who told Goins that you were angry with Brennan?"

"It mighta been McLaughlin himself," Rafe said, "if he killed Brennan, and wanted to put the blame on somebody else."

"And if not?"

"Somebody else coulda told McLaughlin that I was pissed at Brennan, and McLaughlin just repeated what he'd been told. Or maybe somebody else went to Goins separate from McLaughlin and mouthed off about me."

"Wouldn't that be in the report?"

"Mighta been off the record," Rafe said. "There are people at the TBI that used to work for Metro. Somebody who was friendly with Goins mighta gone to him and whispered in his ear."

"And Goins didn't put it in the report because it wasn't an official conversation?"

"Something like that," Rafe said.

"I don't suppose Goins is likely to tell Spicer or Truman who that someone might be?"

"No," Rafe said.

"Do you suppose Wendell—?"

But he shook his head. "Wendell's been standing between me and the brass for thirteen years. And I'm sure Goins knows it. Everybody at the TBI knows it. Ain't nobody gonna believe Wendell's anything but biased."

"So what do we do?"

"Nothing," Rafe said. "There's nothing we can do. None of this changes the fact that I didn't do nothing to Brennan and I wasn't here when he died."

He pushed to his feet. "Let's go see Malcolm. Maybe he remembers who stabbed him. If he does, then we can eliminate somebody."

Maybe so. I unwound from the sofa. "I'll get the baby ready."

We headed out ten minutes later, because that's how long it takes to get a baby ready to travel. It took less time to drive to Skyline Medical Center than it did to get Carrie ready to go in the first place. Practically as soon as I'd gotten her loaded into the car, we were there and I had to unload her again.

This time we didn't need Wendell to get us through security. Rafe must have taken the time to charm some of the nurses when he was here this morning, because they just waved us through, with appreciative looks his way.

That ended when we got upstairs. Another young cop, this one female, was standing in the hallway outside Malcolm's room. She gave Rafe a hard look. "Detective Goins says you can't come in again."

"Detective Goins ain't in charge here," Rafe told her. "And unless you're prepared to shoot me, I don't see how you're gonna stop me."

I didn't, either. He towered over her. I'm five-eight in my bare feet, and I often feel small and slender standing next to him. (I'm neither.) She was several inches shorter than me, and wasn't carrying any extra weight. He could pick her up and move her out of his way without flexing anything but his biceps.

Not that he would. A smart man doesn't touch a woman who hasn't invited him to touch. He especially doesn't touch one with a gun on her hip and the power to arrest him just for breathing. But to make sure of it, I took a step to the side, so I was halfway between them. The young cop—the name plate pinned to her uniform said her name was Moyer—glanced at me.

"We just want to see how he's doing," I said. "We found him after he was stabbed. My husband kept him alive until the ambulance got there. We have a vested interest. And he's a neighbor. We just want to see that he's OK."

"Unless Goins is here," Rafe added, "he'll never know."

"I'm supposed to keep a list of everyone who goes into his room."

There was a clipboard with a sheet of paper leaned up against the wall next to her.

"Then put my name on the list," Rafe said. "Goins ain't got no legal right to keep me from going where I wanna go. And if you try to point that gun at me, you won't like what happens."

No question. "We'll just be a minute," I told her, calmly, as he ducked through the door and inside Malcolm's room. "Feel free to come to the door and make sure we don't do anything we shouldn't do. But I really wouldn't recommend trying to keep him out. Especially since Goins doesn't have a legal leg to stand on."

Moyer chewed her lip, but eventually she nodded. I entered the room after Rafe, and Moyer came in behind us. For a second, it crossed my mind that she might try to do something stupid, like pulling the gun and trying to arrest us both for trespassing, but if the thought had crossed her mind, she discarded it. All she did was take up station inside the door and keep an eye on things.

The room was empty except for Malcolm. Vera must have gone home for a break, or maybe she'd had to go to work today.

Malcolm was dozing, but opened his eyes when he saw Rafe. For a second, he looked scared, and then he relaxed. "Oh. Ss'you."

His voice was slurred, probably from the medication they had him on. I imagined it was strong stuff. He would have been in a lot of pain without it, or so I assumed.

Rafe nodded. "We just wanted to come back and check on you. Savannah brought the baby."

Malcolm tracked his eyes to me, and I smiled and wiggled my fingers. "Hi. I'm sorry about what happened."

"Me too," Malcolm managed, with something resembling a

laugh. It must have hurt, because he winced.

"D'you remember any more about it?" Rafe wanted to know. "Get a look at whoever stabbed you?"

Malcolm moved his head back and forth on the pillow. "S'all blurry. Can't remember what I wanted to talk to you about."

"You came to the house to talk to me?"

Malcolm nodded. "Think so."

"And somebody was there?"

"Musta been," Malcolm said. His brows furrowed as he tried to remember, but after several seconds, he shook his head. "Can't remember. Sorry."

"Don't worry about it. We'll figure it out." Malcolm's brows smoothed out, and Rafe changed tactics. "You worked late the night before, your grandma said."

The brows drew together again, but then Malcolm nodded. "Yeah. Late shift on Friday."

"D'you remember driving home in the dark? Past our house?"

Malcolm's brows drew down again. He had very expressive brows. I'd never noticed that before. Usually he talked more with his hands, and now he couldn't, so maybe that was why. "Yeah?" He didn't sound sure. "Maybe?"

"There was somebody in our yard. Over by the bins. D'you remember seeing someone?"

Malcolm's face smoothed out. "Yeah. Somebody digging in one of the bins. I figured maybe it was a homeless guy, you know? They look for food sometimes. But when I turned the car around the corner, and the lights hit him, he ran."

"Are you sure it was a man?" Rafe asked.

Another few seconds passed while Malcolm struggled with the idea. "Maybe not?" he said eventually. "Looked like a guy. Black pants and a black jacket. But I didn't see him up close."

So it might still be Christina Pavlova. Maybe. Depending on

how she looked. Nobody would mistake me for a man, or my sister Catherine, or Yvonne McCoy. But take someone like Detective Grimaldi or our sister Darcy—tall, lean, not particularly buxom women with short hair—and they could probably pull off looking male. Especially in the dark.

"Pavlova looks like a guy," Rafe nodded ten minutes later, after we'd left the hospital—Officer Moyer looked quite relieved to see the backs of us—and were back in the parking lot. Rafe had taken the car seat with Carrie from me, and was carrying it toward the Volvo. "She keeps her hair short, and whenever I've seen her, she's been wearing a business suit with pants, the way Tammy does, or jeans if it's Casual Friday."

"The TBI has Casual Friday?"

"The brass has Casual Friday," Rafe said with a grin. "It's Casual Everyday for the rest of us."

Then his voice changed, and he added, "Oh, shit."

"What?" I followed the direction of his gaze and saw Detective Goins come toward us. "Oh, no. He'll know what we've been doing here, won't he?"

Rafe nodded. "Let me handle this."

No problem.

Or at least I didn't think it would be a problem until Goins stopped ten feet away and pulled out his gun. And pointed it at Rafe. "Hands on your head."

"I'm carrying my daughter," Rafe said, his voice even, but brimming with ice cold fury. "You're pointing a fucking gun at my six-week-old daughter."

"Put the baby down. Now!"

"Do it," I said, so scared that my voice was threatening to get caught in my throat. "Put her down, Rafe."

He glanced at me. "Take her when I do."

I nodded. As soon as he bent to put the car seat on the ground next to his feet, I scooted over and grabbed it, and scooted back out of range. And was able to draw a breath again.

Not that it was any more pleasant to have that gun pointed at Rafe, really. Especially as I felt pretty certain that Goins wouldn't shoot the baby. He probably hadn't even noticed that Rafe was carrying her until Rafe said something.

But I wouldn't put it past him to shoot Rafe. He—Goins— seemed to sincerely believe that my husband was some sort of danger. Goins would shoot him and feel justified. And Rafe would bleed out in the hospital parking lot, just another unarmed black man with a criminal record shot dead by a trigger-happy cop.

I took a breath. And then another one. And then I put the car seat down, safely out of the way, and stepped in front of the gun. In front of Rafe.

It wasn't the first time I'd put myself between him and someone pointing a gun at him. It was the first time, that I could recall, that I'd done it when neither one of us was armed. But I was pretty sure Goins wouldn't shoot me. He might not think much of me—not the way he kept calling me 'missy'—but I didn't think he'd shoot me. I wasn't so sure he wouldn't shoot Rafe.

For a second nothing happened. Then—

"No, Savannah." Rafe's hands descended on either side of my waist, and he moved me aside. It might have taken a bit more than just flexing his biceps, but he did it.

I scrambled back where I'd been, in front of him. "Have you lost your mind? I'm not moving until the gun's gone."

"Carrie," Rafe began.

"Is fine. Nothing's going to happen to Carrie. Or to me. It's you I'm worried about."

Shooting a young white mother and her infant daughter would get a whole different reaction in the media and the courts than shooting Rafe would. No, we weren't in danger here. He was.

"He ain't gonna shoot me," Rafe said calmly. "Are you, Goins?"

Goins sneered.

"Sorry." I shook my head. "I'll believe it when he puts the gun away. Until then I'm staying right here."

I waited. Goins didn't lower the gun. On the upside, Rafe didn't try to move me out of his way anymore, either.

Into this impasse came the arrival of a black and white squad car. It squealed to a stop next to us, and two uniformed cops tumbled out. Suddenly two more guns were pointed our way.

"We've got it, Detective," a voice said. "You can put the gun away."

Goins hesitated, but after a few long, very long, seconds, he holstered his weapon.

Rafe relaxed, and so did I. Until Spicer said, "We're gonna need you to come downtown with us, Mr. Collier."

"Why?"

Rafe and I said it at the same time, and glanced at one another.

"There's been another death," Spicer said, shoving his gun back into the holster. On the other side of the car, young Truman did the same thing.

"Who's dead?"

"We'll talk about it downtown," Spicer said. He opened the door to the back of the squad car and gestured with his head. "Mr. Collier?"

Rafe hesitated for a second, but I guess he didn't see the point in making a fuss. Or maybe he wanted to know what was going on, and figured this was the best way to find out.

"What about me?" I asked, as he walked the few steps over to the squad car and prepared to get in.

Spicer glanced at me. "You're free to go, Mrs. Collier. We'll bring your husband back to you after we've finished talking."

"Unless he gets arrested and charged," Goins added, smirking.

I ignored him. "Can you at least tell me who's dead?"

"James Foster," Spicer said, closing the door behind Rafe. "We'll see you later, Mrs. Collier. Detective."

He gave Goins a barely civil nod before both he and Truman got back in the squad car. Goins gave me a final sneer and galloped back to his own vehicle to follow the squad car out of the lot. I was left standing in the middle of the rows of cars, alone, reflecting that it was almost like old times. The only difference was the ring on my finger and the baby staring up at me from the car seat.

And the fact that this time, I knew my husband hadn't been involved in whatever Detective Goins was trying to pin on him.

I picked up the seat with the baby and headed for the Volvo.

I called Tamara Grimaldi as soon as I'd walked through the door at home, and had put the baby down. I didn't even take the time to wrench out of my coat first. And when she picked up, I didn't waste any time in telling her, "You've got to talk to somebody and put a stop to this. Spicer and Truman just hauled Rafe downtown for questioning."

"Still going on about Douglas Brennan?"

"Yes." I took a breath and tried to calm down. "No. Someone else is dead. A guy named James Foster. He also worked for the TBI."

"And he's dead?"

"That's what Spicer said. And that's all he said. Rafe probably knows more, but he's downtown, probably shackled to a table in an interview room somewhere, and I can't ask him!"

"We don't shackle people to tables in downtown," Grimaldi said. "And Lyle and George would know that your husband didn't have anything to do with this."

"They pointed their guns at him! All three of them. In the parking lot at Skyline Hospital. I thought Goins was going to shoot him!"

After a second I added, "He was holding the baby, too."

"That was really stupid of Rick," Grimaldi said. "Did your husband hurt him?"

"He had a gun!" I took a breath. "No, Rafe didn't do anything to him. Or to Spicer and Truman. Just got in the car and let them take him away."

"They'll bring him back," Grimaldi said.

"They said they would. And then Goins said, 'Unless he gets charged.' Can he charge him?"

"He can do anything he wants," Grimaldi said, "but he's not stupid enough to risk a wrongful arrest charge." After a second she added, consideringly, "At least I don't think so."

"That's encouraging." Not.

"Did your husband have anything to do with Doug Brennan's death, Ms.... Savannah? Or this other guy's? Foster's?"

"Of course not!"

"Then don't worry about it. If there's no evidence, nobody's going to charge him."

"Easy for you to say," I said, finally sitting down on the sofa, still with my coat on. Carrie blinked at me from the car seat in the middle of the table. It was good she was such an easy baby, because I certainly wouldn't win any awards for taking care of her at the moment. "I don't trust Goins. He's a nutcase."

"He can be trying," Grimaldi agreed, "but he gets there in the end. Is there anything I can do?"

I thought about it, more calmly. When I'd called, I'd wanted her to fix things. Things she probably wasn't in any kind of position to fix from where she was. "Is there anything you can do?"

"Not much," Grimaldi said. "I'll contact Lyle and find out what's going on. If there's anything you need to worry about, I'll let you know. But it's probably nothing. They'll talk to him. He'll tell them what he knows, or that he knows nothing. Rick will throw his weight around, and then they'll let him go."

I hoped she was right. "How are things where you are?"

"Fine," Grimaldi said. "First time I've gone a week without having to investigate a murder in my career."

Must be nice. "Up here they're dropping like flies. First Brennan, then someone tried to kill Malcolm, and now Foster."

"I heard about Malcolm," Grimaldi said. "The kid from up the street, right? How's he doing?"

I told her he was awake and mostly aware, but couldn't remember the attack itself. "But he saw someone in our yard the night before. Rooting in the trash. Malcolm thought it might have been a homeless guy looking for food, but it was obviously whoever left the knife in the recycling bin for Goins to find."

Grimaldi made an encouraging sort of noise. I guess she agreed.

"But it was late, and dark, and the guy ran when Malcolm turned his car down the street. He couldn't even tell if it was a man. He thought it was, but he didn't rule out the possibility that it might have been a female."

"Do you suspect anyone female?" Grimaldi wanted to know.

I explained about Pavlova, and then, for good measure, I also explained about McLaughlin, Hammond, and Grant. "The other most obvious suspect was Foster. But if he's been killed, too, I guess it wasn't him."

"Unless he wasn't killed and killed himself," Grimaldi said. "How did he die?"

"No idea. Spicer and Truman didn't say anything beyond

the fact that he's dead. I'm sure Rafe will tell me when he gets home. If he gets home."

Over in the car seat, Carrie scrunched up her face and made a sound.

"I know," I told her. "I don't like that idea, either."

"What?"

"Nothing," I told Grimaldi. "Just talking to the baby. She's starting to fuss."

"Go take care of her. I'll see what I can find out and call you back."

I told her I appreciated it. "Did you have a good time with Dix and the girls yesterday?"

"Disney princesses," Grimaldi said. "What's not to love?"

She hung up before I could say anything else. I shrugged out of my coat and went to take care of my own small princess.

By the time Rafe got home, it was late. Grimaldi had let me know that she'd left a message for Lyle Spicer but hadn't heard anything back from him, and she would contact me when she did. By the time Rafe walked through the door, I still hadn't heard anything else.

I had completed the evening ritual for Carrie, and put her to bed, but I was too wired and worried to sleep myself, so I was sitting in the living room with the TV on. I was even sort of watching it, although I couldn't have told you who the House Hunters were, and what they were looking for in a house. It was all just a blur of colors and lights and noise, while my own mind churned over the same ground. Someone else was dead. The MNPD—or at least Detective Goins—thought Rafe had something to do with it. Goins was going to arrest Rafe. I'd be a single parent until he could prove that he hadn't done anything wrong, and what if he couldn't prove it? It was all well and good for Grimaldi—and for that matter Rafe—to say that he wasn't guilty, so he didn't have to worry, but innocent people are convicted every day. What was to keep them from doing it to my husband?

By the time I heard the crunching of gravel outside, and then a car door slamming and footsteps on the stairs and porch, I had worried myself into a semi-trance. It wasn't until I registered the key in the door, that I realized he was home.

I made it to the foyer before the front door closed. He kicked it shut with his foot while his arms came around me and he buried his nose in my hair. "Hi, darlin'."

"I was worried," I said into the soft leather of his coat. "I wasn't sure you'd be back."

For once he didn't give me a facile answer along the lines of, "Of course I was coming back." Instead, he just held me. "Sorry."

"They kept you a long time."

"We had a lot to talk about."

"I called Grimaldi," I said, finally pulling away. "She said she'd contact Spicer and see what she could find out, but she hasn't gotten back to me."

"Lyle's been a little busy, wielding a rubber hose." He grinned, but it was a tired grin.

"Surely Spicer, at least, knows better than to think you did anything to James Foster."

He shrugged out of the leather jacket and tossed it onto the coat tree. "Sure. But he still had to make it look good for Goins."

Who did believe that Rafe had done something to James Foster. Right.

"What happened?"

"To Foster?" Rafe looked around. "Baby in bed?"

I nodded. "You can look in on her later. For now, let's sit down so you can tell me what happened. Are you hungry?"

He shook his head. "We swung by a fast food place on the

way home. I'm good."

"Beer? Something stronger?"

He grinned. "No, darlin'. Let's just get it over with."

Fine. I walked into the parlor, around the sofa, and dropped down. "What happened to James Foster? And why would Goins think you had something to do with it?"

Rafe skirted the sofa and sat down in the chair opposite. "Foster's dead. Carbon monoxide poisoning in his fancy new garage, courtesy of his fancy new car."

"So he did it to himself?" And as a side note, that would make the house so much harder to sell. Nobody wants to buy a house where someone died an unnatural death. People aren't that keen on natural deaths, either, but suicide or murder beats heart attack in bed every single day.

"No way to know," Rafe said. "Goins thinks I did it."

"Why, for God's sake?"

"Talked to somebody up the street who described the Volvo. Figured that meant I was on my way to Foster's house to do him in."

Of course he would think that. "I suppose you told him I was with you, and we never stopped and never left the car?"

"Course," Rafe said. "It didn't matter to him. I was there, so I did it."

"Did it happen while we were there?" We hadn't rolled down the windows, and even if we had, I wasn't sure we would have heard the engine of Foster's car running inside the garage. But it was disturbing to think about what might have been happening in the garage while we'd been a few yards away, out on the street.

"I don't imagine it did," Rafe said, whether that was true or he just didn't want me to think there was anything we could have done.

"Did he leave a note?"

"Nobody mentioned one," Rafe said, "I imagine, if there'd been a note, they wouldna given me the third degree."

Probably not. "But he still could have done it himself."

Rafe nodded. "I floated the idea that maybe Foster was the one killed Brennan, and maybe now he killed himself so he wouldn't get caught for it."

"I don't suppose Goins liked that idea."

"Not as much as he liked the idea that I did it to throw suspicion off myself." He got up. "I'm gonna get a beer. Want something?"

I shook my head. And waited until he came back. "So what happens now?"

"We go to bed," Rafe said, "and hope that Malcolm's memory comes back. And that Foster has information somewhere, on his computer or in a drawer, that proves he killed Brennan and I didn't. Then we go to Sweetwater and forget about all this."

I could get behind that. Unfortunately, I had a feeling it wasn't going to be quite that easy.

Sixteen

I've been working for Lamont, Briggs, and Associates since I first got my real estate license more than a year and a half ago. It was called Walker Lamont Realty back then, and I chose it because it was conveniently located, close to the apartment I rented on Main Street in East Nashville.

But after Walker Lamont ended up in prison—long story—Timothy Briggs became broker, and he changed the business name to LB&A, to try to avoid association with Walker. Or to make the association less obvious, anyway. I have no idea why he didn't change the company name to something else entirely, and avoid the Lamont name altogether, but maybe Walker still owns the company and Tim couldn't. I've never asked.

At any rate, it's been my place of employment for a while. In that time, I haven't brought in much money. Selling real estate is a lot harder than I thought it would be when I came up with the idea of doing it. In my defense, I've also had a few other things to think about over the past year. Like Rafe, and keeping him alive, and all the dead bodies that seem to follow him around.

Or follow me around, since I've been responsible for my own share of them.

All of which is to say that when I walked through the door of the conference room for the sales meeting on Monday morning, Tim was flagrantly surprised to see me.

"Savannah! What are you doing here?"

"I still work here," I said, "don't I?"

"Yes, of course. But we haven't seen much of you lately."

Well, first I'd had a baby. And before I was fully recovered from that, there was Christmas. And then New Year. And now I was here.

"There's a chance we're moving to Sweetwater," I said. "I wanted to talk to you about it."

Tim straightened, a well-manicured hand pressed to his chest. "Sweetwater? You and Rafael?"

Obviously. "He got a job offer from the Columbia PD when we were down there over Christmas. He's thinking about taking it." Since he now didn't have another job. But there was no need to mention that.

"But…" Tim said.

"I know you enjoy seeing him." What's not to enjoy? "But we're thinking it would be good for the baby to be in Sweetwater, so she'll grow up with family around."

"Dear me," Tim said, flapping that same hand back and forth in front of his face like a little Victorian lady having palpitations.

I shook my head. "Come off it. You have a boyfriend now. Don't you? I saw you and Kenny Grimes at some restaurant or other not too long ago. You don't need my husband to be happy."

"Kenneth and I are seeing each other socially," Tim said demurely, "but I need your husband to be happy, Savannah. I really do."

I'd walked right into that one. "Well, you can't have him. He's mine. And I'm taking him to Sweetwater. At least I think so."

Tim made a moue. "Well, you'll have to do what's best for your family, darling. But I hope you'll reconsider. The loss would be great. Not just for me, but for all of Nashville."

No arguing with that.

As the other agents filed in around us and got comfortable at the table, I changed the subject. "Remember that house you had listed in The Nations over the summer? Big three-story with a rooftop deck?"

"Of course," Tim nodded. "I never forget a house."

"Well, the owner died yesterday. Killed himself in the garage, apparently."

Tim tsked. "That'll make it hard to sell."

No doubt.

"Not that I'm likely to get the job," Tim added. "How do you know?"

"He was a colleague of Rafe's. A supervisor at the TBI. Name of Foster."

Tim nodded. "I remember. Nice-looking guy. Made my heart go pitter-patter at the final walk-through before closing." He put that hand to his heart again, and mimicked swooning. For a second before he added, prosaically, "Not as handsome as your husband, of course."

Of course. "I've never met him," I said. "Did he seem depressed to you?"

Tim shook his head. "Happy and on top of the world. Flush, and planning the parties he was going to have on his rooftop deck. It was a cash deal, you know."

Was it really? "It was an expensive house, wasn't it?"

"Highest price in the neighborhood until then," Tim said, looking pleased. "Might still be the highest price in the neighborhood. I haven't checked."

I hadn't, either. Although it probably didn't matter, anyway. It was enough to know that Foster had spent a lot of money on his house, on a law enforcement salary that maybe didn't stretch that far without some supplementation.

And not just that, but without a loan. Somehow, he'd ended up with half a million dollars in cash he could use to buy an expensive house.

Of course, he could have inherited the money. Or played the stock market and struck it rich. Or maybe he had a sideline business—not related to the TBI—that brought in extra money. Just because a guy bought an expensive house with cash, didn't automatically mean he was dishonest. He could be leveraged to the hilt, with maxed out credit cards, and have killed himself because he'd gotten into living a lifestyle he couldn't afford. Because in a few weeks another credit card payment would be due, and he didn't have the money.

Or he could have been skimming money from the undercover operations of his subordinates at the TBI, and used the proceeds to buy his expensive house and his expensive car, and when Doug Brennan came along and began to suspect something, Foster had done the only thing he could think of, and had killed Brennan. And once word got out that Goins was on the case and wasn't buying the fact that it had been an accident—even if his focus was on my husband and not Foster— Foster had realized it was only a matter of time before the whole house of cards would come fluttering down, and he'd taken the only way out that he thought he had.

The meeting started, and I sat back in my chair and listened. As usual, I had nothing to contribute. I had no new listings and no new clients, and hadn't sold anything lately. This was the first meeting of the new year, so Tim was all about pumping up the employees to get off to a great start and do amazing things in the coming twelve months.

I waited until things had quieted down a little before I posed my question. "Does anyone know what's going on with real estate in Ridgetop?"

Everyone turned to me. "Is something going on in Ridgetop?" someone asked. And someone else added, "Do you have property for sale in Ridgetop? Because I've got someone looking for something with a view."

Doug Brennan's house had a lovely view, and was likely to come on the market at some point. But it wasn't likely to be my listing. I shook my head. "Just curious. No rumors about some big corporation putting a fulfillment center up there, or anything?"

There was shaking of heads all around the table.

"Do you know something we don't, Savannah?" Tim wanted to know.

I shook my head. "Not at all. Sorry. What about Hermitage?" Might as well ask, right? Just in case Wendell decided to go through with his plan to sell the townhouse and buy that shack on a river somewhere, and enlisted me to help. "Townhouse just off Lebanon Road. Not new but well maintained."

We spent a couple of minutes talking about it—or they spent a couple of minutes talking while I listened—and then the conversation went on to other things.

At the end of the meeting, I told Tim I'd let him know whether we decided to move to Sweetwater or not. "I guess if we do, I should find a brokerage down there to work with."

Tim nodded. "That would be easier for you. Although if you can't find one, or it takes some time to find one and you want to keep your license here for a while, you can commute up when you want to, and do the rest remotely."

I suppose I could.

"And no offense, Savannah," Tim added, "but you may want to consider a different line of work. This one doesn't seem that well suited to you."

"I'll take it under advisement," I said. "I guess I'd better get back to my husband and baby now."

Tim smacked his lips. "Give your husband my love."

Oh, sure. "How about you leave that for Kenny," I suggested, "and I'll just tell Rafe you said hello?"

Tim grinned. He has a lot of teeth, all white and pretty. "You can do that. But Kenny would understand. Believe me."

He probably would. Especially since the chances of Tim getting to do anything with Rafe, other than admire him from a safe distance, are very remote indeed.

So I put my coat back on and walked out to the Volvo for the trip home.

Only to come face to face with Detective Goins in the parking lot.

I stopped like I'd walked into a wall and looked around, suspiciously. "Detective."

He showed teeth. Maybe he thought it was a friendly smile, but it missed by a mile. "Mrs. Collier. Your husband told me I'd find you here."

My eyes narrowed. "You've spoken to Rafe? What about?" Had Goins pulled a gun on him again? And put our baby in danger?

"On the phone," Goins said. "I'd like you to come downtown with me for an interview, Mrs. Collier."

Oh, he would, would he?

"And you spoke to Rafe about this?"

He nodded.

"Then I'm sure you won't mind if I call him and verify that?"

He shook his head. "I understand you've been at police headquarters before." This insinuating statement, which was in no way a question, was accompanied by a smirk. "You can probably find your own way there."

I told him I could. I have, in fact been at police headquarters more than once. Both for interviews and other things.

Goins nodded. "I'll see you there. Shortly."

He got back into his Toyota and peeled out of the lot. I waited until he was gone, around the corner toward downtown, before I got into the Volvo. Before I turned the key in the ignition, I pulled out my phone. And dialed Rafe. "Are you all right?"

"Fine. Why?"

"Goins just showed up here. He wants me to drive into downtown for an interview."

"He called," Rafe said. "I told him where to find you."

"So you're OK with this?"

I imagined the shrug I could hear in his voice. "Not like I can be otherwise. He's got the right to ask. And it's better to cooperate."

I guess it was. "Are you going to be all right with Carrie for however long this takes?"

His voice turned amused. "I don't imagine it'll take all that long. The baby and I'll be fine. We're on the sofa watching the Shopping Network."

Of course they were. "You have enough milk?"

"Plenty of milk," Rafe confirmed. "If you're planning to stay gone a couple days, we could be in trouble, but otherwise, we'll be fine."

And they had enough diapers. He knew how to put them on. If Carrie sprung a leak, it wasn't a big deal. She had plenty of clothes he could change her into. "I probably don't have to worry that he's thinking of arresting me, right?"

"Not less'n you've done something I don't know about," Rafe said. "Go find out what he wants, darlin'. We'll be here when you get back."

No doubt about that. I had the car with the car seat, and Rafe wouldn't put Carrie on the back of the Harley for any reason. "I'll get there as soon as I can."

"Take your time," Rafe said and hung up. I turned the key

in the ignition and set off.

The first time I visited police headquarters in downtown was the morning Rafe and I discovered Brenda Puckett's body. Spicer and Truman drove me there in the back of their squad car, and I was shaking like a leaf, both from the discovery and from the upcoming interview. I hadn't done anything to Brenda, but I was still nervous.

I've been back plenty since. Enough that I totally lost the fear of being interviewed. Once Tamara Grimaldi and I became friends, the police station became a much less uncomfortable place.

Until now. When I parked in the lot behind the building and made my way through security, I was quaking. While I trusted Grimaldi, and knew she liked Rafe and wouldn't do anything to trip him up, I had no such convictions about Rick Goins. As soon as Grimaldi figured out that Rafe worked for the TBI, she backed off him, and treated him like a fellow law enforcement officer. Rafe's eleven years of service to the TBI seemed to make no difference to Goins.

And I guess maybe that wasn't so surprising. I mean, weren't we contemplating the very same thing? That some trusted servant of the TBI wasn't what he appeared to be, and had in fact killed Doug Brennan to cover up something else he was doing?

If we were considering it, why wouldn't Goins?

Of course, we weren't thinking that Rafe had anything to do with it. We were looking for someone else. But Goins didn't know Rafe, so maybe it made sense that he'd suspect my husband. Even if, to me and everyone else who knew Rafe, that made no sense whatsoever.

I was deposited in an interview room, the kind with a two-way mirror where someone could see in but you can't see out, and left to cool my heels. It might even have been the same interview room I'd been in once before. Unless they all looked the same, and they probably did.

Time passed. It was extremely annoying, especially taken into account that Goins had been so pushy about me coming into downtown right away. He'd said he'd see me 'shortly,' yet here I was, and where was he?

"You understand that I have a six-week-old baby at home?" I asked him when he finally wandered in after at least thirty minutes. "I don't have time to sit here and twiddle my thumbs."

He dropped a stack of folders on the table. "I thought your husband was babysitting."

There was a slight sneer in his voice on the word 'husband,' and another on 'babysitting.' As if real men didn't spend any time with their children.

"He is," I said, "but unlike me, my husband doesn't produce milk. So when the baby gets hungry, he can't lift up his shirt and feed her. Only I can do that. And I was only supposed to be gone an hour and a half at the most. Now it's way past that."

And it was supposed to snow this afternoon. Like most Southerners, just the thought of snow puts me into a panic. Traffic gets snarled and impossible to navigate, and it could take hours to get across the bridge and home.

"Then let's get to it," Goins said and opened the top folder. He glanced at what was inside and then at me. "Tell me about your husband."

"Seriously?" Did he have all day? "He's from Sweetwater. Small town a little over an hour south of here. We went to high school together. After he graduated, he went to prison. I was still—"

"Prison," Goins interrupted. "For what?"

"Don't you have that in the folder? It's common knowledge."

He didn't answer, and I added, "Assault and battery. Or something like that. I don't remember the exact wording. He had a fight with someone and put the guy in the hospital."

Goins smirked and made a note.

I continued, since this was all stuff he probably knew anyway. "He was sentenced to five years and served two. While he was in prison, the TBI recruited him and got him released early, and then they put him into undercover work. He spent ten years working his way into Hector Gonzales's South American theft gang, and finally broke it up last year. In February, the TBI offered him a job training new recruits. He did that for the rest of last year, until they eliminated the program on the first of this year and let him go."

Goins nodded. "Let's go back to the assault and battery for a moment."

Lord. "If you're trying to make the point that he's capable of hurting someone, let's just take that as said. He is. But he doesn't have a habit of hurting people who don't deserve it."

"Maybe he thought Douglas Brennan deserved it," Goins said mildly.

I ground my molars together for a second before I opened my mouth again. "When I said they deserved it, I meant that they actually deserved it. The man my husband fought with when he was eighteen, was forty-five and had hurt Rafe's mother. In any county but the one where we grew up, he would have gotten off with time served."

"That's not in the file," Goins said.

"I'm aware of that."

He tilted his head. "So how do you know?"

"How do you think I know? He told me!"

"And how do you know he told the truth?"

"How do I...?" I bit it back. Goins obviously wasn't going to take Rafe's word for anything, and in his position I guess maybe

I shouldn't expect him to. But it was frustrating, since it all seemed to add to the picture he had of Rafe. The very misshapen picture. "Does your file happen to include the fact that that same man—whose name was Billy Scruggs—ended up killing LaDonna Collier a year and a half ago?"

"No," Goins said.

"Well, the sheriff said he'd make sure the file reflected that."

Goins smirked. "I guess he must have forgotten." The implication was that the sheriff had never said that, and if he had said it, he'd never intended to do it.

I fought back the desire to scream, and channeled my mother's upbringing and a year at finishing school in Charleston to calm down. It took all of that. "What exactly am I doing here, Detective? Because this is a waste of my time. My husband had nothing to do with Doug Brennan's murder. Brennan didn't even give him the news that his position was eliminated. Ben McLaughlin did. Brennan's the one who tried to get him reinstated."

"And when he couldn't," Goins said, "maybe your husband killed him."

"He'd have to know that Brennan couldn't, for that to make sense. And he didn't. By the time he got to the TBI on Friday, Brennan was already dead."

"Maybe Brennan told him on Thursday," Goins said.

I shook my head. "He didn't. I heard the conversation."

Goins smirked. "So you say."

I rolled my eyes. "I was there. I know what Brennan said. And all it was, was that he wanted Rafe to stop by and talk to him when we came back to town on Friday. By then, someone else had killed Brennan. While Rafe was in Sweetwater."

Goins didn't say anything to that, and I picked up the thread from where I'd been earlier. "He had nothing to do with James Foster's death, either. It might have been a suicide, anyway. It sounded like a suicide. Maybe Foster killed Brennan and then himself. Did you know that Foster was living well above his means? New car. New house. The most expensive house in the neighborhood. One he paid for with cash!"

Goins didn't write it down, of course. He didn't even acknowledge it. "Let's get back to your husband."

"Let's not," I said, "OK? We can say we did, if it makes you happy. But my husband was in Sweetwater when Doug Brennan died. I can attest to it. So can my mother. So can Detective Grimaldi. He didn't get Malcolm to help him compromise Brennan's brake cables. If you look into it, I'm sure Malcolm has an alibi. He was at work on Thursday, after all. But Rafe had no reason to want Brennan dead. Killing Brennan wasn't going to get him his job back. He has another job offer, anyway. And he's been working for the TBI for eleven years. He's a law-abiding citizen." Mostly. "Whatever he did at eighteen doesn't matter anymore."

"It all matters," Goins said.

"You know, it really doesn't. He's spent the past eleven years sweating and bleeding and risking his life for the TBI. That's what matters." That's what made him who he was today. Not some crazy, chivalrous, misguided defense of his mother almost fourteen years ago.

Goins looked pleased. "Exactly."

He agreed with me? "Exactly, what?"

"That's it," Goins said. "He's sweated and bled and risked his life for the TBI for eleven years. And when the TBI fired him, he couldn't handle it. So he snapped and killed Brennan."

I threw my hands up. "He didn't snap, for God's sake. He came home on Tuesday night and told me it had happened. Then he went to the TBI on Wednesday and handed in his badge and gun. Then we went to Sweetwater on Thursday morning. Brennan didn't die until Thursday night. Almost three days after McLaughlin told Rafe he was no longer employed by the TBI. Nobody snapped."

Not even whoever had killed Brennan. Snapping means you pick up a blunt object and whale away, spur of the moment. Cutting someone's brake cables and waiting for them to drive away at the end of the day isn't snapping. It's cold and calculated.

But I could see that nothing I was saying had any effect on Goins. He had made up his mind, and was in the phase where he was trying to prove his hypothesis, no matter how misguided.

"Is there anything else?" I asked. "Because if there isn't, I'd like to get back to my daughter and my husband. Before the snow starts, and before the baby starves to death."

There was no chance of that, of course. Rafe had told me they had plenty of milk. But I was annoyed.

"One more thing," Goins said. "Your husband admitted to being at James Foster's house yesterday."

"I doubt that very much," I said. "We were outside Foster's house—the operative word there being 'outside'—for a span of maybe ten seconds. Neither of us left the car. Neither of us went into the house, or even up to the door. We didn't step foot on the property. And you have no proof we did."

"What were you doing there?"

I told him what we'd been doing there. "Someone killed Brennan and stabbed Malcolm. And it wasn't Rafe. So we came up with a list of suspects and drove around to take a look at them."

"Leave the investigating to the professionals," Goins said.

I snarled at him. Actually snarled. Mother would have been aghast.

Or maybe not. Under the circumstances, maybe even my mother would have snarled. "My husband *is* a professional,

Detective."

Goins looked like he'd bitten into something sour. "You may leave, Mrs. Collier. I can see I won't get anything helpful from you."

"You wouldn't know anything helpful if it bit you," I said and got up from the table. "Don't bother to see me out." Not that he'd made a move in that direction. "I've been here before. I know the way."

I sailed toward the door. And through it. And down the hall and across the lobby and out the door to the parking lot. Where I located Goins's Toyota and relieved my feelings by kicking the back tire violently several times. The only thing that resulted was that I bruised my toes, but it felt good in the moment. Then I limped over to where I'd parked the Volvo, got in, drove out of the parking lot, across the bridge, and home.

Seventeen

Wendell stopped by on his way home from work. We live in the opposite direction of the one he'd take home, so it wasn't quite as casual as it sounds.

I was in the middle of cooking dinner, and Rafe must have surmised that I didn't want to miss any of the conversation, because he invited Wendell to have a seat at the kitchen table instead of in one of the more formal rooms where we'd normally be entertaining guests—at least if we stood on ceremony—but where I wouldn't be able to hear what they were talking about.

"You're welcome to stay for dinner," I told him, as I stirred diced tomatoes into ground beef at the stove. "There's plenty." Or would be, once I was finished with it.

He shook his head. "Thanks, but I have plans."

OK, then. "Rafe drove me by your townhouse yesterday. He told me you might be thinking about selling it."

"Maybe," Wendell allowed.

"Let me know if you need any help. I asked during the sales meeting today, and somebody who's familiar with the area told me that those condos are popular. They sell quickly, and for good money."

"Good to know," Wendell said.

"I'll let you talk." I turned back to the stove, but kept my ears peeled.

At first there wasn't much to hear, just the companionable

popping of beer caps and the sound of swallowing. Then Rafe said, "Goins dragged Savannah downtown for questioning this morning."

"No kidding?" Wendell looked at me.

I shook my head. "None. He wanted to talk about that old business with Billy Scruggs. Like that isn't a decade old and forgotten already."

"Depends on who you ask," Rafe said dryly, and I guess that was true. Sergeant Tucker in Columbia certainly hadn't forgotten. Good thing Goins didn't know Tucker existed, or vice versa, or Goins would never get over his suspicions of Rafe.

"He brought up how we'd been outside Foster's house in The Nations yesterday," I added. "I pointed out that since we'd stayed in the car and hadn't so much as stepped foot onto Foster's property, it was hard to make anything of that."

"Any information on Foster?" Rafe asked Wendell.

Wendell shrugged. "Lotta speculation about what's going on. No real information. I don't think it's conclusive that it wasn't suicide, but everyone assumes it had something to do with Doug Brennan."

Rafe nodded. So did I. It was a logical assumption.

"I had a meeting with Ben McLaughlin," Wendell added. "He wanted to know what I thought of this rumor that you had something to do with it."

"I hope you told him that Rafe had nothing to do with it," I began, at the same time as Rafe asked, a lot more calmly, "That going around the TBI, too?"

Wendell nodded. "Hard to say where it came from. I tried to track it back to the beginning, but everybody I asked said they'd heard it from somebody else. I got it from Jamal, Jamal got it from Kirk, and Kirk said he got it from Foster. Could be that Foster started it, but since I can't ask him, there's no way to know. But people are talking."

"Course they are."

I looked from Rafe to Wendell and back. "You're taking it very calmly."

He slanted me a look. "Not like I ain't used to taking the blame for everything that goes wrong, darlin'."

When he put it like that... "That doesn't make it OK." And Sheriff Satterfield had mostly stopped putting the blame for everything that went wrong on Rafe.

"I don't care," Rafe said. "I don't work there no more. They can think whatever they want."

He turned back to Wendell. "McLaughlin say anything else?"

"Not about you. And I didn't wanna ask straight out if there was something going on in his command that mighta caused someone to wanna murder Doug Brennan."

No, that was probably best. Especially since Ben McLaughlin himself was one of the suspects.

"What about the others?" I asked. "Pavlova, Hammond, and Grant? Did you talk to any of them?"

"All of'em," Wendell said. "McLaughlin called a meeting. Two of his people have died in the past couple days. He's upset. Understandably. And so is the upper brass."

"Does he suspect that something's going on in his command that might account for it?"

"If he does, he didn't say," Wendell said. "Just went over the facts and told us all the MNPD and Goins are in charge, and to answer any questions they ask. If anyone has information, to tell Goins."

"How did that go over?"

"Fine," Wendell said. "Larry Grant grumbled about Metro investigating one of our cases, and shouldn't it be us investigating our own, but everybody else seemed to understand why we can't."

"And nobody said or did anything suspicious?"

Wendell shook his head.

"They wouldn't, darlin'," Rafe told me. "They're professionals. Or at least too professional to let slip something like that, that easy."

Wendell nodded. "McLaughlin and Pavlova both did some undercover work before they moved into command. They're used to keeping a straight face."

"Hammond and Grant didn't?"

They both shook their heads. "Grant's support," Rafe said. "He never moves outside the office. His background's in tech. I guess he thought the TBI would be more exciting than working for some IT outfit."

"Hammond came to the TBI from the PD," Wendell added. "When his wife got pregnant, he wanted a job where he could work regular hours."

Or he wanted a supervisory job where he could skim money, because with a kid on the way and one more in the works—he had at least the two we'd seen—he needed more than he was making.

I didn't say it. I didn't have to. Rafe and Wendell knew as well as I, maybe better, that all these people were still under suspicion, no matter their background or ability to keep a straight face.

Rafe glanced at the kitchen window. "The snow's starting."

Wendell did, too. "Guess I should think about getting home. Before it gets any worse." He pushed his chair back from the table.

"Before you do," Rafe said, "let me run something by you."

Wendell sank back down on the chair.

"I was thinking," Rafe said, "that maybe I oughta call these people."

These people… as in McLaughlin, Hammond, Pavlova, and

Grant? The suspects? "Why would you want to do that?"

"To see what'll happen," Rafe said. "Three of'em may wonder if I had something to do with what happened. The fourth'll know better. If I call'em all, and give each of'em the idea that I know what they're up to, the three that didn't do nothing are prob'ly gonna contact Goins and complain, and then at least we'll know which three that is."

"If Goins shares the information with you, and he probably won't. And they may not call him, either. Maybe they'll think you've lost your mind because they aren't doing anything they shouldn't be, and they give you the benefit of the doubt because they feel bad for you. And anyway, why would you do something to make Goins even more suspicious of you?"

"Not sure it's possible to make him more suspicious," Rafe said.

"Fine. It would certainly not make him any less suspicious. Which is sort of the point. We want Goins to realize you had nothing to do with this. Not give him the idea that you know something you don't."

"If we can prove who did it—" Rafe began.

"Goins still won't believe you. If he caught one of them in the process of chopping at Brennan's brake cables with their nail scissors, he still wouldn't believe that you didn't have anything to do with it."

"Then it can't get any worse than it is," Rafe said. "I think it's worth a shot. If we can rattle one of'em sufficiently, he might do something stupid. And if everyone but that one goes screaming to McLaughlin or Goins, at least we know who didn't do it. Whoever's guilty ain't gonna say nothing. He ain't gonna wanna draw any attention to himself."

It made sense. I had to admit that. At least to myself. But... "I don't like you putting yourself in danger."

"I ain't in any danger," Rafe said. "These people live in

Nashville. They ain't gonna go out in the snow."

I glanced at Wendell, who said, "Just in case, maybe I oughta spend the night after all."

Rafe rolled his eyes. "You're as bad as she is. When did you start worrying about the chances I take?"

"I always worried about the chances you took," Wendell told him evenly. "Many a time, I told you not to do it. Whatever it was. You usually did it anyway. I figure it's gonna be the same thing now."

"Are you telling me not to do this?"

There was a pause. Wendell didn't say anything.

"It's worth a shot," Rafe insisted.

"I'm not saying you don't have a point, boy. But this ain't your job to do. Let Goins do it."

"If I leave it to Goins," Rafe said, "I'll be behind bars tomorrow."

And it was hard to dispute that. But that didn't make it any easier to see him take stupid risks.

He shook his head when I said so. "It ain't stupid. And not much of a risk. All I'm gonna do is call each of 'em and put a little bug in their ear. Make 'em wonder whether maybe I know something they don't want me to know. Something that maybe I haven't realized, or done anything about, until now. When it's in my own best self-interest to mention it."

"So you'll make yourself look like you're willing to look the other way in exchange for some money. Since you've lost your job and all."

He nodded. "Makes sense, don't it? And whoever's doing this would believe it. If he's doing it for the money, he'd believe that I'd care about the money, too."

He probably would. I sighed. "I should have married Todd. He wouldn't have kept me up at night with crazy, hare-brained schemes like this."

"I keep you up at night with other stuff," Rafe said, and there was no denying that. I turned toward the stove to stir the ground beef—and to hide the warmth in my cheeks from Wendell—while Rafe chuckled.

So I stirred the green chiles and the seasoning into the ground beef and turned down the heat to let the chili simmer while I pulled shredded cheese and sour cream and little tortilla crumbles out of the fridge and cabinets. Meanwhile, Rafe dug his phone out of his pocket and dialed.

I listened while I shook the shredded cheese into a bowl and the tortilla crumbles into another, and scooped the sour cream into a third. I guess I could have just left it all in the containers it came in—and had it been just Rafe and me here, I might have—but we had company, and that meant making sure the food didn't just taste good, but was presented properly, as well.

"Agent Pavlova?" He must have started with her. Very chivalrous of him. Unless he suspected her more than he did the others. "This is Rafe Collier."

There was a faint quacking from the other end of the line, and I wondered why he didn't put it on speaker so Wendell and I could hear, as well.

On the other hand, if it was on speaker Pavlova might wonder why, since it's usually possible to tell, and then she might wonder whether someone else was listening in, as well. Maybe he was trying to avoid that.

"This won't take long," Rafe said, from which I deduced that Christina Pavlova must have told him how busy she was. "I was thinking maybe we oughta get together sometime. To talk."

There was more quacking. Pavlova must be asking what he wanted to talk about, because he said, "Better if we leave that till we got some privacy, don't you think?"

As far as sinister implications that said nothing specific, it wasn't bad at all.

Pavlova quacked. I thought I could hear a sort of frantic note in the tone of her quacking, but it could have been my imagination.

"Tell you what," Rafe said. His voice was nice and even, but he'd coated it with an edge of steel. "How about you just sleep on it? And let me know in the morning? Not something you wanna wait too long to deal with, I imagine, but we can take a few hours for you to think about how you wanna handle it. And what might happen if you decide not to call. Let me know. I'll be here."

Pavlova said something, but I have no idea what it was. I don't know that Rafe did, either. He hung up in the middle of it. And arched his brows at Wendell.

Who nodded. "Sounded good."

It had. Certainly like he knew something he didn't. Something the person he spoke to might not want him to know.

He was already dialing the second name on his mental list. I waited. Until— "Grant? This is Rafe Collier."

His lips curved. "Exactly. That Rafe Collier."

Wendell smirked. I did, too.

Rafe started going through much the same spiel with Grant that he had with Christina Pavlova. He'd only gotten halfway through it when Wendell's phone rang. He pulled it out, glanced at it, and muttered an apology before he took himself and his phone into the hallway.

Rafe finished his conversation with Grant with the same vaguely threatening air—like Pavlova, Grant wasn't ready to admit anything, and wanted to sleep on it—and arched his brows at me.

"Good job," I said. "I have no idea who called Wendell. I guess he'll tell you when he comes back in."

Rafe nodded and polished off the call to Hammond while he waited. There was no answer, so maybe Hammond was having dinner with his wife and small children and turned the phone off while he did. Rafe ended up leaving a brief message laced with vague not-quite-threats and innuendo, before he hung up. By the time he had, Wendell was back in the kitchen. "Pavlova called McLaughlin."

Rafe nodded. "No need to call him myself, then. If it's him, he knows I don't know nothing. If it ain't him, it don't matter."

"He said if you have something on Pavlova, you need to tell him," Wendell said, "and not go behind his back to try to work an angle of your own."

"Which is exactly what he'd say if it's him and he doesn't want you to know it," I said.

They both nodded. "Grant's sleeping on it," Rafe told Wendell, "same as Pavlova, and Hammond didn't pick up. I left a message. Anybody else on the list?"

Wendell rattled off another dozen names. The list started with Johnson and ended with Kirkegaard. I didn't think I'd heard any of them before. "Who are they?"

"Undercover handlers and agents," Rafe said. "Some of Brennan's, some of Foster's." He glanced at Wendell. "You got numbers?"

"I can get 'em." Wendell started punching buttons on his phone.

"Why—?" I began, and Rafe explained it to me.

"If Foster was dirty, somebody helped him skim merchandise and money. If Foster was murdered, somebody killed him. The most likely suspect is somebody who worked under him."

Obviously. "So now you're going to call all of them, too?"

"Might as well," Rafe said, and dialed the first number Wendell gave him.

Ten minutes later, with the phone calls out of the way and the chili done, we settled down to eat. Wendell, too. He must have decided to stick around. I'm not sure whether it was the weather, or the fact that Rafe was sticking his neck out, but Wendell made no more noises about wanting to leave. After dinner, I headed upstairs to put clean sheets on the bed in the lavender room that used to be Mrs. Jenkins's, while Rafe and Wendell took Carrie to the parlor to watch basketball while they waited for someone to call back with a confession, or at least with a desire to meet and talk.

No one did, though. Grant and Pavlova must still be thinking about what to do—or maybe Pavlova wasn't, since she'd dumped the metaphorical mess in McLaughlin's lap—and Hammond didn't call to ask what the hell Rafe meant by making such an insulting, slanderous suggestion on his voicemail. I figured he either hadn't gotten the message, or he knew it was neither insulting nor slanderous, and he was planning what to do about it. Of the handful of undercover handlers Rafe had called—not like he could call the agents themselves; he knew better than to put them in danger—two had cursed him out, one had threatened to have him up on charges, and one had snarled at him to do his worst. All four had hung up in his ear. The other two hadn't picked up.

After the basketball game we went to bed. Rafe rustled up a pair of pajamas for Wendell—a bit too big for the older man, who is neither as tall nor as muscular as Rafe, at least not anymore—and he even pulled on a pair of pajama bottoms of his own, too. There was no hanky-panky in the bedroom before we fell asleep.

Eighteen

I guess I should be grateful we had a baby. Without Carrie, who knows what would have happened?

As it was, I was already up and awake in the middle of the night, sitting in the rocking chair in the nursery with the baby on my lap, when something crashed through one of the windows downstairs. A second passed, during which I was frozen in shock. Then came a whoosh, at the same time as I screamed. "Rafe!"

"On it." He was already moving, coming through the doorway on the other side of the hall toward the top of the stairs. A moment passed, then— "Shit!"

It isn't often I hear panic in my husband's voice—he's faced things the rest of us will never face without batting an eyelash— but I heard it then. "What?!"

"Get the baby." His voice was tight, and by now I could hear crackling behind it. Meanwhile, he pushed Wendell's door open fast enough that it knocked back against the wall. "Move!"

Wendell must already be moving, because his voice was almost as close to me as Rafe's. "What the hell was that?"

Rafe said something I didn't catch, both because the crackling was getting louder and because the baby was crying. I'd had to unlatch her from what she was doing, and she wasn't ready. I rocked her—"Shhh! Shhh!"—as I ran for the door. Since she was full of milk, and I hadn't burped her properly, and I was bouncing her as I ran, she threw up on me. Of course.

At the moment, it was the least of my concerns. I stopped at the top of the stairs with an echo of Rafe's exclamation from earlier. "Shit!"

It was no wonder he'd sounded panicked. At the bottom of the stairs, the foyer was already engulfed in flames. They licked at the walls and the old wood of the newel post. Our winter jackets, on the coat rack beside the door, were burning like bonfires.

Rafe headed down the stairs toward the flames, and I found my voice. "No! What are you doing? You can't—"

He glanced at me over his shoulder. His very bare shoulder. He'd put on a pair of drawstring pajama pants in deference to the fact that Wendell was in the house, but he was barefoot and bare-chested and quite a sight with the light from the flames flickering over his torso.

"We can't stay here."

He kept going. I had my mouth open to scream, but then he stopped, halfway down the stairs. A second later he'd grabbed the handrail and vaulted over the open side of the staircase into the hallway to the kitchen. A second later Wendell did the same thing, a little less gracefully, and landed with a grunt. He was twice Rafe's age, so there was nothing surprising about that. I probably wouldn't be able to vault at all, and since I had the feeling I'd be asked to, I'd better get used to the idea.

"Gimme the baby," Rafe's voice said from the dark beside the stairs.

I crept carefully down the top few steps. The flames were already getting closer, and the heat was intense. But I went as far down as I thought I safely could, while the flames crackled and the heat seared half of my body, and held the baby over the railing. She was still squalling, and more so once she left what she probably felt was the safety of being held close to my body.

Rafe lifted his hands, and I dropped the baby into them. It wasn't a far drop, and when she landed, she let out a surprised squawk and then was silent.

For a second before the screaming started again, more loudly than before.

Rafe passed her to Wendell, and turned back to me. "Now you."

Great. But there was no other choice, of course. I couldn't go down through the flames. They'd engulfed the bottom of the stairs and the whole area in front of the front door. The jagged hole in the window was probably helping to fan them. And while I could run two flights up to the third floor and hope that someone would come to put out the flames before I suffocated or burned to a crisp, it didn't seem like a good idea.

I climbed over the railing, grateful I had started wearing pajama pants and camisole tops to bed since Carrie was born. The short tops were so much easier to deal with when it came time to feed her than the full length nightgowns I used to wear, and now there was the added benefit that Wendell wouldn't be able to look up the bottom of my skirt while I was balancing on the outside of the staircase, waiting to jump.

You can thank my mother—or I can—that a thought like that even crossed my mind at a time like this.

"C'mon," Rafe said. His voice was calm again, all the panic gone now that he was in the middle of the situation and dealing with it rather than just looking at it. "I'll catch you."

Of course he would. And my daughter was down there. I jumped. And was caught halfway down, my fall broken, so by the time I landed—a little heavily, but with plenty of help—my feet didn't bang painfully against the hardwood floor, but floated down almost like a feather.

He let me go again immediately. "Take the baby. Go out the back."

I grabbed the baby from Wendell. "What about you?"

"I spent too much time working on this house to watch it burn," Rafe said grimly, giving me a push down the hallway. "Go."

I went, with Wendell right behind. Directly through the kitchen to the back door. The old skeleton key was in the lock, along with a new and shiny deadbolt Rafe had installed when he came to live here. I turned the key and flipped the deadbolt and pulled on the door.

It didn't budge.

"Rafe!"

This time the panic was in my own voice, and he turned from where he was rooting in the area under the sink for the tiny fire extinguisher we keep there. I had no idea what good he thought that would do against the ocean of flames currently occupying our foyer, but I didn't say anything about it. I had more important things to worry about.

He looked from me to the door. After a second he left the pantry and waved me aside. I moved out of the way so he could throw himself at the door.

There was the splintering of wood from outside—whatever had kept the door closed was gone—and then he stumbled through the opening. Straight into another fire.

I screamed, and in the foyer, the original fire roared higher as more oxygen flooded into the house. Flames from the back porch licked at the edges of the kitchen door. Wendell plunged through the opening and grabbed Rafe by the arm and dragged him back inside. And slammed the door behind him, leaving the second fire—currently engulfing the small wooden porch attached to the back of our brick house—burning merrily.

"Fuck." Rafe's voice was weak.

"Did you get burned? Did you get hurt?"

I couldn't drop the baby, or I would have been all over him

to see for myself.

"Not so much it matters." Which wasn't exactly a no, but whatever had happened didn't slow him down. He swung in a circle, and then zeroed in on the basement door. "Down here."

He yanked it open and flipped on the light. By some miracle it still worked. I guess the flames hadn't devoured the whole electrical panel yet. "Get in the tunnel."

"It's boarded up!"

"We'll take the boards off first," Rafe said.

We? "You're coming?" Instead of risking his life trying to save the house he'd spent too much time working on?

Not that I was happy to see all the original woodwork and plaster and Victorian finishes—and our furniture and clothes and everything else—go up in flames. But it was wood and plaster and stuff. It could be replaced. He couldn't.

He nodded. "Hopefully somebody's called the fire department and they're coming, but this is too much for me to deal with. We gotta get outta here before we can't."

Thank you, God.

I scrambled down the stairs with Wendell behind me. Rafe shut the door—one more barrier between us and the flames—before he followed. Wendell was already digging through the tools on the bench in the corner, and Rafe armed himself with a crowbar, and the two of them disappeared into the dark space under the stairs.

I stood on the cold dirt in my bare feet clutching the baby and waited. And while I tried to listen for sirens, I couldn't hear anything but the sounds of the tools, and the two of them cursing, and the muted roar of the flames.

It felt like an eternity. I imagine it was really just a couple of minutes before Rafe stuck his head around the stairs. "C'mon. Wendell's already in. You go next."

I scrambled under the stairs and over to the small opening.

There was no part of me that wanted to make this trip again. I'd made it once before, nine months pregnant, and it had been the stuff that nightmares are made of. I'd dreamed about suffocating and being buried alive for weeks afterwards. But I'd rather do that than burn to a crisp. So I got on my knees, while I clutched the baby to my chest with one arm. "Bring the crowbar. You're going to have to bust through the wood at the top of the shaft when we get there. You nailed that shut, too, remember?"

"Wendell's got it," Rafe said. "Gimme the baby."

I wasn't proud. I handed her over. He was better equipped to hold her and crawl on one arm than I was. Or at least that's what I told myself.

He gave me a nudge. "Go on, darlin'. I love you."

"I love you, too," I said. And started crawling. Without a single thought as to how big my derriere was going to look to the man behind me.

I won't lie. The trip through the tunnel was worse this time. I didn't have to worry about getting stuck, so that was a good thing. Last time I'd made this crawl, I'd been worried at every turn that my pregnant stomach would be too big to make it to the end, and I'd be stuck down here and would starve to death before anyone found me. Rafe had no idea where I was, or even that the tunnel existed, and Mrs. Jenkins—who was with me— was too weak to unstick me if I did get stuck. And if she had to leave me behind in the tunnel, I wasn't sure she'd remember that I was there, so she could tell anyone.

I didn't have that problem this time. I was smaller all around, and wearing less, so getting stuck wasn't an issue. If I'd made it through pregnant, I could make it through now. But I was cold, in my bare feet and bare arms. I'd been wearing a coat last time.

Not that I was the only one of us in that predicament. Rafe

was wearing less than I was, and Wendell wasn't wearing much more. He'd slept in both pajama jacket and pants, or had taken the time to shrug them on before he came out of his room, but that still wasn't a lot of clothes for early January.

And unlike last time, I had to worry about the fire behind us. I kept getting this vision of what would happen when the fire—or fires—combined in the kitchen. When the one from the foyer burned down the hallway and the one on the back porch burned through the door, and they engulfed the kitchen. And burned through the door to the basement and then the wooden stairs.

When Wendell burst through the floor of the pavilion and reached the back yard, would the influx of oxygen through the tunnel act as a sort of funnel, and we'd get a ball of flames sucked through behind us, before Rafe and Carrie and I could make it up and out? Would the three of us burn to a crisp at the bottom of the shaft before we could make it safety?

I didn't know enough about the physics and chemistry of it to know for sure, and I didn't want to ask, since I might not like the answer. So I just kept crawling, while the worst case scenario looped, over and over in my head.

"I'm here," Wendell's voice said in front of me. It felt like it had taken a year, but it's actually not that long a trip. We were still on our own property. I can walk from the house to the pavilion in less than a minute. Crawling through a narrow hole in the ground takes longer, but it hadn't taken the eternity it felt like.

"There are wooden slats on the side of the shaft," I said, and coughed. "Sorry. You have to climb, and then hang on while you break through."

He was already moving, and it was the little particles of whatever—dirt, dust, earth—raining down that made me cough. I buried my mouth in my elbow as my chest heaved.

"You OK, darlin'?" Rafe's hand descended on my back,

warm and hard through the thin cotton of the camisole.

I nodded. Not that he could see me in the dark. So I cleared my throat. "Yeah. Just a cough. You?"

"Fine. Not the best night's sleep, but we'll make it."

We would. "What'll happen when the air from outside hits the tunnel?"

"We'll climb up," Rafe said.

"It won't pull the fire through the tunnel?"

He shook his head. I couldn't see it, but I felt the displacement of the air. And heard the negation in his voice. "I don't think the fire's made it to the kitchen yet. It wasn't burning that fast."

It looked like it had burned plenty fast to me, but who was I to argue? The last thing I wanted to believe, was that we were about to go up in flames, just as we thought we'd made it to safety.

"Someone set that fire," I said. And changed it to, "Set both of them."

He nodded. For good measure he added, "Yeah. Set the one on the back porch, boarded up the back door so we couldn't get out that way, and threw a bottle with something flammable through the front window."

"Deliberately. Someone tried to kill us."

He nodded again. "We should figure out who dug this tunnel, so we can pay our respects."

We should. If it hadn't been for the tunnel, and the lucky break of Mrs. Jenkins showing it to me the week Carrie was born, we'd still be standing in the kitchen wondering what to do. "First thing tomorrow I'll call the Historical Commission and ask." If we made it out alive, and it looked like we might.

"I figure we'll have other things to do first thing tomorrow," Rafe said. "But sometime after that."

He raised his voice. "You need help up there?"

Wendell grunted. "You nailed 'em in good, boy."

Rafe grinned. By now Wendell had removed one or two of the boards from the opening, and there was enough light for me to see his face.

"I love you," I said.

"Love you, too." He leaned in to kiss me. The baby was squished between us. She wasn't crying anymore, but sort of gently hiccupping. Hopefully she was too small for this experience to have scarred her forever. But if she grew up and developed a fear of the dark and tight places, I knew what to blame.

"I'll take her," I said. "You can climb up and help Wendell."

"He's got it." And with no fireball bursting through the tunnel to fry us to a crisp, either. "And I'll keep the baby. Give you both hands free to hold on."

Fine. "Go up before me, then. You can probably climb faster than me, anyway." Even with one hand. "I'll just slow you down."

He shrugged. But when Wendell knocked away the last of the wood covering the exit from the shaft and clambered through, Rafe didn't insist on going last. Instead, he wiggled past me and headed up, hauling himself from step to step with one hand and cradling the baby to his chest with the other.

I stood at the bottom of the shaft and watched. I hadn't said so, but if anything happened—if for some reason he couldn't hold on to the baby—I wanted to be down here to catch her if she fell.

I should have known better. He made it to the top with no problems, still holding the baby. Once he was over the edge, he turned to peer down at me. "C'mon, darlin'. Almost there."

I remembered this climb from last time, too, and there was no 'almost there' about it. Last time, I'd been crying by this point. But I climbed, with splinters digging into my palms and the bottoms of my naked feet from the rough, wooden boards. Climbed, toward my husband and baby girl cheering me on from the top of the ladder.

It took another eternity, but I made it. And came out into a world of craziness.

Wendell had already left the pavilion by the time I got to the top of the ladder. There were two big fire trucks outside the house, one in the driveway on the front, directing water from big hoses through the windows of the parlor and dining room, and one around the corner, still on the street, with a hose snaking over the fence and across the grass to the back of the house.

The wooden back porch sheltering the kitchen door was almost completely gone. A few smaller flames licked here and there, but the porch itself was just ash and charred timbers.

Flames were still flickering behind the windows in the dining room, which was the room closest to us. But they were smaller than I'd been afraid of, and the firemen, in heavy protective gear with boots and helmets, were directing a steady stream of water through the broken panes. The original hand blown glass from the 1880s was history, but I guess that was a small price to pay.

It wasn't the only price we'd be paying, of course. It looked like the front of the first floor would be almost a total loss. The gingerbread trim on the porch roof was gone. The roof itself sagged, with only one porch post holding it up, and that one looking the worse for wear. But the flames hadn't broken through the heavy security door in the back, and there were no flames in any of the upstairs windows, either. And we were all alive and mostly well. It could have been a lot worse.

Wendell had gone to talk to the fire crew, and was standing by the big rig in conversation with a tall guy with an impressive handlebar mustache. Probably the captain of whichever fire station the trucks had come from, or at least some sort of supervisor.

Hell—heck—he might have been an arson investigator, although it was a little early for one of those to be on the scene.

Rafe was sitting on the wooden floor of the pavilion next to me, barefoot and bare-chested and in nothing but a pair of plaid sleep pants with a drawstring waist. He had me in one arm and the baby in the other, and we were all trying to catch our collective breaths as two EMT's—I recognized them from two nights ago, when they'd come to pick up Malcolm—hurried across the grass toward us, bags in hand.

"We're fine," I said, as they thundered up the couple of steps to the pavilion floor on heavy boots. "Just shaken up."

"Watch the hole," Rafe added.

They ignored both of us. "Would you like us to take a look at that, sir?"

That?

And then I remembered. Rafe had burst through the kitchen door into the burning back porch, and Wendell had yanked him back inside. And when I'd asked if he'd been hurt, he'd told me it wasn't bad enough to worry about.

I twitched out of his arm and scrambled a few feet away. "Oh, my God, Rafe. What did you do?"

He shot me a look. "I told you, it ain't bad. Just some blisters."

On the arm he'd kept around me as we sat here. The same arm he'd used to hold Carrie to his chest the whole way through the tunnel.

The paramedics went to work slathering the burns with salve and bandages, and I shook my head. "Why didn't you say something? I wouldn't have let you carry the baby all that way if I'd known you'd hurt yourself."

"Easier to carry her than hold myself up," Rafe said with a

shrug. The female EMT watched the way his muscles moved with what I can only call appreciation, and then seemed to realize what she was doing, and shot me a slightly sheepish look.

"Don't worry about it," I told her. "It happens all the time. I'm used to it. So is he."

Rafe winked at her, and she blushed. Her partner smirked, but didn't say anything. "How about you, ma'am. You OK?"

"I'm fine," I said. "We were up and moving as soon as the fire started, so we didn't inhale a lot of smoke. And I was nowhere near the flames."

He nodded. "What about the baby? Its lungs are smaller than yours."

I hadn't thought about that, and now I realized, with a sick feeling curdling in my stomach, that she could be hurt.

Not that she was acting hurt. She'd wailed lustily the whole way down into the basement, and had dissolved into sniffles and hiccups while Rafe carried her. Now she was blinking up at us with big eyes. There didn't seem to be anything wrong with her. But I didn't draw a deep breath again until both of the paramedics had taken a look at her and declared her good to go.

There was certainly nothing wrong with her lungs. She starting using them as soon as they began poking at her.

I took her back after they were finished, and she calmed down. "Any chance we could get our hands on some clothes?" I asked Rafe, since now that the adrenaline had left me and I had been out here a while, I was starting to feel the chill. He was wearing even less than I was, and had a burn on one arm; he was probably feeling the chill even more than I was.

"Our winter coats are history."

I nodded. I'd seen the coat rack go up in flames. "It doesn't look like the flames reached the second floor, though. We have more clothes there. Do you think someone might go up there if we asked, and would bring us something?"

"I'll do it," Rafe said and rolled to his feet. He used the uninjured arm to push himself up, but otherwise there didn't seem to be anything wrong with him.

"Make sure you're allowed to go inside first," I called after him as he set off across the grass. The little bit of snow that had fallen earlier had been churned into slush and mud by the water and all the feet tramping across our yard, but I'm sure it was still burning cold on the naked soles of his feet.

He lifted a hand—the uninjured side—to let me know he'd heard me, but he didn't turn around. I lifted my camisole—Carrie was trying to find milk through it—and let her find her way to food while I watched him cross the yard to where Wendell and the station chief were still in conversation. A minute passed, and then all three of them headed toward the back of the house. I guess they'd decided that it would be easier to get in that way.

I watched them boost themselves up and through the kitchen door—the wooden porch and stairs were gone—and I'm sure the movement hurt Rafe's arm, but he sidelined the pain and did it anyway. Wendell followed, a little less gracefully, still wearing Rafe's blue pajamas, and then the fire chief clambered through. They all disappeared inside.

I stayed where I was. Once the paramedics had cleared me and left, no one else bothered me. The firemen were busy doing their own thing. And Spicer and Truman must not be on duty on the graveyard shift, because after a few minutes a black and white squad car came up the driveway, but the two officers that stepped out were people I'd never seen before. And they didn't seem to notice me, just exchanged some words with the paramedics and firemen—to make sure that everything was under control, I guess—and then they reversed out of the driveway the way they came and drove off again.

I wondered whether they'd file a report, or whether our address would come up as being of interest in the case Rick Goins was working.

He must not be working the graveyard shift, either, or he probably would have been on hand, trying to prove that Rafe had set fire to his own house, with his own wife and infant inside, just to prove someone else was out to get him.

I closed my eyes and sent a prayer heavenwards with a heartfelt plea that the two cops who had just left wouldn't knock Goins up and send him over here, because this night was already traumatic enough, and we didn't need that on top of everything else.

Nineteen

It might have been ten minutes or so before Wendell and Rafe and the fire chief came back out of the house. Wendell and Rafe had both changed into street clothes. Wendell was wearing what he'd been wearing yesterday, minus the overcoat that was now nothing but ashes on the floor of the foyer. But he'd worn his shoes upstairs last night, so his feet were covered. So were Rafe's. They weren't the boots he'd left in the hallway downstairs, along with his jacket, before retiring to bed last night, but a pair of sneakers he wore to the gym sometimes. The jeans were faded and snug and fit him very nicely, and he'd thrown on a cable knit sweater over what was probably a T-shirt. The black leather jacket he usually wears was history, of course.

They were all carrying bags. I guess they'd taken the time to throw whatever they could fit into the suitcases they could find so we'd have something to wear for the next week. Rafe was carrying Carrie's diaper bag across his chest, and one of my coats—not the puffy one I'd had on yesterday, but a demure (and warm) wool I'd had since I was Bradley Ferguson's wife— over his arm. A pair of my boots dangled from his hand.

"Here, darlin'." They dumped it all on the floor of the gazebo, and Rafe put the coat around my shoulders. I smiled up at him. "Thank you. How bad is it?"

He dug in the diaper bag and pulled out a small blanket he

draped over Carrie. "Could be worse."

"The front of the house is a total loss," the fire chief said after nodding a greeting to me. He kept his eyes very carefully away from the nursing baby. "You'll have to do some work in the dining room, but not much. The rear of the house is all right." So the library and kitchen and powder room, I assumed. "The staircase is destroyed. The heartwood survived, but the sapwood all burned. And there's a lot of damage from the water and smoke. I'm afraid that can't be helped."

No problem. We were here and alive and hadn't lost most of the house or most of our belongings, so it was all good. "The upstairs is OK?"

They all nodded. "Other than some smoke," Rafe qualified.

So we could fix it. If we wanted to. The insurance would cover it, surely. Although we probably couldn't live here for a while.

The thought was still making its way through my mind when Rafe said, "You should take the baby and the car and go stay with your mama for a few days."

It would take more than a few days to fix this. But what he meant was probably that I should take the baby and car and go stay with my mother for a few days while he didn't. While he stuck around here until the case was solved.

I shook my head. "If you're staying here, I'm staying here."

"I'm gonna spend a couple days with Wendell," Rafe said, after the fire chief had excused himself and wandered off. I guessed he didn't want any part of the argument he heard brewing.

"If there's room for you at Wendell's house, I'm sure there's room for me, too. We sleep in the same bed."

"It's a twin," Rafe said.

OK, so that might be a little tight. And then there was Carrie. But I wasn't about to give up that easily. "Then why don't you come to Sweetwater, too? You can take a couple of days to recover and then go to work for Grimaldi."

"I wanna finish this," Rafe said, with a glance over his shoulder.

He wasn't talking about the house, of course. He was talking about whoever had thrown the Molotov Cocktail—or whatever the current term was—through our window. Whoever had tried to kill us in our sleep.

I lowered my voice. I'm not sure why, since no one else was close enough to us to hear what we were saying. The fire chief was back by the fire truck by now. "You think this is because of those phone calls you made last night."

It wasn't a question, and I didn't make it sound like one.

He nodded. "It was stupid. I just didn't think anybody'd do something like this."

Who would? Doug Brennan's death had probably been designed to look like an accident, and Foster's like a suicide. When Brennan's accident was questioned, Foster's suicide was supposed to explain it. The person who had set it all up had been hoping to get away with it.

But this was murder. There was no way anyone could look at this and think it was accidental.

Unless we weren't supposed to know what had happened. If we'd slept through the missile through the window, and the house had gone up—or down—in flames, with all of us inside it, maybe it would be chalked up to old wiring in a very old house.

With the way things had worked out, that wasn't a possibility. I'd been awake, and had heard the glass break. There was no coming back from this. Whoever had done it was on the hook now, with no way to wiggle his way—or hers—off.

"Do you know who it is?" I asked Rafe.

He hesitated. Glanced at the house. Glanced at Wendell.

Looked back at me. "Not for sure. I have an idea. But it's too soon to tell."

"Do you know who it isn't?"

He looked like he wanted to roll his eyes at my persistence, but he didn't. Or maybe it was just frustration. His answer made it sound like it could be. "It ain't Foster, and he was at the top of my list until yesterday."

"Unless he was involved," Wendell said, "and whoever he was involved with took care of him."

Rafe nodded. "Then it's either Hammond or McLaughlin, or one of the handlers Foster had under him. One of'em coulda struck a deal with Foster, prob'ly with the help of the undercover agent, and between the three of'em—the agent, the handler, and Foster—they got busy playing the players in whatever field they were working."

"Until Brennan talked to Foster about you," Wendell nodded, "and Brennan figured out what Foster was up to, and Foster killed Brennan. And when he told his partners what he'd done, they decided they might as well take Foster out, too."

I looked from one to the other of them. "Why would they do that?"

"The game was up anyway," Rafe said, "if Brennan had figured it out. They couldn't keep going. This way they take the suspicion off themselves and put it on Foster. Who prob'ly did kill Brennan."

"What about McLaughlin or Hammond?"

"Foster coulda been working with one of them, too," Rafe said. "Hammond's Foster's opposite in narcotics the way Pavlova's Brennan's."

All the possessives and contractions—and job descriptions—confused me, and he dumbed it down. "Foster was to undercover narcotics like Brennan was to undercover organized crime. Both of'em dealt with undercover agents and handlers. Hammond's narcotics and Pavlova's organized crime, but none of'em deal with undercover agents."

Got it. "There's plenty of money to be made in organized crime, though." As he very well knew. He'd been winding his way through every aspect of it for ten years.

He grinned, but didn't take the bait. "No reason for Pavlova, if she's dirty, to involve Foster. And Foster's involved. Or was."

Or why kill him? I nodded. "That makes sense. Besides, when you called her, Pavlova called McLaughlin. If she was planning to do something to you—if she was planning to do this," I glanced at the house, "chances are she wouldn't have drawn attention to herself by calling him."

Always assuming McLaughlin wasn't dirty, too, and the two of them weren't working together.

I put that thought aside for now. This was complicated enough without that. "So it's more likely that whatever's going on was going on on the narcotics side of McLaughlin's department. Brennan wasn't dirty—at least we don't think so—and chances are, if something had been going on in organized crime, even under just Pavlova, the two of you, as well as Brennan, would have noticed it."

They both nodded. "Too much activity in organized crime," Rafe said, "with me and the boys and the gang unit and all that. Hard to slip anything past anyone."

"Brennan did notice," Wendell added, "and that's how come he's dead."

"So for now, we're putting Pavlova on the bottom of the list, because she's in organized crime, and we don't think this was happening there. We think it was happening in narcotics."

The both nodded, and Wendell averted his eyes politely while I moved Carrie, pulled my camisole down, and put the baby against my shoulder so I could burp her.

"Any reason we can't take this conversation to Wendell's

place for the rest of the night? We can't stay here."

"You go on," Rafe said. "I wanna make sure the place is boarded up before we leave. Don't want nobody thinking it's a good idea to walk in and help themselves to whatever's in there."

"I'm sorry," I said. "I'm sure your TV is history."

He shrugged. "There's a TV in your mama's house."

There was. It wasn't the size his had been, but if he didn't care, I certainly didn't. And we could replace it with something bigger, if he wanted.

I got to my feet, a bit stiffly, because it had been cold sitting there on the hard wood floor of the gazebo, without much in the way of clothes on.

Wendell peeled a key off his keychain and handed it to me. "The guest room's at the top of the stairs on the right. Make yourself at home."

"We'll be there as soon as I get this squared away," Rafe added, and picked up a suitcase and some of Carrie's paraphernalia for the walk over to the Volvo. "An hour. Maybe a while longer. Then we'll finish talking."

I would absolutely hold him to that. "Take care of yourselves. Both of you."

"He ain't here," Rafe said with a disdainful look around. "Prob'ly waited long enough to see the flames take hold, but there's too much activity now for him to risk being seen. He's home, in bed, congratulating himself on how clever he's been."

No doubt. I got Carrie situated in the car—the seat had survived mostly intact inside the house, and Rafe had brought it out—while the men dumped the bags and suitcases into the trunk. "Don't worry about hauling'em inside when you get there," Rafe told me, and I figured he'd tell me he'd help me later, but instead he said, "You'll just have to put'em back when you take off for Sweetwater."

Which I wasn't planning to do until he was coming with me, but I didn't argue, just nodded. "Be careful."

"You, too." He kissed me, and stepped back to wave me off. I got into the car and cranked the key in the ignition. The Volvo didn't seem to have been damaged at all by anything that had happened, and purred just as sweetly as always down the driveway. I headed down Potsdam to Dresden, and from there over to Dickerson and the entrance to the interstate.

The streets were all quiet this time of night. There'd been so much activity outside our house that I hadn't really thought about how early it was, but the lighted numbers on the dashboard told me it was just going on 4ᴬᴹ, and the streets were mostly deserted. The little bit of snow that had fallen had already blown off the interstate, and it was an easy drive out to Hermitage. It was just past a quarter after when I pulled up outside Wendell's townhouse and found a spot marked *Guest Parking*, where I pulled the car in. And then I turned off the engine and dropped my hands to my lap and just sat there for a few minutes, shivering.

It wasn't because I was cold. I'd had the heat going in the car, and it was nice and toasty. I was wearing the wool coat on top of my pajamas, and boots on my feet, so I was in no danger of freezing.

No, it was reaction, pure and simple. I had held it together during the trip down the stairs and into the basement. I'd had a few moments of quiet panic in the tunnel, but I hadn't said anything about it, because Rafe had Carrie to deal with, and he needed me to be strong, because he couldn't take care of me too. And once we got up the shaft and outside, there were people there, and I couldn't break down into a gibbering mess in front of them. Not only would it be unbecoming, but I was sitting there in my pajamas, with no makeup and no bra, and it wasn't the time to draw attention to myself.

And I'd focused on keeping the car on the road during the drive. But now I was here, safely parked outside Wendell's townhouse with the engine and lights turned off. The baby had gone back to sleep in the back seat, and I didn't want to disturb her, because the sooner we got her onto a working day/night schedule, the better for everyone involved. And yes, six weeks was probably a little soon to be worrying about that. But she was asleep. I didn't want to do anything to change that. So I sat there in the dark, and had my little meltdown very quietly, in the front seat of my car, while around me, everyone was sleeping. Caroline was making soft little snuffling, sucking noises as she slept, and the thought that, if things had gone differently I might never have heard those small snuffling, sucking noises again, was heart breaking.

Who'd throw a firebomb—or whatever it was—into a house where there was a six-week-old baby, for God's sake? Who had that little respect for human life as to be willing to kill a baby in order to get her father off their tail?

Probably not Christina Pavlova. If she rescued animals, she probably had a somewhat soft spot for babies, too. Maybe not as soft—animal people tend to value animals above humans, even tiny humans—but I'm sure she liked babies better than she liked adults. And anyone who rescued animals surely wouldn't deliberately kill a baby, even as collateral damage.

McLaughlin and Hammond both had children. McLaughlin's were grown, or close to grown. Hammond's were still small. We'd postulated that either one of them might do something illegal to get money to provide for their children's needs. Did that extend to not wanting to harm anyone else's child, too?

I would tend to think it did. But of course I could be wrong.

That left Grant, the bachelor, and the unknown undercover operative or handler we thought might have been in business with Foster, and who had killed Foster after Foster killed Brennan.

Wendell had a daughter, Rafe said. An adult daughter now. But he certainly wasn't a family man, not the kind with a wife and a kid at home. And I was willing to bet his opposite number, the hypothetical narcotics handler, didn't, either. It was even less likely that the undercover narcotics agent did. People with a lot of hostages to fortune, women and children at home, didn't tend to go into that kind of work. Too much risk. Too much time away from the people they loved.

That's as far as I'd traveled down the convoluted byways of my mind when something happened. The door to Wendell's townhouse opened, and someone came out.

My first instinct was to question whether I'd made a mistake in identifying Wendell's townhouse. Maybe what I thought was Wendell's townhouse wasn't really Wendell's townhouse at all. Maybe it was Wendell's neighbor's townhouse, and now the neighbor was off to an early start at work.

But no. What I was looking at, was what Rafe had told me yesterday was Wendell's townhouse. It was unadorned except for a prosaic black doormat, and was stuck between two other townhomes, identical but for the fact that one had a leftover Christmas wreath still on the door, and the other some sort of sign that said—I threw my mind back to when I'd seen it in the daylight—*Welcome to the... Masons*, was it?

Wendell's door had neither. The guy was coming out of Wendell's door.

He—definitely a man, too tall to be female, and dressed all in black—pulled the door shut behind him. Wendell hadn't turned the light next to the door on—probably because he hadn't been home since yesterday morning—so I couldn't see his face, but the shape was male. A lot less muscular than Rafe, but with male shoulders and male hips. Broader on top than on the bottom, inverse to most women.

There wasn't much light in the parking lot, and he kept his head down as he walked between the cars. He didn't cross close to mine, and I moved my head slowly to watch his progress. Any kind of movement in a world that's otherwise sitting still is very noticeable, and I didn't want him to notice me. Wendell hadn't mentioned that there'd be anyone else at his home, and if someone was supposed to be there, I felt sure he'd have let me know when he gave me the keys.

Ergo, this guy didn't belong. And since he didn't, I didn't want him to notice me.

He crossed the small patch of grass between where I was parked and the parking area on the other side. He must have left his car door open, because there was no sound of him unkeying the lock remotely. He just opened the door and got in. And the dome light didn't come on when the door opened, so he must have disconnected or otherwise turned it off. Yet another reason to suspect he was here doing something he shouldn't be.

He sat behind the wheel for a second—maybe doing the same thing I was doing, taking a breather after his experience—and then he turned the car on and reversed out of the space. He didn't flip the headlights on until he was sitting at the exit, waiting to turn onto Lebanon Road.

I turned my own car on and hurried after, just as quickly as I could. And while I wasn't worried about any of the residents looking out the window and noticing my car, I didn't want him to see me exiting the subdivision right on his heels, so I kept my own lights off, too, until after I'd turned onto Lebanon Road.

We were headed in the direction of downtown. Of home. My home. It obviously wasn't Christina Pavlova in the car ahead of me, so it made sense that we weren't going toward Mount Juliet and Wilson County.

I didn't think it knocked any of the other suspects out of

contention. Hammond lived near the lake. He could have gone left out of the subdivision, but he could also turn left closer to town. Grant lived in East Nashville. McLaughlin lived in Brentwood. And any of them could be on his way to the TBI.

Or it could be someone I didn't know, the hypothetical handler or undercover narcotics agent we'd been talking about earlier. If so, he could be going home, or going to work, or going somewhere else entirely.

Hell, he could be going out for breakfast, to reward himself for a job well done.

I could see the taillights of the car up ahead. It was still early, and the roads were still pretty deserted. I didn't want to move too close to him for fear he'd notice me. As a result, every time he moved around a curve or crested a hill, I was afraid I'd lose him by the time I got there myself.

I could call Rafe, though. He'd saved my cell phone from the bedside table, and had put it in the pocket of the coat he'd brought me from upstairs earlier. I dug it out and dialed.

He picked up immediately. "What's wrong?"

"Nothing," I said, and amended it to, "Nothing much. There was a guy at Wendell's place when I got there."

"Scuse me?"

"When I got there, I stayed in the car for a minute or two."

He didn't answer, and that made me feel I had to explain. "I was a little shaken up from everything, and Carrie was asleep, and I didn't want to wake her, and it's weird to walk into someone else's house anyway, when they aren't home..."

Although I should be used to that, being a real estate agent.

"What happened?" Rafe said, and I reined myself in.

"Nothing. I was sitting there, as I explained, outside, and the front door opened. And this guy came out."

"Can you describe him?"

I could, but I didn't do a very good job. "Maybe six feet,

maybe not. Not too muscular. He was dressed all in black, with a black hat. The kind you wear when it's cold. And it was dark. I didn't see his face."

"White guy? Black? Latino?"

That I could answer. "White. If he was anything else, he was very light-skinned."

"Young? Old?"

Um… He hadn't moved like someone young, but not like he was feeling his age, either. "Somewhere in the middle? Older than you, but younger than Wendell? Forties, maybe?"

If he was disappointed in my powers of observation, Rafe didn't say so. "Then what happened?"

I described how the man had gotten into his car and left, and how I was following him down Lebanon Road toward town. "We're just passing the Donelson YMCA. The turnoff toward the lake is just around the corner. If he goes that way, maybe it's Hammond."

"How close are you to him?"

"Not close enough to see him clearly. I don't want him to notice me. But I'll see if he turns."

Once I caught up and made it around the curve.

"What kinda car?" Rafe asked.

"Oh. Um… SUV. Not too big. Dark. Smaller than Goins's Toyota. Darker in color, too."

"I didn't think it was Goins," Rafe said. And added, "You woulda recognized Goins, right?"

Probably. "Sure. This isn't someone I've seen before. At least I don't think so. He didn't look familiar."

"What's he doing now?"

I peered through the windshield. "Not turning. Going straight on Lebanon Road. We're approaching Donelson Pike. If he wants the interstate, that's the way he'll go."

But he didn't. Just zoomed across that intersection, too. It was early enough that the main roads, like the one we were on, had flashing yellow lights at every intersection, all the way into town. The smaller, merging roads had red blinking lights and had to stop before merging. But so far, it had been smooth sailing for the two of us, and the two or three other cars on the road.

Up ahead, the SUV started up the hill over the railroad tracks where the commuter train runs. I could see the taillights crest the incline and then disappear over the top. I pushed down on the gas so I'd catch up sooner. And headed up the hill, too, to the top.

And— "Damn!"

Twenty

"What?" Rafe said.

"I don't see him."

We'd reached the part of Donelson where all the stores were. And some of them were open this early. There was a gas station with its lights lit, the donut place, a couple of twenty-four/seven drugstores and grocery stores. And more cars. Some people shop this early to avoid the rush.

I cruised along, peering left and right, while I kept the phone to my ear. "There are more cars now. There are residential neighborhoods on the left and right out here, and more cars merging onto the main road." Not that many, admittedly, but where there had been two or three, beyond the two of us, now there were five or six. Maybe seven. "I can't see him. He must have turned off. Do you want me to go back and look for him?"

"Would you recognize him if you saw him?"

He didn't wait for me to answer. "No. Just go back to Wendell's place and get some sleep. See what damage this guy did inside."

That made sense. "What's going on where you are?" I asked, while I made a highly illegal U-turn I felt comfortable making, since there were so few cars on the road. Then I headed back the way I'd come. "Are the firefighters still pouring water on the house?"

"They're mostly done by now. Still standing around

shooting the breeze. I'm gonna use some of the wood from the gazebo floor to bar the front and back doors on the house."

"What about the gazebo?" Not only could someone fall in, but if they did, they could make it into the house that way, which seemed to defeat the purpose.

"If anybody's determined enough to push loot ahead of 'em back and forth through that tunnel, they're welcome to what they can carry," Rafe said, and I guess he had a point. "I'll go to the hardware store in a couple hours and get some plywood. For now we gotta make do with what we have."

That made sense, too. "I'm crossing Donelson Pike now, going in the other direction. Still no sign of the SUV. But… shit." I mean… shoot.

"What?"

"Blue lights. In my rearview. It must have been that U-turn I made earlier."

I hadn't noticed any police cars, or I wouldn't have done it, but they aren't always marked and easy to see. Someone had obviously seen me, though. Someone who was now flashing blue lights at me from behind.

Maybe there'd been a cop parked outside the donut place, and I just hadn't noticed.

"I'll pull over," I told Rafe, "and call you back later."

"Don't—"

I didn't wait for him to finish what was probably an admonition to behave and not do anything stupid. As if I would. I don't often get pulled over, but when I do, I do know how to behave. And anyway, I'm a white woman with a baby in the backseat. My chances of getting out of this without a ticket—and with my life—were a lot better than Rafe's would have been.

So I disconnected the call before I heard the rest of what he'd been planning to say, and dropped the phone in the console. Better not to be on the phone, anyway, when you're pulled over.

It isn't against the law—texting while driving is illegal, talking isn't—but I wanted all my attention free to talk myself out of the ticket if I could.

The car—just a dark bulk I couldn't see well because of the flashing blue light and the headlights, although it was clearly unmarked and not your usual white and blue squad car—pulled in behind me. A second passed, then the door opened. I guess he hadn't bothered to run my license plate before approaching. Sometimes they do.

I powered my window down, and kept both my hands visible on the wheel. Carrie was still asleep, bless her, and didn't seem bothered by the cold air flooding into the car. It bit at my own nose, but there was nothing I could do about that. At least I was wearing a coat over my pajamas.

The cop ambled up to the window. He didn't lean down, just stood there, so that all I saw when I turned my head, was the bottom of a black windbreaker, zipped, and the top of a pair of black pants. Plus a belt with, among other things, a holstered gun on his hip. "Are you aware you made an illegal U-turn back there?" his voice inquired from above.

"I'm sorry," I said humbly. Nothing else I could do, after all. I mean, everyone knows that U-turns are illegal. And I couldn't very well claim that I couldn't remember doing it.

His voice was not impressed. "License and registration, please."

"Of course." I reached for my purse, which is usually next to me on the passenger seat, and stopped. "I don't have a license."

"You don't have a license?"

"On me. I don't have a license on me." Or at all, really. It had been in my purse, and my purse had been downstairs in the foyer, and anything that had been in the foyer was now reduced to ashes. "It's a long story. See, we had a fire in our house last night, and—"

"A fire?"

I nodded. "Someone threw something through the window, and it sort of exploded, and the whole foyer burned, and the parlor, and some of the rest of the downstairs, including my purse with my license and all my credit cards and everything else I own…" And Lord, the extent of what I was going to have to deal with tomorrow just hit me. All those credit cards and debit cards I'd have to replace, all those phone calls I'd have to make, not to mention a trip to the DMV, which is always a time-consuming and annoying task…

"Your name?"

"Savannah Martin," I said. "Collier."

"And you survived a fire?"

"By the skin of our teeth. See, we live in this old house in East Nashville, and at some point someone dug a tunnel from the basement to the gazebo in the yard—I'm thinking maybe there was another house there at some point, because why would anyone dig a tunnel to a gazebo?—but when the fire started, and we couldn't get out the front door, and there was another fire on the back porch so we couldn't go out that way either, we went into the basement and through the tunnel and ended up in the gazebo. And that's how we made it out."

It was quite an exciting story. I had expected better than a "Wait here," delivered in a sort of choked voice. Maybe he was trying not to laugh, although I didn't think my recounting had been that funny.

"Sure," I said, but he was already on his way back to his own car. And that was when, as I watched him walk away in the rearview mirror, his back to me, I realized that there was something familiar about him.

That I had, in fact, seen this guy get into his car just a few minutes ago.

That this was the same guy who had come out of Wendell's

house. The same guy I'd been following.

He must have noticed me, and turned off somewhere where I couldn't see him, and when I'd turned around, he'd doubled back behind me, and then he'd turned on his blue lights—which it wasn't surprising that he'd have, if he worked for the TBI— and had used my U-turn as an excuse to figure out who I was and what I was doing, following him.

By now he had figured out that Rafe was alive. I mean, I'd told him as much, with my story about crawling through the tunnel to safety.

He must have gone to Wendell's house after he threw the Molotov Cocktail through our window. He'd probably seen and recognized Wendell's car parked outside our house, which he would if they worked together, and had realized that Wendell's place would be empty. And I guess he'd been worried that there might be something there that would incriminate him. He wouldn't realize that Rafe's phone calls last night had been a shot in the dark, made to more than one person to see who'd react. He'd thought we knew who he was, and what he'd done, and he'd reacted.

And now he'd react again. If I stayed here, he might do something to hurt me. He had a gun on his hip, after all. I'd seen it.

All this went through my mind rather quickly. He was just reaching for his door handle when I yanked the Volvo into gear and floored the accelerator, and took off down the road in perfect Rafe-like fashion, like a bat out of hell.

The sound was enough to wake Carrie, who made a couple of startled sounds before starting to scream.

"Sorry, baby. Sorry."

I couldn't worry about it at the moment. If I could get far enough down the road, fast enough, maybe he wouldn't bother chasing me. Maybe he'd just let me go. I hadn't seen his face, and couldn't actually identify him. And so far he hadn't done anything to harm me. Maybe he'd just leave it at that, and let me go.

But no. The SUV took off from the curb with a roar and fell in behind me, blue lights flashing. For a second I wondered whether I'd lost my mind, whether I was actually trying to run away from a legitimate cop who'd just pulled me over because I'd committed a traffic violation earlier. I could wave goodbye to a simple ticket if that was the case. I'd end up in jail.

But no. It was him. The guy from Wendell's townhouse. As we roared through the intersection at Stewarts Ferry, under the flashing yellow lights, I recognized the SUV. And it didn't look like any official MNPD car I'd ever seen.

He was still a couple of car lengths behind, and I aimed to keep it that way as we approached and then passed the Donelsen Y going back toward Hermitage. A small shopping area was coming up on the right, along with the Hermitage House Smorgasboard, a little family restaurant that's been in the same spot for close to fifty years. After that, there would be the bridge over the Stones River, and then Hermitage proper, with more houses and apartments, with Wendell's townhouse and more people.

The car behind me was gaining, and I pushed down on the gas pedal. The small brick building housing the Hermitage House came and went in my side window. Carrie kept squalling. "Sorry, baby," I muttered. "I can't get you now. Sorry."

The SUV and my Volvo were the only two cars going in this direction. Everyone else was headed the other way, toward downtown, and there still weren't many cars. We were at a pretty deserted stretch of road, between the more densely populated neighborhoods of Donelson and Hermitage. As we approached the river, the SUV made its move. It put on a burst of speed and came up on the side of me. The driver turned the wheel to the right and started pushing me toward the side of the road.

I could see the bridge coming closer as I fought to keep the car moving forward. It was only a few months since I'd ended up in the water. It had been the Duck River in Sweetwater, and I'd still been pregnant with Carrie. For a few eternal minutes I hadn't thought I was going to be able to squeeze through the car window to get myself to safety.

That wouldn't be a problem this time. I'd fit through the window. But this time I'd have to get Carrie out of her seat and take her with me when I went. And there was a very long drop from the bridge to the water here. Not like the gentle boat ramp I'd gone down into the Duck, where the car I'd been inside had ended up half in and half out of the water.

No, if Carrie and I went off the road and into the river here, it would be straight into the deepest part of the Stones River, and I wouldn't give much for our chances of survival.

The SUV kept pushing me closer to the edge of the road. I kept trying to resist, but it isn't easy. His car was heavier than mine, bigger and bulkier. The bridge kept coming closer.

I stepped on the brake, and the SUV overshot and went past me, onto the bridge itself. I couldn't stop in time, either, so I ended up following him. And had to wait until we'd gotten past the bridge and out on the other side before I could wrench the wheel to the left and turn the Volvo onto the grassy median that would take me to the other side of the road, going in the opposite direction, where there were more cars and where maybe someone would notice what was going on and would intervene.

The SUV followed, though. And its higher chassis and bigger wheels traversed the bumpy ground easier than I did, in my sedan that was much closer to the ground. When I made my way into the lane going the opposite way—back toward Donelson again—he was right behind me.

I had to dodge another car that was zooming by on its way toward downtown. The driver shot me a middle finger out the window.

"Yes, yes. Same to you." I straightened up and headed back onto the bridge, on the north side this time.

But behind me, the SUV was doing the same thing, and hadn't been hindered by the pickup truck with the finger. By the time we made it to the other side of the bridge again, he was up on the side of me. And nudged me into the small parking lot that's there, at the trailhead of the Donelson Greenway that runs along the river.

It isn't my part of town, so I wouldn't have known that if I hadn't seen the signs.

Because the SUV's blue lights were still flashing, nobody stopped to inquire what was going on. Everyone who went by swung to avoid our two cars as we made our way into the small parking lot. I cursed myself for not being able to keep the car on the road, for not just driving straight into the ditch and at least taking my lumps in plain view of everyone driving by—that had to be better than being back here, in the dark above the river—but I still kept going. That need to try to flee, to get away from danger, is quite powerful.

And then the edge of the bluff came up, and he kept pushing me closer and closer. One of my wheels left the ground and went out into nothingness, and then another. And then the car tipped forward and started rolling down the incline to the dark river below.

We ended up going about twenty feet before the front of the car fetched up against a tree trunk, and we stopped sliding.

It might be a momentary respite, but I'd take it. Up at the top of the incline, the blue lights disappeared. I strained my ears, but it was hard to hear anything above the water. Even with the window down, it was hard to discern whether the SUV was leaving, or whether the driver had just turned off the lights and was waiting to see whether I'd keep going into the river before he left. Maybe he was planning to come down and give me a hand. Not up, but farther down.

I was afraid to even breathe. One wrong move, one redistribution of weight, and the Volvo might lose its tenuous grip on safety and start rolling again. I moved very slowly when I turned the key in the ignition. There was no sense in keeping the engine running, after all. That wouldn't help me. There was no way I could reverse back up an incline like this.

I did keep the lights on, just in case someone happened to see me. I could use some help. Both to get away from here, and to get away from the man who might, even now, be on his way down the incline to finish me.

I risked a look in the mirror. There was no one coming.

That didn't mean he wasn't still up there, waiting. Hoping the car would start rolling again on its own, so he wouldn't have to come down here and push it.

Before that could happen, maybe I should try to attract some attention, and some help. If someone came, they might not be able to haul us up and out, but if they were paying attention, they could at least keep the man in the SUV from finishing us.

I moved my hand to the horn and pushed down. And kept it there.

The sound cut through the silence like a tornado siren. It startled Carrie into silence for a moment. Until she started screaming again, louder than ever.

"Sorry, baby. Sorry." I moved my head—only my head, while I kept my hand on the horn—to look into the back seat. She seemed to be fine. Still strapped into her carrier, but at a very awkward angle now. The blanket I'd put over her when I strapped her in had fallen when the car tilted, and was almost covering her face. Maybe that was why she was screaming.

She wasn't in danger of suffocating, anyway, or she wouldn't be able to make the noises she did, so I could afford to not worry about it. We had bigger concerns. Any second the skinny tree holding the car in place could decide to bend or break, and we'd fall forward toward the water. And at that point, a blanket would be the least of our troubles.

I wondered whether I dared to open my door and get out. Maybe I could make it around the car to Carrie's side, and could save her. I couldn't do it from where I was. She was too far away, and the angle was awkward, and I didn't want to contort myself too much, or redistribute my weight too far, for fear that I'd upset the gentle equilibrium of the car and we'd skew sideways, off the tree, and end up in the water.

And then the loveliest thing happened. A pair of headlights appeared at the top of the incline, and a dark figure started scrambling down, sliding in the scree.

My first thought was that it was our pursuer, who had gotten tired of waiting for the Volvo to make the final trip into the Stones River. But a quick look in the mirror told me that no, this was a young man in jeans and a green jacket, and no one I'd ever seen before.

The window was still open from earlier. I'd never taken the time to close it after the cop—who I now knew wasn't a cop at all—had pulled me over in Donelson. All my attention had been focused on driving the car. I don't think I'd even noticed the cold wind slapping my cheeks.

My rescuer slid to a stop a couple of feet away, his eyes wide in shock. "You OK, lady?"

He was Hispanic, and his accent reminded me of José's. I nodded shakily. "There's a baby on the other side of the car. Get her."

He didn't hesitate, and didn't ask any questions, just scrambled down the slope far enough that he could go around the front of the car. Maybe it was easier, or maybe he thought it would be safer than trying to go around the back, in case he accidentally slid into us and started us moving down the slope, or something. If we'd moved forward while he was in front of the car, we would have pushed him ahead of us into the river, but it worked. He got around to the other side and started making his way up toward Carrie's door. It was hard work—one foot back for every two he gained—but he got there. I pushed the button—carefully—to unlock the doors, and heard the locks disengage.

The young man said something. I couldn't hear him over the roar of the river with the doors closed and all but my own window closed, so I powered down Carrie's window, as well. She glanced up at him, a stranger just outside her window, and fell silent with a startled squawk.

"Excuse me?"

"I said," the young man said, "that the car could tilt when I pull the baby out. Maybe you should get out at the same time. Keep the weight even."

Maybe I should. I nodded and reached for my door handle. "On three. Two."

He pulled Carrie's door open, and I pushed on mine. And threw myself out of the car on my side while he yanked Carrie's seat out on his.

I landed on my hands and knees, and scrambled up the scree a few feet, the hard pebbles biting into my knees through the soft pajama pants. On the other side of the car, Carrie's seat swung in an arch from the momentum, and then settled down. The car shifted. Pebbles rolled. Metal screamed against wood for a second as the tree decided whether to stay on the job or not.

And then everything calmed down. The tree stayed where it was. The car did, too. My rescuer glanced at me across the back of the car. "Can you make it up?"

I nodded. It would be on hands and knees the whole way, but I could make it. Especially if the alternative was to fall into the rapid current below me.

I won't claim it was an easy trip. It really was two feet forward and one back, and it felt more like two forward and two back, climbing the whole way with the sound of the river below. My rescuer was having an even worse time of it, having to haul not just himself but the seat with Carrie up the hill. But at least she'd stopped screaming. All we could hear, apart from the river and the occasional sound of a car going by on the road up above, was our own labored breathing. My rescuer would mutter occasionally in what I assumed was Spanish. He was probably cursing me, and himself for stopping to help me.

"I appreciate it," I told him breathlessly. "We would have probably ended up in the river if it hadn't been for you."

He glanced over at me. "I saw you trying to get away from the other car. At first I thought he was a cop. The blue lights. But he didn't act like a cop. When I pulled in to see if I could help, he took off."

Good. At least he wasn't still up there, waiting for me to stick my head over the top of the incline so he could shoot me.

"I don't know who he was," I said, since it was more or less the truth. "He stopped me down the road. I thought he was a cop at first, too. But when I realized he wasn't, I tried to get away from him. And this happened."

It was a fine story. It made sense. And was mostly true. Or all true, really, if you disregarded a few omissions.

We climbed another few minutes in silence. The top of the hill did get closer, but not as fast as I'd like.

"I'm sorry if I'm keeping you from work," I added.

"They'll wait." He lifted the carrier with Carrie and put it down two feet farther up. And scrambled up until he was even with it. And did it again. "Save your breath. Climb."

Good advice. I saved my breath, and climbed.

We were a few feet from the top when there was the sound of a car taking the turn into the small parking area on two wheels. My heart skipped in my chest, sure he was back, ready to kill us.

But then I heard the sound of a car door opening, and a familiar voice. "Savannah!"

I pulled myself the last couple of feet to the top of the hill and stumbled into my husband's arms.

Twenty-One

"How did you know where to find us?" I asked a little later. It was the second time in just a few hours that I was feeding Carrie *al fresco*, still in my pajamas, after a traumatic experience. It had, not to put too fine a point on it, been a hell of a night.

"I knew where you'd been," Rafe said, leaning an arm on the top of Wendell's car and looking down at me, "and I figured he wasn't gonna let you get far. So we started back there—" He gestured toward Donelsen, "and came looking."

He glanced around, at the steep hill and the empty parking lot and the water rushing below us. "I figured we'd end up here. It's where I'd go, if I wanted to get rid of somebody."

Good to know. Or maybe not.

The young man who had rescued Carrie and me had disappeared. He just handed Carrie to Wendell, who had come with Rafe in the Town Car, and got back into his truck and left. He never even told us his name.

"He saved us," I told them both later, for the second time, as we stood and watched the tow truck Wendell had called haul the Volvo to safety in the predawn light. "I might have made it up myself, and I might have been able to get Carrie out. But the car might have tilted, and she would have ended up in the river. He got her out and got her to the top of the hill. He saved her."

Neither of them said anything. There was nothing to say. We could advertise for the young man, I supposed, and maybe find him, but he obviously hadn't wanted any attention.

"Mighta been illegal," Rafe said, and I nodded.

"Might have. And that makes it even nicer of him to risk stopping. Especially considering the guy who pushed me off the road was sporting blue lights."

"Did you get a good look at him? Or the car?"

This was Wendell's question, and I had to admit I hadn't. "The car was a dark SUV. I already told Rafe that. And I described the man after I saw him the first time. I didn't get a better look at him later. He didn't bend down to look into the car when he pulled me over, so I never saw his face. I was talking to his gun belt. I didn't actually recognize him until he was walking away again, back to his car, and I watched him in the mirror, and I realized I'd seen him walk away before."

They nodded. "And you took off," Rafe said.

"And he followed." We'd already been over this once, but I guess it couldn't hurt to go over it again. "He tried to force me off the road on the other side, before we got to the bridge. I got away from him then, and crossed the median to this side. But then he followed and got me down into this little parking area and over the edge of the hill. And after I'd sat there for a bit, the young Hispanic guy showed up. He said the SUV left when he pulled in to see if he could help."

And by now it could be anywhere. "He knows you're still alive," I added. "I told him about the fire and how we got out. I was trying to explain why I didn't have a license. That was before I realized who he was, obviously. And that was why he sounded funny and excused himself to go back to his car. He found out you weren't dead."

"But then he tried to kill you." Rafe's voice didn't bode well for this guy whenever we found him.

I nodded. "And Carrie. Although I'm not sure he knew she was there."

Rafe glanced at her, at the back of her dark, curly head as she was nestled against my chest, and the look in his eyes didn't bode well, either.

"My money's on Grant," Wendell broke the silence. He was standing in front of the door Rafe was holding open, with his back against the car as he watched the movements of the winch. Careful not to look at me. "Hammond and McLaughlin have kids. They wouldn't try to kill a baby. No matter how much they wanted her father dead."

Rafe nodded. "Once we get the Volvo up outta this predicament, I say we go back to the TBI and kick some ass."

"Can I come?" With everything that had gone on, I didn't like the idea of being left alone again. Besides, I wanted to watch.

He glanced at me. "No way I'm leaving the two of you alone again till this is over. Yeah, you can come."

Good. I went back to watching the tow truck slowly winch the Volvo up the hill while Rafe and Wendell discussed how best to approach the situation once they got to the TBI. What they'd do if he was there, how they'd handle it if he wasn't.

The front of the Volvo crested the hill, and the truck started driving forward to get the whole of the car safely onto the pavement. That done, we all moved to the edge of the scree to inspect the damage. Rafe directed a glower down the hill, where the tire tracks of the Volvo, coming and going, were very obvious in the slight dusting of snow we'd gotten last night. That small tree, looking a little the worse for wear now, had shown up in the nick of time. Just a yard or two below that point, the edge of the hill crumbled away to an almost straight drop into the water.

I shuddered and turned my attention in the other direction, to the Volvo itself.

My car looked perhaps a little worse for wear, too. It had a small dent in the middle of the hood, where it had made contact with the tree and been held by it. Other than that, it didn't look bad. As I'd said once, the safest car on the road.

"See if she starts," the tow truck driver called out of his window.

I was still holding Carrie, so I let Rafe do it. "The key's in the ignition."

He walked the couple of steps to the door and yanked it open. "It's safe," I asked Wendell, "isn't it? The car isn't likely to blow up, or anything like that?"

He shook his head. "It's fine."

The car started right up, with maybe a slightly louder than usual purr of the engine—something a little out of alignment under the hood, probably as a result of the meeting with the tree—and the tow truck driver hopped down from the cab to unfasten the big hook he'd used to pull the Volvo up the incline. "Y'all got it from here?"

"As long as it drives," I said, "we'll just take it to a shop ourselves." No need to incur the towing fee on a car that would make the trip on its own. This little excursion to pull the car up the hill would cost plenty. We didn't need to add to it unless it was necessary.

The driver nodded and went back to his cab. The tow truck executed a neat three-point turn, and exited the lot. Rafe executed a turn of his own, with more than three points—more to see how the car would handle than because he needed all those points, I thought—and then nodded. "She'll do. We'll get her to a body shop when we get to Sweetwater."

"We're going to Sweetwater?"

"Later," Rafe said. "First we're going to the TBI." He nodded to Wendell. "We'll see you there."

Wendell nodded back, and headed for his own car, while I put Carrie back into the car seat, and the car seat back into the car, before I buckled myself into the passenger seat next to Rafe.

Who just sat there for a second without saying anything.

"Are you all right?" I asked.

He shook his head. "I coulda lost both of you. Just like that. This ain't worth it. I'm going into home renovation when we're done with this."

"You'd be bored out of your mind," I said. "Just go to work for Grimaldi. It's nice and quiet down there."

Not exactly true, since we'd gotten into plenty of trouble in Sweetwater, too. But for now it seemed to do the trick. He nodded, and put the car into gear. And followed Wendell's Town Car out of the lot and back onto Lebanon Road just as the sun peeked over the horizon behind us.

The trip to the TBI went quickly and painlessly. It was still early enough that there were very few cars on the roads, and Wendell had a blue light of his own, that he stuck out the window and onto the top of the Town Car. We followed in its wake the whole way to Inglewood.

Once we exited the highway at Hart Lane, in sight of the TBI building and its antennae, Wendell shut the light off and pulled it back inside the car. We drove up Gass Boulevard toward the TBI quietly, past the fancy old shell of the building that used to house some sort of orphanage back in the old days, and past the Medical Examiner's office to the top of the hill and the big, brown building housing the Tennessee Bureau of Investigations.

There are people at the ME's office around the clock, just as there are at the TBI. Someone's always on duty. There were a handful of cars in front of the Office of Forensic Medicine, and when we drove into the lot at the TBI, there were a few there, too. Including a dark SUV parked under a tree.

I pointed to it, and Rafe nodded. He pulled the Volvo over to it, got out, and put his hand on the hood. "It ain't warm anymore. But with the temperature being what it is, maybe it wouldn't be."

Maybe.

"And there's no ice on the windshield, so it ain't been here all night."

No, it hadn't. Not that that thought would have occurred to me, but now that he'd mentioned it, it made sense. Someone had driven that car here recently, albeit not so recently that the engine was still warm.

We parked the Volvo next to Wendell's Town Car, and I pulled the carrier with the baby out of the back seat. "Now what?"

"Now we go in," Wendell said, "and the first thing we do is go see McLaughlin. He's gonna need to know what's going on, if we're gonna take down one of his employees inside the TBI."

"Are you sure it isn't McLaughlin himself we're looking for?"

"I don't think it's McLaughlin," Wendell said, "but that's why you're coming. You'll recognize the guy you saw?"

I had to hope I would. "As soon as he starts talking, I'll recognize his voice, if nothing else."

"Good enough," Wendell said, and led the way into the TBI.

We had to stop at the security desk, of course, where Rafe and I, and even Carrie, were issued visitor passes. The guy on duty didn't seem quite sure that it was OK for him to give Rafe one, but when Wendell got in his face and told him to, he didn't dare disobey. I felt pretty certain that the guy was on the line to somebody the second we hit the elevator, though, and that supposition was borne out when we got off the elevator on the second floor and were hailed by a stocky guy in his early fifties, with brown hair going gray at the temples. "Craig! What the hell d'you think you're doing?!"

Wendell glanced at me. I shook my head. Not only was this guy an inch or two shorter than the man I'd seen, and a bit stockier, but the voice was wrong. He was also about ten years older, unless I missed my guess, and was dressed in a suit and tie.

"Ben." Wendell's voice was calm. "You know Rafe. This is his wife, Savannah."

Ben McLaughlin's eyes snagged on the pajamas he could see through the opening in my coat, and on the baby, still in her sleeper, before they returned to Wendell. "Craig…"

"It's a long story," Wendell said. "Let's take it into your office."

And McLaughlin must have been curious enough to hear what was going on, because rather than argue, he just did an about-face and led the way down to a door on the right.

"Have a seat." He gestured to two chairs in front of the desk, while he himself took a seat behind it. Rafe deposited me in one chair and left the other to Wendell, while he walked over to the wall and leaned on it, arms folded across his chest. He'd shrugged out of the sweater while we were still in the car, so in spite of the January weather and sprinkling of snow on the ground, he was in a T-shirt with the bandage around his arm and over his shoulder on display.

McLaughlin nodded to it. "What happened?"

I let Wendell explain. He had been there for everything that had gone on at the house overnight, and he had more official standing than either of us.

When he was finished, McLaughlin turned to Rafe. "This true?"

Rafe nodded.

"I received Christina Pavlova's call last night. No one else has contacted me."

Rafe shrugged.

"*You* didn't contact me," McLaughlin added.

"You were on the list," Rafe said coolly, "but after you heard from Pavlova, I figured there wasn't any need to call you myself. You already knew what I was doing. And you weren't gonna fall for it."

McLaughlin's lips twitched. "You're not afraid of saying what you think, anyway."

"For what it's worth," Wendell said, maybe because he was afraid McLaughlin was angry with Rafe, in spite of the almost-smile, "you were at the bottom of the list. Foster was at the top, until he died."

McLaughlin nodded.

"Now we're down to Hammond and Grant for the short list. It was a man who attacked Savannah, so Pavlova's off the hook. She pretty much was anyway, after she contacted you yesterday. Whoever killed Brennan and Foster wouldn't have done that."

McLaughlin nodded again. "Someone attacked you?" he asked me. "Tell me about that."

I told him about it. And ended with, "It wasn't you. He's younger than you, and the voice was different."

He looked surprised for a moment, and then I guess he accepted it. "That's what you were doing in the hallway," he said to Wendell. "Checking if it was me."

Wendell nodded. "And it wasn't. So now we check Hammond and Grant."

McLaughlin didn't move from the desk. "Why them?"

Wendell laid out our reasoning. McLaughlin nodded. "I don't see Josh Hammond trying to burn anyone alive. Especially not a family with a baby. I don't see him trying to push a woman with a baby into a river, either. He's a family man."

"What about Grant?" Rafe wanted to know. "You see him doing it?"

McLaughlin hesitated. "I wouldn't have thought so. But at least he doesn't have children of his own. I don't see anyone who has children being able to do this."

Since this was something we had thought of ourselves, it didn't come as a surprise. On the other hand, it wasn't conclusive evidence, either. Some people do horrible things to their own children, while some treat their own like gold, but couldn't care less about anyone else's. Either way, being a parent wasn't proof one way or the other.

"Let's just let Savannah talk to'em both," Rafe said, "and see what she says."

McLaughlin nodded. "Grant's already at work. I saw his car in the lot when I came in."

So had I, if he happened to drive a dark SUV. But before I could ask, McLaughlin reached for the phone on his desk. "I'll just call him up here."

We all waited while he punched a button or two on an old-fashioned phone. A voice answered. "Yeah?"

Rafe and Wendell both looked at me. I shrugged. I couldn't say for certain that this wasn't the voice I'd heard, but I couldn't say for certain that it was, either. It's hard to tell from just one word, especially on a speaker phone.

McLaughlin issued the request that Grant come to his office, and Grant said, "On my way."

Rafe and Wendell looked at me again. I shrugged again. I still wasn't sure.

We waited in silence for Grant to arrive. McLaughlin turned a pen over and over in his hands. I crossed my legs in the other direction. Wendell sat so quietly he'd practically stopped breathing. And Rafe pushed off from the wall next to the window and moved across the room to the wall next to the door, I guess in case Grant was the person we were looking for and he tried to make a break for it once he realized we knew.

McLaughlin watched, his brows arched, but he didn't saw anything. When Rafe leaned his other shoulder against the opposite wall and folded his arms again, he gave a sort of approving nod.

There was a knock on the door, and McLaughlin called, "Come."

"Boss?" A head with mousy brown hair and glasses appeared around the door. "You wanted to see me?"

McLaughlin nodded. "Come on in."

I already knew this wasn't the guy we were looking for, though. Too skinny—the guy in the SUV, the guy who had pretended to be a cop—was more muscular than this. Not as built as Rafe, not as stocky as McLaughlin, but not as lanky as Grant, either. And the voice was wrong. So was the attitude. When he came into the room and saw us all, especially Rafe leaning against the wall looking menacing, he looked a little confused, but not guilty. Certainly not afraid, and anyone who had hurt Rafe's wife and child, and who was facing a Rafe looking at him like that, would have been terrified. It's sexy as hell if you're not on the receiving end of it, but if you are, it's enough to make a hardened criminal pee his pants.

And this was no hardened criminal, nor anyone with anything to hide. Grant just blinked at us behind the glasses. "What's going on?"

"Nothing," McLaughlin said. My lack of reaction must have told him everything he needed to know, unless it was Grant's own lack of reaction that did it. "Have you seen Josh Hammond this morning?"

Grant looked surprised. "He's in. He was at his desk when I walked by."

"Would you tell him to come see me? Don't mention that anyone else is here."

"Sure," Grant said. He made to withdraw, and then he hesitated. And stopped in front of Rafe. "I was sorry to hear you were let go. For what it's worth, I never thought you did anything to Brennan."

Rafe nodded. Grant blushed and disappeared through the door. McLaughlin arched his brows, and Rafe shook his head.

No, much better not to ask. But I could see what Rafe had been talking about when he mentioned the way Grant looked at him. Clearly, somebody had a crush, even if he was a lot more polite about it than Tim.

Less than a minute passed, and then there was another knock on the door. Hammond didn't wait to be asked to enter. He just knocked and pushed the door open and his head inside. "Boss? Something the matter?"

McLaughlin glanced at me. Rafe shifted his weight like he was getting ready to pounce. And Hammond stuck his head around the door jamb and looked from Wendell to me to Rafe. His brows went up. "Hell."

It wasn't a guilty hell. Just a surprised one. And although he was the right height and weight—slimmer than McLaughlin, more muscular than Grant—he didn't have the right voice, either. "It's not him," I said.

McLaughlin dismissed him the same way he had Grant, and Hammond made to leave.

"One second," Rafe said, and McLaughlin's brows went up. So did Hammond's. He glanced at McLaughlin, but when the latter didn't interfere, he halted his retreat. He wasn't happy about it, though.

"Yeah?" His eyes were narrowed, and it was clear he didn't like Rafe as much as Grant did. Or maybe he just didn't like him the way Grant did. Either way, he didn't like being questioned by him.

"You used to work for Metro PD."

Hammond nodded. "So?"

"You know Goins?"

"Sure," Hammond said.

"Seen anything of him lately?"

"Not since I left," Hammond said.

"You ain't spoken to him this week? Maybe about Doug Brennan?"

Hammond shook his head. "I have nothing to do with what happened to Brennan. We weren't close. He worked undercover organized crime, I work narcotics. We have our own undercover department. And besides, it's a waste of time to talk to Rick Goins. When he makes up his mind, it's hard to change it. Easier just to let him work things through on his own till he figures out where he went wrong. It takes time, but it beats trying to reason with him."

No question. I'd beat my own head against that particular wall a time or two, so I could attest to the absolute verity of this.

Rafe nodded. "Thanks."

Hammond glanced at McLaughlin. "Everything OK?"

McLaughlin nodded. "Fine. You can go back to work."

Hammond withdrew.

"Now what?" McLaughlin said. He glanced at me. "You're sure it wasn't either of them?"

I nodded. "Positive. Hammond had the shape but not the voice. Grant didn't have either. And either one of them would have wet his pants when he came face to face with Rafe, anyway, if he were guilty."

McLaughlin's lips twitched. Rafe's eyebrow arched. He pushed off from the wall by the door, sauntered over to put a hand on my shoulder for a second and drop a kiss on the top of my head, before he continued over to the wall by the window again.

The conversation stopped until he was in place. Then McLaughlin picked it back up. "Any other ideas? Could Foster have killed Brennan and then himself?"

"Of course he could have," Wendell said. "But someone set the fire last night and pushed Savannah off the road this morning. And it wasn't Foster."

No, it wasn't. "The person we're looking for might not have killed either Foster or Brennan. But he tried to kill all of us in the house fire, and then he tried to push me and the baby into the Stones River. So even if he isn't a murderer right now, it isn't for lack of trying."

McLaughlin nodded. "What more can we do?"

There was a moment's silence. "We thought it made sense for it to be Hammond or Grant," Wendell said. "Hammond's also in narcotics, and Grant knows a little about everything. But if it isn't either of 'em, maybe it's someone that's under Foster. Maybe Foster was the top of the chain and the rest of the operation was in the tiers below."

McLaughlin allowed as how that made sense. He pushed off from his desk. "Better we go down to Foster's department than call them up here one by one. There might not even be anyone there yet."

I guessed there might not. The undercover guys wouldn't be coming in to the office at all, and the handlers might not keep regular hours, either. Rafe and Wendell certainly hadn't been keeping a nine-to-five schedule back when they were doing undercover work.

So I picked up the baby carrier, in deference to Rafe's arm and to the fact that it's hard for a man to look menacing when he's carrying a baby, and we trooped out in the hallway behind McLaughlin.

Foster's department was situated one floor up, but when we got there, it was deserted. It consisted of a room full of cubicles, and there wasn't a single person at any desk. McLaughlin looked around with a frustrated expression on his face.

"Someone's been up here," Wendell said, pointing to a takeaway container of coffee on a desk. It had leaked a little, and was sitting in a ring of coffee that was slowly spreading across the desktop. If nobody had been here this morning, and the cup was from yesterday, the coffee would have been dry by now.

A jacket hung over the back of the chair in front of the desk, and I pointed to it. "That's the kind of jacket the guy in the SUV was wearing."

Your basic dark windbreaker, with extra padding for the winter. No identifying marks anywhere, but the kind of thing that identified the wearer, very obviously, as being in law enforcement.

"Gym?" Rafe suggested. And it was a good suggestion. Whenever he'd gone in to work extra early, it was so he could work out.

Granted, this guy might have other things on his mind this morning, but he might also have thought that a nice workout, after pushing a car with a woman and her infant into the river, would be just the thing to relieve tension and make him relax.

We headed back to the elevator.

The workout facilites at the TBI are in the basement. I'd been there once. Rafe was trying to teach me self defense—I can't even remember off-hand who I needed to defend myself from—and I'd ended up on my back on the mat with him on top of me, and a very enjoyable interlude had ensued.

But I digress. Rafe either didn't remember, or he also had other things on his mind, because he didn't look at me as we approached the gym doors. His expression was grim.

The elevator had made a noise as the doors opened, and I'd been a little worried that the man we were after, if he was down here, had heard it and realized we were coming. But it must have been lost in the sounds inside the gym. Feet moving and grunts and the occasional breathless curse. Our man, if he was here and this wasn't someone else, wasn't alone.

We stopped outside the doors. They had windows in the top, but the glass was covered with brown paper, so it wasn't possible to see in. McLaughlin tried the handle. It moved in his hand.

He looked back over his shoulder. "Ready?"

Rafe and Wendell nodded. Wendell pulled his gun. Rafe's eyes glinted with annoyance when he remembered that he didn't have one.

Then McLaughlin pushed the door open and we all slipped inside.

It wasn't as quiet and orderly as all that, but we also weren't trying to be stealthy. There were four of us—five if you counted Carrie, although you probably shouldn't, and you shouldn't count me, either. That left three of us—and McLaughlin and Wendell were armed—against one.

Except the one wasn't alone. He was inside the sparring ring on the opposite side of the room, mock fighting with someone. Tall, lanky, with brown skin and black hair…

"Rafe!" Jamal stopped in the middle of his attempt to drive his opponent back against the ropes, and grinned widely from ear to ear.

I squinted, as the light caught on something in Jamal's hand. And in that second, Jamal's opponent made his move.

He had an arm around Jamal's throat and his knife against the underside of Jamal's jaw in the time I went from realizing that they weren't just mock fighting, they were mock fighting with knives.

Knives with real blades.

Twenty-Two

For a second, everything stood still. Nobody moved. We all just stood frozen. Until Jamal let out a shuddering breath and dropped the knife he was holding. It hit the plastic with a sort of dull thump and the man holding him gave it a kick. It went flying off the mat, out of the ring, and onto the floor.

"Kirk," McLaughlin said, his voice rough. I recognized the name from when Alexandra had told me who Jamal's new handler would be. "What the hell are you doing?"

And between you and me, Alexandra had been right. Kirk wasn't near as hot as Rafe. He had some decent muscles, and blond hair in a crew cut, but there was just the hint of a potbelly, now that I saw him without the windbreaker.

Yes, he was absolutely the guy who had tried to run me into the river earlier. I didn't even need to hear him speak to know it.

He didn't acknowledge McLaughlin's question, just kept his knife at Jamal's throat and his eyes on Rafe and Wendell. "Don't come any closer, or I'll gut him like a fish."

There was no doubt in my mind that he would. Or at least that he'd try. This was probably the same guy who'd stabbed Malcolm. Given that Malcolm was still holding his own and would survive what happened to him, Kirk might not manage to kill Jamal if he tried, either.

But it wasn't a risk I wanted to take. Nor did Jamal, I'm sure.

"Let him go," McLaughlin said. "Put the knife down and let him go. We can figure this out."

Kirk laughed. It wasn't a pleasant laugh. "It's too late for that."

"You haven't killed anyone yet. Foster killed Brennan and then himself…"

But Kirk either didn't realize that McLaughlin was giving him an out, or he didn't care. He snorted, as if this was an insult to his own abilities instead of a way to claim himself innocent of murder. "I killed Brennan and Foster. Me. Nobody else."

No one spoke, and he added, disdain in his voice, "Foster called me in a panic after Brennan had spoken to him. Foster said Brennan figured out that Foster was being paid to look the other way while my boys and I creamed off some of the take on our deals. He even went down to the parking lot and tried to get at Brennan's brakes. Hacked away on the underside of Brennan's car with his knife. It's a miracle Brennan was able to get it to drive at the end of the day!"

It was clear from his tone that he could have done a much better job of cutting someone's brake cables than Foster had.

"So if Foster didn't cut Brennan's brake cables," McLaughlin asked, "what happened?"

"I followed him," Kirk said, "and pushed him off the road. It went a lot smoother than when I tried to do the same thing to the Collier bitch this morning. Brennan went right over the edge and down."

He gave me a scowl. I'd clearly disappointed him by not doing the same.

I opened my mouth to apologize—sarcastically, I swear; my good upbringing doesn't extend so far that I'll actually apologize, sincerely, to my would-be murderer for surviving— and then I thought better of it. No need to upset him unnecessarily. Not while the point of that knife was at Jamal's throat.

"Why d'you put the knife in my trash can?"

Kirk turned his attention to Rafe. "I wiped the handle first. Figured there might be some traces of Brennan's car on the blade. Thought Rick Goins would find it and test it and match it. But I guess he was too much of an idiot for that."

Or there was nothing on the blade to test. Which was also a possibility.

"How do you know Rick Goins?" McLaughlin wanted to know. I did, too. Kirk hadn't come to the TBI from Metro PD. Or if he had, no one had mentioned it.

He smirked. "High school buddies. He called me for the inside intel when he got the case. It was no problem to whisper in his ear how Brennan had fired Collier. I didn't even have to suggest that with Collier's background, he was a likely suspect. Rick's the same racist asshole he was in school; he figured that out right quick on his own."

"And Malcolm?" Rafe said.

"That the black kid? He saw me put the knife there. When I saw him again the next day, I decided to teach him a lesson."

Kirk's voice was chillingly unemotional, like he was talking about taking away Malcolm's video privileges instead of stabbing him repeatedly with a knife and leaving him to die.

"One less young, black male on the street," he added, with a smirk that no doubt included both Rafe and Wendell. "No loss to anyone."

Sounded like there might be a bit of a racist asshole in Kirk, too, if you'll excuse my French.

"For your information," I said, "Malcolm's going to be all right. He survived, too. Just like I did. Just like we all did."

With the way he was talking, I figured we might as well get the fire out on the table, too. He'd been willing to admit to— even brag about—how clever he'd been about everything else, so it was likely he'd cop to that, as well.

"You threw an accelerant through the window of my house," Rafe said, his voice conversational, but with an undertone of icy fury that was clear as day to me, at least. "Where my wife and my baby were sleeping."

Kirk smirked. "You got out."

"No thanks to you." He took a step forward, and Kirk did something with the knife that made Jamal squeak. Rafe stopped, frustration on his face and in the way his hands clenched at his sides. If it hadn't been for Jamal, he would have thrown himself at Kirk by now, knife be damned.

"We're gonna leave now," Kirk said. His eyes flicked from side to side, assessing the room. "Through this door back here." There were two, apparently. One on one side of the room, where we'd come in, and one on the other.

There must be a staircase up and out of the building over there, or he wouldn't get far, seeing as our door was between him and the elevator.

He pulled Jamal backwards a couple of steps. It must have been awkward, because Jamal was several inches taller than Kirk. Kirk probably weighed more, or at least they weighed about the same, but Jamal is practically as tall as Rafe, but with the build of your average distance runner. Tall but lanky. "And you're gonna stay here and let us."

Nobody spoke. Kirk took another step back, still dragging Jamal. But Jamal's heel must have gotten caught on something, and suddenly he was falling.

Except not really falling. He was executing some complicated sort of twist in Kirk's grip, rotating away from the knife, at the same time as he somehow managed to hook a foot around one of Kirk's legs, and dump him on his butt. Kirk let go of Jamal, probably because he didn't have any other choice, and although he tried to hold on to the knife, Jamal swung a size fifteen shoe and kicked it out of his hand.

All in one beautifully choreographed move.

The knife went flying, and ended up hitting the wall with a clang.

By then, while Jamal was still finding his balance, Rafe was halfway across the floor. A second later, he was on top of Kirk. I turned away so I wouldn't have to watch what happened next. Not because Kirk didn't deserve it, but because it wouldn't be pretty. Someone would haul Rafe off fairly soon, I was sure, if he didn't rein himself in and remember who and where he was, but the first couple of seconds while he gave vent to his temper were bound to be pretty ugly.

It didn't take long. Maybe twenty seconds, maybe less. Enough time for me to hear a fist connect with flesh and bone a couple of times, before it turned silent.

I swung back around.

Nobody had had to pull Rafe off. They were all still standing where they'd been, not interfering, and Rafe was pulling himself off Kirk, who was flat on his back on the mat. There was a little blood at the side of his mouth, but nothing else. Rafe got to his feet and shook out his fist.

"We'll call that justified," McLaughlin said calmly, "under the circumstances." He glanced around the room. "Anybody got a pair of handcuffs?"

"He ain't going nowhere," Rafe said, and wiped at his own mouth with the back of his hand. Maybe Kirk had gotten in a shot. "Not for a while. You OK?"

He glanced at Jamal.

"Gotta scratch on my face from the knife," Jamal said. "Nothing to worry about. Chicks dig scars." He grinned.

And while he was right—he did have blood on his cheek from the knife—it didn't seem to be a big deal. It probably wouldn't even need stitches. Just a shallow scrape he'd sustained in trying to get away. While Alexandra would probably make a big deal out of it if he showed her—and told her what had happened—he wasn't likely to have to deal with lasting ramifications.

"Nice kick," I told him, and I have to admit my voice was a little shaky. These episodes are always a little scary, and anyway, I enjoy seeing my husband in action.

McLaughlin nodded. "Nice moves altogether."

"Rafe trained me," Jamal said.

McLaughlin glanced at him. At Rafe. And at Wendell, who had unearthed a pair of handcuffs from somewhere—maybe he'd had the foresight to bring them in from the car earlier, in the hopes that he'd get to put them around someone's wrists this morning—and was in the process of putting them around Kirk's. "Maybe we should discuss this termination in more detail."

Yes, if I'd been watching Rafe and Jamal in action, and had the power to hire or fire them, I'd keep them on the payroll, too. Especially as McLaughlin's department was now three men short, with Brennan and Foster in the morgue and Kirk on his way to prison. And they were likely to lose more, too, when they interrogated Kirk, as he'd probably be induced to share the names of those of his 'boys' who had been in this with him.

McLaughlin's department wasn't going to look good after this. But if he could talk Wendell into withdrawing his resignation, and talk Rafe back into the fold, that would go a little way toward mitigating some of the damage.

He must have been thinking the same thing, because he waited until Wendell had finished handcuffing Kirk and had straightened before he said, "It looks like I'm gonna be short two supervisors and a handler, not to mention several undercover operatives, from this week's mess. How would you like to take over Doug Brennan's position? Or Foster's?"

Wendell looked at him. And looked at Rafe. And looked at McLaughlin again.

McLaughlin sighed. "Yeah, yeah. If you take Brennan's job, or Foster's, Collier gets your job, or Kirk's."

There was a moment of silence.

"I already have a job offer," Rafe said.

McLaughlin nodded. "From the Columbia PD. I know."

"My wife wants to spend more time with her family, now that the baby's here. And Chief Grimaldi needs my help."

And while all of that was true, I had a feeling Rafe, if he could choose, would prefer to stay with the TBI, and with Wendell and Jamal.

"Why don't we take some time to think about it?" I said. Everyone turned to look at me, and Rafe's eyebrow rose. "We can't live in our house right now, anyway. The fire damage has to get fixed, and that could take a while. First the insurance company has to investigate and then decide whether to pay the claim, and then the work has to be done. We could be into spring by the time the house is livable again."

Rafe nodded, the corner of his mouth curling up. I guess he knew where I was going with this.

I turned to McLaughlin. "Maybe the TBI could loan Rafe to the Columbia PD for the time we have to spend in Sweetwater? You've done it before. He went down there to help Sheriff Satterfield with a case just a few months ago, and last May, the MNPD sent him down to interview the ADA about his ex-wife's death." Todd Satterfield, as it happened. A very uncomfortable experience for everyone involved. "There's precedence."

"I can live with that," Wendell said, while Jamal looked like an overgrown choir boy with his hands folded in front of him and a pleading expression on his face.

Rafe looked from them to me.

"I'm fine with it if you are," I said. "I told you, I don't care where we live. Carrie and I just want to be with you."

"But you were looking forward to spending time with your family."

"And I will. For the next couple of months, at least. At the end of it, you can decide whether you want to stay in Sweetwater and work with Grimaldi, or if you want to come back here and work with Wendell and Jamal. But at least you have choices."

Rafe nodded. Down on the mat, Kirk groaned.

"I better start the paperwork," McLaughlin said with a sigh. "I'll copy the MNPD and Goins. He won't be happy, I imagine."

I imagined he was right. "Make sure you tell him you heard Kirk confess to both murders." I glanced around the room, at Rafe, Rafe's handler, Rafe's protégée, Rafe's baby—who was being very quiet in her car seat—and me, Rafe's wife… "He won't believe that any of us are telling the truth, and without some independent proof, I'm not sure he'll ever believe Rafe didn't have something to do with it. Even if we all heard Kirk confess."

"The recording'll take care of that," McLaughlin said, and fished a small voice recorder out of his breast pocket. When he saw my expression, and mine might not have been the only one, he added, "I engaged it when the security desk told me you were on your way up. Just in case. It's been running for a while."

If he'd engaged it before we'd even laid eyes on him this morning, it had been. "Is that legal?" fell out of my mouth.

"One-party consent state," Rafe told me. "As long as one party to a conversation agrees to record it, the other party don't have to."

"And doesn't even have to know it's being done?"

He shook his head.

"Wow," I said.

"All legal," McLaughlin assured me. As Kirk emitted

another moan down on the mat, he added, "I'll go find someone to drive him downtown."

"Until you know who you can trust and who you can't," Wendell suggested, "might be just as well to have us do that."

McLaughlin thought for a moment, and then nodded. "Take him outside and load him up. Make sure you read him his rights first. I'll call Goins and tell him to expect you."

"You'd better stay here," Wendell told Rafe as McLaughlin headed for the door. "It won't help for Goins to see you."

Rafe shook his head. "Savannah can drop me at the house. I'll board up the doors like we talked about, and then I'll head down to Sweetwater for a while. See what I can do to help Tammy clean house."

"You had a good practice run up here," Wendell said and slapped him on the back before he turned to Jamal. "C'mon, boy. Let's take out the trash."

The two of them hauled Kirk to his feet. He was awake enough by now to walk on his own, even if he wasn't entirely steady on his feet. They marched him to the door—the one he'd planned to use for his escape—and out. "Matthew Kirkegaard," I heard Wendell intone as they passed out of hearing, "you're under arrest for the murders of Douglas Brennan and James Foster…"

I turned to Rafe. He turned to me. And looked at me for a moment before he said, "You sure you're OK with this?"

"I told you. I'm OK with anything that makes you happy." After a second I added, "Almost anything. I draw the line at sharing you with Yvonne McCoy."

He chuckled. "No need to worry about that. The only person you have to worry about sharing me with is Caroline."

Not quite. There was David. And Wendell. And Jamal. And in the immediate future, Grimaldi. But for right now he was mine, and that was good enough.

"Let's go home," I said.

He nodded. "I'll take the baby." He picked her up, and we walked out of the TBI gym hand in hand.

# # #

ABOUT THE AUTHOR

New York Times and *USA Today* bestselling author Jenna Bennett (Jennie Bentley) writes the Do It Yourself home renovation mysteries for Berkley Prime Crime and the Savannah Martin real estate mysteries for her own gratification. She also writes a variety of romance for a change of pace.

For more information, please visit Jenna's website:
www.jennabennett.com